A BODY IN THE COTTAGE

A gripping Welsh crime mystery full of twists

P.F. FORD

The West Wales Murder Mysteries Book 5

JOFFE BOOKS

Joffe Books, London
www.joffebooks.com

First published in Great Britain in 2023

© P.F. Ford

Cover art by Dee Dee Book Covers

ISBN: 978-1-83526-094-4

To my amazing wife, Mary — sometimes we need someone else to believe in us before we really believe in ourselves. None of this would have happened without your unfailing belief and support.

CHAPTER ONE

'What do you mean you want to stop? You've barely started work.'

The burly red-faced man banged his fist on his desk.

Tom Fletcher, the building site foreman, shrugged. 'None of us wants to stop work, Mr Harding, but what else can we do?'

'Can't you find some way to work around that house?'

'When I called the police to say we'd found a body, they said the whole site could be a crime scene. We're not to touch anything until they get here.'

'Police? You've called the bloody police?' Harding kicked out at his waste bin, sending it flying across the room. 'I can't believe this. And which bright spark ordered a search of the houses in the first place?'

'That was me,' said Fletcher.

'You're not even supposed to be in charge, for God's sake. Where is Watkins anyway? Why isn't he here?'

'Graham's away until tomorrow. If you recall, we were only supposed to be doing general site clearance this week.

You said you didn't expect to get planning permission until the end of the week at the earliest, so Graham decided to spend some time at home while he could.'

'If you'd spent over ten years arguing for planning permission to get this project off the ground and it was suddenly granted earlier than you expected, you'd want to get started as soon as you could in case the buggers change their minds. Wouldn't you?' The glare intensified.

'I understand that, and it's what we were trying to do,' said Fletcher.

'But now you're telling me we've got to stop,' roared Harding. 'So in fact, you've done sod all today.'

'Er, yes, I suppose that's right.'

'So, what you're saying is, I'm paying a team of workers to sit around drinking tea, right? And tell me, why did you order a search of the houses in the first place?'

'Houses like these often attract homeless people looking for somewhere to shelter, so you should always make sure the houses really are empty before you start demolishing them. It's basic health and safety procedure.'

'There's a damned great sign outside saying this site is private and people should keep out. As far as I'm concerned, if they want to ignore it that's their problem, and they enter at their own risk.'

Not for the first time, Fletcher was appalled at Harding's callousness. 'That might be how you see it, but I'd rather not have a death on my conscience,' he said. 'And I'm sure you wouldn't want your company being investigated by Health and Safety before work has even started, all because we ignored the rules.'

Fletcher could see Harding was struggling to contain his anger, but he knew what he was talking about. He wasn't a man to be easily bullied.

'Now, if there's nothing else, I'll go and wait for the police to arrive.'

'Yes, you do that,' said Harding.

* * *

Detective Sergeant Norman Norman stared blankly at the words Detective Constable Judy Lane had written down for him.

'I'm not even going to try to pronounce this, Frosty,' he said to DC Winter, who was driving.

'It more or less translates as "homes for miners",' said Winter.

'Yeah, Judy told me that much,' said Norman. 'But knowing what it means doesn't make it any easier to pronounce.'

Winter smiled. 'Well, since Catren has the day off, that's what I'm here for.'

Catren Morgan was the other DC in their team.

Norman sighed. 'I'll certainly be relying on your translation skills today.'

'Catren warned me about that. She also tells me you don't do running,' said Winter. 'Is that right?'

'Well, hopefully there'll be no need to run today. No, I gave up running years ago after I put on so much weight, and I've managed to avoid it ever since.'

'I can't imagine you ever being overweight,' said Winter.

'It's flattering of you to say so,' said Norman. 'But the fact is I was once twice the man you see before you now. I was depressed and I just kept eating, with the result that I suffered a heart attack, hence the no running.'

'No shit!' said Winter. 'Was it a bad one?'

'It was bad enough to scare some sense into me,' said Norman. 'I mean, I wouldn't wish it on anyone, but it was certainly a wake-up call.'

'Is that why you originally left?'

'At the time I had a boss who wanted me out but had no reason to fire me. She saw my heart attack as the perfect opportunity to push me into early retirement on the grounds of ill health.'

'That doesn't sound right.'

'I didn't think so at the time but, looking back on it now, I think she did me a favour.'

'Really?'

'Sure. I was stuck in a rut back then. It took a while for things to work themselves out, but I'm really happy working with you guys, and with my new life here in Wales. In fact, I can't recall ever being happier, and what more can a man ask for? Anyway, enough about me. What do we know about this place we're going to?'

'It was originally built to house miners. It was a nice little community until the pits closed in the eighties and there was no work. People began to move out, and by the turn of the century the houses were considered derelict. A developer bought the site in the early noughties and he's been fighting for permission to redevelop it ever since.'

'How come it's taken so long?'

'A local history group have been campaigning against the redevelopment. They think the site should be preserved as a museum.'

'A museum? Do they seriously think people would come and see it?'

'They see it as an important part of Welsh heritage,' Winter said.

'You know a lot about this for someone who was still a twinkle in his daddy's eye at the turn of the century.'

'I had a grandfather who used to work down the mine. He lived in one of those houses for a while. I heard a bit about it as I was growing up, so I guess I tend to listen whenever I hear it mentioned.'

'How come someone found a body if the place is derelict?'

'They must have finally got planning permission, because the message we got was that they were just about to start demolishing the houses when they found it.'

'What time was that?' asked Norman.

'About midday, I think.'

'Your background knowledge might come in handy,' said Norman.

'I'm afraid you've probably exhausted my knowledge already, sarge.'

'What about your grandfather? Maybe he can help,' Norman said.

'He died ten years ago.'

'Oh. I'm sorry.'

'Don't be. It was a long time ago, and I don't miss him.'

'What about your parents?'

'Mum's from Carmarthen, and Dad's family moved away from the mining community when he was about ten. From what I can make out he hated the place and couldn't wait to get away.'

'But you do know where it is?'

'Yeah, it's where that turning is up ahead. Um, I've never actually visited it before.'

'Don't sound so worried,' said Norman. 'This isn't a test, and you haven't failed. If I was on my own I wouldn't have a clue, so any knowledge you have will be of help.'

Winter indicated, slowed the car, and turned right through a row of trees onto a narrow lane. A hundred yards ahead a six-feet-tall chain-link fence emblazoned with the name *Harding Redevelopments Ltd* stretched off in both directions. A uniformed PC was standing guard at the gate.

Winter wound down his window, identified himself to the PC, and drove in through the gates.

'He says we have to take the first left, then second right,' Winter told Norman. 'The builders have a portacabin where they make tea. They've been asked to wait there until we give them the all clear.'

'Are there many of them?' Norman asked.

'About a dozen, I think, but not all of them actually saw the body.'

As Winter drove, Norman gazed at the terraces of tiny redbrick houses that lined the narrow streets, and imagined what it must have been like to live here. Some people might consider a place like this to be squalid, but Norman had grown up in similar housing and he could well recall the community spirit that existed, in spite of its perceived faults.

Winter parked the car and Norman led the way towards the crime scene. They ducked under the blue and white cordon tape stretched across the end of this final street, a terrace of ten houses each side. The other end of the street was sealed off by a makeshift wooden fence. All the activity seemed to be centred around the fifth house along on the left-hand side.

'That'll be number nine then,' said Norman as they approached the house.

'Do you think the number's significant?' asked Winter.

'I have no idea, son. Right now, your guess is as good as mine.'

An officer handed them a couple of forensic suits, which they donned along with overshoes, before going inside.

'Dr Bridger is upstairs,' she told them. 'And watch how you go, the stairs aren't too clever.'

Norman led the way to the staircase.

'Wow, she wasn't kidding,' said Winter, peering over Norman's shoulder. 'Look at that damned great gap. Is it even fixed to the wall?'

'It must be okay if Bridger and the forensic guys went up,' said Norman. 'But, just to be sure, let's go up one at a time so we don't overload it.'

Gingerly, Norman made his way up the stairs, to the sound of ominous creaks and groans.

'Is it the staircase making all that noise, or is it your knees?' asked Winter.

'We'll find out when you come up,' said Norman. Winter began his ascent. 'Well, there you go. Unless yours are just as bad, of course, but at least I can put mine down to age.'

They found Dr Bill Bridger, the pathologist, on his knees examining the back of the head of the prone body.

'Morning, Bill,' said Norman.

Bridger looked up at him. 'What's this? No boss this morning?'

'Sarah's in a meeting. She'll be along as soon as she can. I'm afraid you'll just have to make do with me and Frosty for now.'

Bridger smiled. 'I suppose you're the make do and mend option.'

'Yeah, always second choice, that's me,' Norman said wryly. 'So, what have we got here?'

'What we have here is the body of a Caucasian woman, probably in her mid to late thirties.'

'Was she a squatter?' asked Winter.

'Looking at the designer labels on her clothes, I'd say not,' said Bridger. 'Of course, it's possible she was the best dressed squatter in Wales but somehow, I doubt it.'

Norman pointed to a pair of shoes lying near the body.

'Are those her shoes? Why did you take them off?'

'They're Jimmy Choos, so they go with the rest of her outfit, but why they're lying there I have no idea,' said Bridger. 'I certainly did not remove them.'

'Any ID?' asked Norman.

'Not that we've been able to find. There's no handbag, phone, purse or anything else. There's no watch or jewellery on her either, but there's an old callus at the base of her ring finger and an indentation that suggests she wore a wedding ring.'

'It's missing? This is starting to sound like a mugging that went wrong.'

'Not necessarily. It doesn't look as if it's been yanked off hastily. It could simply be the case that she stopped wearing her wedding ring, and there could be all sorts of reasons for that. And if it was a mugging, why not take the shoes? They must be worth a goodly sum.'

'Cause of death?'

Bridger grimaced. 'I'm not sure. She's pretty bruised and battered, and there's what appears to be a blunt force trauma wound to the back of her head, but at this stage it's difficult to say what caused it, or even if it was responsible for her death.'

'Was she raped?' asked Norman.

Bridger shook his head. 'No sign of any sexual activity.'

'Perhaps she fought back and the mugger beat her up,' suggested Winter.

'Maybe,' said Bridger.

'But you don't think so, right?' asked Norman.

'I'm doubtful, but I can't say for sure until I get her on the slab.'

'I wonder what she was doing here,' said Winter.

'One thing I can say with a degree of certainty is that she didn't die here. As I said, there's a blunt force trauma wound to her head, and dried blood in her hair, but there's no blood on the floor.'

'So she died somewhere else and was dumped here,' said Norman. 'That means whoever killed her had to know about this place.'

'That won't help us much,' said Winter. 'These old houses are probably known to over ninety per cent of the local population.'

'What about time of death?' asked Norman.

'At this stage I'd say between forty-eight and seventy-two hours ago, but that could change,' said Bridger.

'So we have no idea who she is, or how she died. All we do know is that she didn't die here and it might have happened on Friday night but we can't be sure.'

'I'm sorry, but that's about the best I can do right now,' said Bridger.

Norman winked at Winter. 'Naturally, I would have preferred a full name and address for the victim, a cause of death, and the name of the perpetrator, but I understand you can only work with what you've got. Miracles take a little longer, right?'

'You're all heart, Norm, you really are,' said Bridger with a grin. 'Is it okay if I remove the body now?'

'Sure,' said Norman. He turned to Winter. 'As there's just the two of us, we'd better start by speaking to the builders, especially the guys who found the body. We can come back here later when the scenes of crime officers have finished.'

Norman led the way back down the stairs. As they reached the bottom step he stopped and pointed to a five-litre plastic petrol can standing on the floor.

'Now, what's that doing here?' he muttered.

He reached down and tested it for weight.

'It's full,' he said. 'Can you make sure the SOCOs don't forget to bag it and tag it.'

'Is it important?' asked Winter.

'Maybe, maybe not,' said Norman. 'It just seems an odd thing to find in a derelict house that's about to be demolished.'

'Maybe the builders were planning a bonfire.'

'Yeah, maybe. Perhaps we should ask when we interview them. We need to know everyone's movements from Friday night through to this morning.'

CHAPTER TWO

There were two portacabins on opposite sides of a make-shift car park. Norman guessed the one the builders used was the shabbier of the two, and not the one with a Rolls Royce parked outside. As they walked into the car park a door opened in the posher one. A man in a suit appeared, whistled loudly and called out to them.

'Oi, you there,' he called, beckoning them over.

'Oh, crap,' muttered Norman. 'Here we go.'

'What?' asked Winter.

'I bet this is the developer,' said Norman. 'And he wants to know when they can get back to work.'

'He looks a bit of a twat,' said Winter.

'That'll explain why he's whistling like we're a pair of dogs,' said Norman. 'If there's one thing guaranteed to piss me off, he's just done it.'

'Should we ignore him?'

'You can't ignore people like him,' said Norman. 'He won't allow it because he thinks he's special. I tell you what, you speak to the two guys who found the body, and get a couple of uniforms to help interview the others. And remember, we need to know everyone's movements from Friday night through to this morning. I'll deal with the dickhead.'

Leaving Winter to speak to the builders, Norman trudged over to the angry looking man at the portacabin door.

'Are you with the police?'

Norman produced his warrant card. 'DS Norman. And you are?'

'Joe Harding. I'm the developer. How much longer are you going to take? We've got a job to do here, you know.'

'Well, we have a job to do too, Mr Harding, and I'm afraid ours takes priority. You and your men are just going to have to wait.'

'Yeah but for how long?'

'As long as it takes,' said Norman.

'Can't we work around you?'

'No, you cannot work around us,' said Norman. 'Doing so could destroy vital forensic evidence. You can start work again when we have finished our investigation of the area, and not before.'

'I've been waiting years for permission to knock these bloody houses down.'

'Then a day or two more won't make a great deal of difference to you, will it? But it could make a huge difference to the success of our investigation.'

'Are you serious? You're going to make an investigation out of this?'

'Of course we are. This is a suspicious death. Until we have good reason to think otherwise, house number nine is a possible murder scene, which is why we have cordoned off the surrounding area.'

'Murder?'

'Possible murder,' said Norman.

'But it's just a dead squatter, isn't it? She shouldn't even be here. It's private property.'

'We don't believe the dead lady was a squatter,' said Norman.

'What makes you think that?'

'I can't go into details,' said Norman. 'But even if she had been a squatter, she was still a member of the human race, and just as deserving of justice.'

'I'm not sure I like your tone, Sergeant Norman.'

'Well, I'm sorry about that,' said Norman. 'The thing is, just like you, I'm keen to get on and do my job, but at the moment you are stopping me from doing that.'

'I can see you just want to be difficult,' snapped Harding. 'Are you in charge?'

'Detective Inspector Southall will be the senior investigating officer.'

'I don't believe I've come across him.'

'No, you won't have come across him,' said Norman. 'DI Southall is a woman.'

Harding sighed.

'A woman, you say. Well, there we are then,' he said. 'No wonder we're being held up. I suppose this is all about women's rights and that sort of crap, is it?'

'Actually it's my decision. I'm sure DI Southall will agree with my assessment when she gets here. Anyway, are you suggesting that being a woman would hamper her ability to do her job?'

'Well, you have to admit—'

'The only thing I'll admit about DI Southall is that she's one of the best DIs I ever worked for and I've been doing this for more years than I care to mention. I think you'll find she doesn't have an old school tie, either.'

'Old school tie?'

'You know exactly what I mean,' said Norman. 'An old school tie, like you and the rest of your dinosaur friends in the funny handshake brigade wear. It's how you get things done, right?'

Harding snorted. 'Your bloody impertinence is beginning to annoy me, Sergeant. Who is DI Southall's boss?'

'That will be Superintendent Bain,' said Norman.

Harding gave Norman a knowing smile. 'Ah! Now you're talking proper policemen. I know Bain. We've played golf a few times.'

Norman bristled at the implied slight, but he kept his temper because however well Harding thought he knew

Nathan Bain, Norman probably knew him better, and had done so for a lot longer. Bain was not just the boss at Llangwelli station he was also the man responsible for enticing Norman out of retirement.

'If you know Superintendent Bain so well, you won't need me to give you his phone number, will you?'

'I think I'm going to call him and make a complaint.'

'That's a good idea,' said Norman. 'Why not do it now? At least while you're complaining to him I can get on and do my job.'

Harding turned his back and slammed the portacabin door shut behind him.

'Dickhead,' muttered Norman.

As he headed across to the builders' portacabin, Southall drove into the car park.

'Hi, Norm. What have we got?' she asked, getting out of the car.

'Dead woman, found in a bedroom at house number nine. No ID, white, aged mid to late thirties, expensive clothes. Bill Bridger says she's been badly beaten, possible blunt force trauma to the back of the head.'

'A squatter?'

'Too well dressed,' said Norman. 'Bill reckons she was probably killed somewhere else and dumped here. Probably died between forty-eight and seventy-two hours ago. He's already taken the body away.'

Winter was making his way towards them from the builders' portacabin.

'How did you get on, Frosty?' asked Norman.

'Apparently the boss, Joe Harding, wanted them to start demolishing the houses first thing this morning, but the site foreman, Tom Fletcher, insisted they search the houses first, just to make sure there weren't any squatters hiding inside.

'The unfortunate guy who found the body is called Davey Burrows. He called Tom Fletcher as soon as he found her. None of the others saw anything. They're the only two who saw the body, and they're both pretty shaken up.'

'What do you think?' Norman said.

'If you mean do I think either of them are involved in her death, or have anything to do with her body being in that house, then, no, I don't think they are,' said Winter.

'I guess it wouldn't make much sense to dump a body and then tell everyone you've found it, would it?' said Norman.

'What's next?' asked Winter.

'Well, I need to take a look at the murder scene,' said Southall. 'And I think we ought to check all the other houses.'

'The builders have already checked them,' said Winter.

'Yeah, but they were just doing a quick check for people who shouldn't be there,' said Norman. 'We're looking for a possible murder scene, or anything that might provide a clue to what happened.'

'Oh, right. I see what you mean.'

'Me and Frosty can make a start on that,' Norman suggested to Southall. 'When you've finished checking out the murder scene, I think you probably need to have a word with Joe Harding.'

'He's the boss, right?'

'Yeah, that's the guy,' said Norman. 'I told him he would have to stop work until we tell him otherwise, but he's champing at the bit to get his guys working again. He's impressed by rank, so he might take it a bit more seriously if he hears it from a detective inspector rather than a sergeant. There again, he gave me the impression he thinks women should know their place.'

'That should make for an interesting conversation then,' said Southall. 'Where is he?'

'You see where that Roller is parked? That's his, and it's parked outside his portacabin. He's probably on the phone to Nathan Bain. He said he was going to make a complaint about me.'

Southall smiled. 'I find it hard to believe you would upset anyone, Norm, unless, of course, they were being a dickhead.'

'Oh, he was definitely being that,' said Winter. 'Whistled to us like he was calling his dog.'

Southall made a face. 'In that case, you two start searching the houses and I'll have a word with Mr Dickhead,' she said marching determinedly towards Harding's portacabin.

'I wouldn't want to be in his shoes,' said Winter, watching her walk away.

'She's awesome when she gets going,' said Norman. 'Five feet of fire and brimstone, and I've yet to see anything, or anyone, intimidate her.'

He turned his attention back to the houses. 'Come on then, Frosty, let's see if we can find a murder scene.'

* * *

As Southall approached the portacabin, she heard shouting from inside, then what sounded like a phone being slammed down onto its cradle followed by a loud curse and a rapid drumming. She knocked on the door.

'Yes!'

Southall pushed the door open and made her way inside. Harding was sitting behind a huge desk, his face flushed an angry red. His fists were still clenched — he'd obviously been beating his desk in frustration.

'Mr Harding?' she said with a smile, showing her warrant card. 'I'm Detective Inspector Southall.'

'So you've decided to show up at last. If you're the senior investigating officer, shouldn't you have been here from the start, instead of letting that other idiot loose?'

Southall smiled patiently. 'You're mistaken, Mr Harding. DS Norman is not an idiot.'

Harding snorted derisively. 'Well he seems to think you should be wasting your time trying to figure out what's happened to some drug-addled squatter.'

'I don't believe that's quite how DS Norman described the victim, sir,' said Southall.

'It doesn't matter how he described her. I want this mess cleared up now.'

Southall counted to ten in her head. 'You talk about the victim as if she were just a piece of meat.'

'These people are a waste of space. Because of her I've got men sitting around drinking tea when they should be working.'

'Well, I'm sorry if her death is inconveniencing you, Mr Harding, but the law gives us the authority to investigate any suspicious death, wherever it happens, and regardless of your opinion of the victim.'

'I've already made my feelings known to Superintendent Bain,' growled Harding.

'That's your prerogative,' said Southall. 'Can I ask what he said?'

'He agreed with me that you shouldn't be wasting your time on a squatter and that you should get off my site and let my people get back to work.'

Southall raised her eyebrows. 'I find that hard to believe.'

'Are you calling me a liar?' roared Harding.

'Good heavens, no, Mr Harding, of course not. But you must understand I don't take orders from the likes of you.'

Harding was breathing hard, his shoulders tensed, fists clenching and unclenching on the desk.

'Actually, I'm surprised Superintendent Bain hasn't already called me if that's how he felt,' said Southall, producing her mobile phone. 'Perhaps I should call him now, then we can find out exactly what he did say.'

'All right!' he snapped. 'There's no need to call him.'

'Yes, that's what I thought,' said Southall. 'Of course, if Superintendent Bain calls and orders me to close the case and withdraw my team, I'll be happy to oblige. But we both know that's not going to happen, don't we?'

Harding opened his mouth to argue but Southall was too quick for him.

'Look, Mr Harding, I've worked for Superintendent Bain long enough to know how he operates, that's why I know how the conversation would have gone,' she said. 'I knew it when I heard you slam down the phone and beat your fists on the desk as I was about to knock on your door.'

Harding glared at her.

'Let me spell it out for you,' said Southall. 'House number nine, and any part of the surrounding area that has been cordoned off, is out of bounds to you and everyone who works for you. My advice would be to send your men home.'

'You're joking. How long for?'

'I never joke when there's a possibility that someone has been murdered,' said Southall. 'As for how long your men should stay away, that's rather like asking how long is a piece of string.'

'Oh, now, come on,' said Harding, grudgingly. 'This delay is costing me a fortune.'

'I can't help that. My investigation of this site will take as long as it takes.'

'Can't you just take photographs?'

'Of course we will take photographs, but there's a bit more to it than that. It could take the rest of the week.'

Harding muttered a quiet curse. 'I've got a couple of skips loaded with rubbish from the other end of the site,' he said. 'Can I at least get them picked up and sent to the tip so they can be unloaded? They've been ready to go since before the weekend.'

'Are you sure none of the contents is from my crime scene?'

'Scout's honour,' said Harding sarcastically, 'it's all from the other end of the site.'

'Then, yes, I suppose I can allow that,' said Southall.

'Thank God for small mercies,' said Harding.

'Here's another small mercy,' said Southall. 'I'm going now, but I warn you, Mr Harding, if I find you've been trying to intimidate anyone working on this case, I'll be arresting you for obstruction. Are we clear?'

Harding managed a barely perceptible nod.

'Good,' said Southall, heading for the door. 'By the way, we'll need to interview you properly.'

'Interview me?' said Harding incredulously.

'That's right. We'll be interviewing everyone who works here.'

'You can't seriously think I've got anything to do with this.'

'I'm afraid everyone's a suspect until they're eliminated from our investigation,' said Southall. 'It's normal procedure.'

'Well, I demand you eliminate me right now,' said Harding.

'It doesn't work like that,' said Southall. 'You can't just demand to be eliminated.'

'Are you saying my word isn't good enough?' snapped Harding.

'Perhaps you could start by telling me where you've been all weekend,' Southall said.

'I spent the weekend at home. From late Friday afternoon until this morning.'

'Can anyone verify that?'

'No. I was on my own.'

'Unfortunately, that's not good enough as an alibi,' said Southall.

'This is bloody preposterous,' roared Harding. 'Why on earth would you suspect me of murder?'

Her hand on the door, Southall turned to Harding. 'As you were at pains to point out, Mr Harding, this is your site and you've owned it for years. So, who would know it better?' She offered him a sweet smile. 'Now I'm going to give you some time to get that temper of yours under control, but I will be back for that interview, so don't leave town.'

* * *

Just as Norman and Winter reached the end of the street, rain began to fall.

'Well, fancy that,' said Norman. 'I might have known it would rain as soon as we came outside. Let's grab our coats before we get soaked.'

Coat on and hood up against the rain, Norman considered their options. 'It would be fair to assume that whatever happened to our victim could have taken place anywhere, and the body could have been driven here. But we have to start somewhere, so for now we'll assume it happened around here.'

'Okay,' said Winter. 'What do you suggest?'

'Let's say you've just murdered someone and you want to move the body but you don't have a car handy,' said Norman. 'How far would you want to carry it?'

'Not far, that's for sure,' said Winter.

'Right,' said Norman. He pointed to the houses on the left side of the street. 'So, on that basis, we know the victim was found in the middle house of that terrace, so it's quite possible the murder could have taken place in one of the houses on this street. Agreed?'

'Makes sense to me,' said Winter. 'Where shall we start?'

'Let's start at number two, and go up that side. Then we'll walk back to here, have a five-minute break, and do the same on the other side.'

An hour later they reached the last house on the street.

'So much for my brilliant theory,' said Norman, as he pushed open the door of number nineteen.

'Well, we had to start somewhere,' said Winter. 'And as theories go, it makes sense.'

'Only if the victim came here with someone, or came here to meet someone.'

'You mean for sex?' said Winter. 'Seriously? I think I'd rather do it in the back of my car than in a dump like this.'

'Yeah, it's not exactly the Ritz, is it?' said Norman gloomily. 'There again, it takes all sorts, and it's not our place to judge.'

After a quick look at the ground floor, they made their way up a rickety flight of stairs to the two bedrooms. Taking a room each, they pushed open the doors and stepped inside.

'You'd better take a look in here, Norm,' called Winter. 'I think we may have found what we're looking for.'

Norman peered in over his shoulder. There were two thin mattresses, not unlike yoga mats, lying on the floor. What appeared to be a large sleeping bag had been thrown into one corner of the room, and a rucksack stood forlornly beneath the window.

'Quite the love nest,' said Norman.

Winter pointed to another corner.

'There's a dark stain on the floor over there. It could be blood.'

'We'd better tell the boss,' said Norman, 'and we need the SOCOs up here. They'll get everything photographed, bagged up and taken away, and we should ask them to take a sample of whatever that is on the floor. If it's blood and it matches our victim, this could well be our murder scene.'

Five minutes later, Norman led Southall up the stairs and pointed out their find.

'We'll have to get it all taken away for analysis,' he said.

Southall stared at the scene for a full minute before she spoke.

'A couple of yoga mattresses and a sleeping bag,' she said, finally. 'Are you suggesting our victim was on the game?'

'Is it so hard to believe?' asked Norman.

'I don't have a problem believing she was a sex worker,' said Southall. 'But I'm struggling with the idea that she would bring punters all the way out here to a dump like this. And, didn't you tell me there was no evidence that she'd had sex?'

Norman shrugged. 'That's what Bill said. Maybe they didn't get that far.'

Southall didn't look convinced.

'If I'm being honest, I have to admit I find it hard to believe, too,' said Norman. 'But, working girl or not, if that is blood on the floor, and it's hers . . .'

'Yes, I'm not disputing that,' said Southall. 'It's just . . . Didn't you say earlier that she was dressed expensively?'

'Yeah, lots of designer labels.'

'Well then, it doesn't add up, does it? If she was a sex worker making enough money to buy decent clothes to impress the punters, wouldn't she have somewhere better than this to take them to? I would think they'd be a bit disappointed if she brought them out here.'

'Maybe when they got here and the guy saw this place, there was an argument about payment and it got out of hand.'

'That's assuming too much,' said Southall. 'I'm sorry, but I can't see it.'

'Okay, so maybe she wasn't a prostitute. Maybe she was married and she had a boyfriend. Bill said she wasn't wearing a wedding ring when she was found but she had worn one in the past.'

They could hear Winter making his way back up the stairs.

'The SOCOs will be here in a couple of minutes,' he said. 'I've told them you want everything taken away.'

'Make sure they know we need them to check the sleeping bag for DNA,' said Norman. 'However unlikely it might be, we need to know whose DNA is inside it.'

Winter nodded.

'Okay,' said Southall. 'So, the body's gone, and the SOCOs have finished taking number nine apart, yes?'

'They're still searching the wider site for clues, but they've finished at the house, and they'll be over here in a minute or two,' said Winter.

'Okay. Frosty, I'd like you to stay here, make sure they take a sample of that blood, and keep an eye on things,' said Southall. 'I'm going to take Norm back to the ranch and see if we can find out who the dead woman is. And if that idiot Harding gives you any grief, let me know straight away.'

'Yes, boss,' said Winter.

'When the SOCOs have finished, you can use my car to get back,' said Norman, tossing his keys to Winter.

'How did you get on with Harding?' asked Norman as Southall drove them off site.

'He's an arrogant dickhead,' she said.

Norman smiled. 'Yeah. I already knew that.'

'He has a vile temper and he disapproves of women,' said Southall. 'It's a mystery to me how people like him get to be successful.'

'My guess is he's one of the funny handshake mob,' said Norman. 'That's how people like him succeed. It's not what you know, it's who.'

'Whatever it is, I definitely want him checked out,' said Southall. 'He is too keen to get the place demolished, and he has access to the site any time he wants.'

'I couldn't agree more,' said Norman.

* * *

By the time Southall and Norman got back, DC Judy Lane had cleaned and prepared the large whiteboard attached to the wall at the front of the office. A large map of the murder site and surrounding area had been pinned to the wall alongside the board.

'I see you've managed to set the board up ready for us to make a start, Judy,' said Southall. 'Thank you for that. Unfortunately, we can't match your efficiency with much in the way of useful information.'

'I'm afraid I can't offer anything useful either,' said Lane. 'I've spent all afternoon searching through the reports of missing persons, but I can't find anyone even close to being a match for the victim.'

Southall sighed. 'Don't worry, Judy. I have a sneaking suspicion it's going to be that sort of case.'

Norman printed a handful of photographs of the murder scene and victim and pinned them to the board, marked houses number nine and nineteen on the map, added what little information they had and stepped back to admire his handiwork.

Southall came and stood beside him. 'It's not much to start with, is it?'

'I don't think we'll be solving this one in a hurry, that's for sure,' agreed Norman. 'Until we have an identity for our victim, or someone comes forward to report her missing, we're up that famous creek without so much as a hint of a paddle.'

'That's true,' said Southall. 'Though I think that, as our victim is a woman, and until we have reason to think otherwise, we should assume our killer is a man.'

'It usually is,' said Norman wearily. 'But it doesn't really help much, does it?'

'No, it doesn't,' agreed Southall. 'Right now we can't even make an intelligent guess at a motive. I know you said it could be about sex, but I'm not sure I agree that she was a prostitute.'

'Yeah, I've been thinking about that,' said Norman. 'What if I was looking at it the wrong way round? What if she met the guy quite innocently and he took her there against her will? Perhaps he had rape in mind but she put up a fight and he lost control.'

'Or maybe he had murder in mind all along,' suggested Lane.

'We certainly can't rule out either of those scenarios,' said Southall. 'And, frankly, they both work better for me than the first one.'

'Sadly, it doesn't make her any less of a victim,' said Norman.

'There is one thing I'm really struggling to understand,' said Southall. 'Ignore the reason the victim and her killer were in the bedroom at number nineteen and, for a minute, just accept they were there, and for whatever reason he kills her.'

'Okay, I can do that,' said Norman.

'So, having killed her at number nineteen, why would he then move her body to number nine? He would know that all the houses are derelict.'

'Yeah, I was thinking the same thing,' said Norman. 'It would only make sense if he removed all the other evidence as well. I mean, if it wasn't for the mattresses and sleeping bag, would we have even noticed the stain on the floor?'

While they stood talking, Winter arrived back and handed Norman his car keys.

'Everything okay, Frosty?' asked Southall.

'They've bagged and tagged everything, and taken a sample of the blood,' said Winter.

'It's definitely blood?' asked Norman.

'That's what they said.'

'Did you remember the fuel can?' asked Norman.

'Bagged and tagged,' said Winter. 'And while I think of it, the builders said they didn't leave it there.'

'What's this?' asked Southall.

'There was a full petrol can inside number nine,' said Norman. 'It's probably nothing, but I thought it was worth checking out.'

'Goodness. Look at the time,' said Southall. 'I don't know about you guys, but I don't think we can do much more today. Let's call it a day and start again in the morning. Hopefully Dr Bridger will be able to give us something to work with.'

'What do you want me to do in the morning?' asked Winter.

'Joe Harding,' she said. 'I want you to find out everything you can about him.'

Winter nodded. 'Sure. Is he a suspect?'

'They're all suspects,' said Southall. 'And right now, he happens to be the one who stands out the most.'

CHAPTER THREE

Tuesday, 14 March
7.58 a.m.

Six storeys high, the Madoc Building looked incongruous among the surrounding two-storey dwellings, there was nothing of similar height for miles around. Consequently, locals tended to despise it, judging it a testament to planning office corruption, although their claim had never been verified.

The lift sighed to a halt at the top floor. Four passengers spilled out, three of them turning left, heading towards the restaurant and the daily bargain breakfast. The fourth, a teenager in a hoodie, stopped at the lift doors and knelt to retie her shoelace.

After a quick glance to make sure no one was watching, she hurried off in the opposite direction to the restaurant, where a flight of stairs led up to the roof. By the time she reached the last few steps she had begun to wonder why she had chosen this way out. It would probably have been a lot less hard work to have stepped in front of a bus, but that wouldn't have been fair on the unfortunate driver. This way, no one would have to spend the rest of their life with what she was about to do weighing on their conscience.

At last she reached the door to the roof. It was a fire escape door with one of those bars across it, so all she had to do was push down hard and it would open. She stopped for a moment to get her breath back, then gave it an almighty shove. With a satisfying clatter the bar crashed down and the door flew open. The time was exactly eight a.m.

Down in the basement, in the security office, the security guard saw a light on the control panel begin to flash. He took a sip of his tea, put the cup down and flicked a switch. The top left-hand screen on the small bank of monitors flickered into life. The image showed a door up on the roof swinging open in the breeze.

'Now that can't have blown open,' he muttered. 'Someone must be up there.'

He flicked another switch and the screen showed a view of the roof. He rotated the camera slightly and a small figure came into view, walking away from the door. He watched, intrigued, as the figure headed across the roof. His curiosity turned to concern as the figure climbed over the safety rail and walked to the parapet wall, just two feet from the edge of the roof.

'Oh crap,' he said, out loud. 'We've got a jumper.'

He looked at the clock as he reached for the phone: *8:02*.

* * *

DI Sarah Southall was out jogging when she received the call. Even so, it took her less than twenty minutes to get to the store. By that time all the roads around the building had been closed to traffic, and an ambulance and fire engine were on the way. A local police patrol car was parked in front of the store, and a harassed looking PC was doing his best to turn away the early shoppers. Southall flashed her warrant card, made her way into the building and stepped into the lift.

When she reached the top floor, she ran to the top of the stairs and through the door to the roof, where DC Catren Morgan was waiting for her.

Morgan pointed to a small figure sitting on the parapet wall running around the roof. She had her back to them, and with her hood up it was impossible to see her face.

'Has anyone spoken to her?' asked Southall.

'Not yet, boss, but there's a negotiator on the way.'

'Do we know who she is?'

Morgan shook her head. 'No idea. The security guard thinks she's a teenager, but she's been keeping her face hidden, so it's hard to be sure.'

Southall studied the wall around the roof. It was about three feet high and the girl was sitting on it with her back to them, her feet dangling over the side. If she slipped forward from the wall, just one more step would take her over the edge.

'I'll understand if you don't want to come with me,' she said.

Morgan frowned. 'I'm sorry?'

'I'm going to go and talk to her.'

'But I've arranged for a trained negotiator to come,' said Morgan.

'Yes, so you said, but I don't think it's right that we stand here talking while she's over there on her own. At this time of the morning it could take a negotiator hours to get here from Cardiff, and in the meantime she could jump. I don't want to have to tell her parents we stood back and let their daughter jump to her death, do you?'

'You're right,' said Morgan. 'I'm with you.'

Cautiously, Southall made her way towards the girl on the wall, Morgan trailing in her wake. A stiff, cool breeze was blowing into their faces. Southall shivered and pulled the collar of her coat up around her ears. She looked over at the young girl on the wall — she must have been freezing.

'What's the plan then, boss?' asked Morgan, standing beside her.

'Well, according to plan A, one of us would magically transform into Wonder Woman,' murmured Southall. 'Since that doesn't seem to have happened, we'll have to go with plan B.'

'What's plan B?'

'To tell you the truth, there is no plan B. I'm just going to wing it and try to get her talking. I'm sure the expert will arrive and tell me it was the wrong thing to do, but we can't just hang around and do nothing. If I can get close enough, I'll try to grab her.'

'What do you want me to do?'

'Two of us might make her panic, so you stay back — but keep your wits about you. If I do manage to get hold of her, you'll need to get your arse over there as quick as you can.'

Since they were approaching the girl from behind, Southall was careful to make plenty of noise, so as not to startle her. She stopped at the safety barrier, and called out.

'Hello! I'm Detective Inspector Southall but you can call me Sarah. I've got my friend Catren with me. Is it all right if we come over there and talk to you?'

The hunched figure gave a shrug, and turned briefly in their direction.

'If you're some sort of negotiator and you've come to talk me down, you're wasting your time.'

'There is a negotiator on the way,' said Southall. 'I thought we could have a chat while we wait, if that's okay?'

The girl shrugged again.

'Talk if you want to, but don't come too close. If you try and grab me, I'll jump.'

'I only want to talk,' said Southall. 'I promise we won't come any closer than you say. We'll walk over to your right, so you can see us, then you can tell us where to stop. Catren will stay back and I'll come a bit closer, but you get to decide how close we can come. Is that okay?'

Just as she had promised, they gave the girl a wide berth, keeping well to her right, about fifteen feet away. When they reached the perimeter wall, Southall said, 'Catren is going to stay here. Is that okay?'

'As long as she really does stay there,' the girl said.

'I will, I promise,' said Morgan.

Southall slowly approached the girl until she was about six feet away.

'That's close enough,' said the girl.

'Okay. Fine. I'll stop here. Is it all right if I sit down? Only that wind is going right through me.'

'Sit wherever you want, just keep away from me.'

Very slowly, and deliberately, Southall sat down in the lee of the wall, sheltered from the breeze.

'What's your name?' she asked.

'Erin.'

'Does Erin have a surname?'

'Just Erin works for me.'

'Okay, Just Erin. Aren't you cold?'

'Freezing,' said Erin. She swung one leg back over the wall so she was sitting astride it, and pushed her hood back to keep the two police officers in view. She was shivering, and her face was white as a ghost.

'I can get you a coat brought over,' said Southall.

'If you were about to jump off a roof, would you be bothered about getting cold?'

'Well, no, I suppose not,' said Southall. 'But whatever the problem is, this isn't going to help, is it?'

Erin said nothing.

'Why don't you tell me about it,' said Southall. 'Perhaps I can help.'

'No one can help. That's why I'm going to jump off this roof.'

'There must be some hope.'

'Why must there be?'

How trite her words must sound, thought Southall.

'I'm sorry. I know it's what people always say, but I believe things really are never as bad as you think they are.'

'You have no idea,' said Erin, grimly. 'As far as I'm concerned, things couldn't be any worse.'

'What makes you say that?'

Erin said nothing.

'How old are you, Erin?'

'Old enough.'

'I'm guessing sixteen? Maybe seventeen. Am I right?'

Erin ignored the question. 'Honestly, if I knew I'd come up all those stairs just to sit here and listen to you, I'd have stepped out in front of a bus instead. It would have been a lot quicker and easier.'

'So why didn't you?'

'It wouldn't be fair on the bus driver, would it? You know what people are like, he would probably have blamed himself, and then he would have had to live with the guilt for the rest of his life.'

'That's a very mature attitude,' Southall said.

'It would be selfish to do that to someone, wouldn't it?'

'And how do you think I'm going to feel if you jump?' asked Southall. 'I can assure you Catren didn't come up here because she wanted to watch you jump. And what about the poor security guard. How's he going to feel?'

'You're not going to make me feel guilty. You're the police. It's your job.'

'Yes, that's true, but we're not robots. We're human beings with feelings, just like bus drivers are. And, in case you didn't know, it's our duty to protect the public, which includes you.'

'I admit it's not the security guard's fault I'm up here,' said Erin. 'But it's not the same for him as it would be for a bus driver. I mean, he's not going to run me down, is he?'

'Of course it isn't his fault. It's not our fault either but, as you said, people blame themselves, don't they? If you jump off this roof, don't you think we're going to feel guilty? We'll probably spend the rest of our lives wondering what we could have done differently. Is that fair?'

Erin's mouth opened once or twice, but no sound came out.

'I don't think you want that to happen,' said Southall. 'Do you?'

'I hadn't thought of it like that,' admitted Erin.

'Anyway, what's the big rush?'

'Huh? How d'you mean?'

'You seem to be in a hurry to die. I'm wondering why.'

'I already told you, because things couldn't get any worse.'

'But look at you,' said Southall. 'You're young, and you're beautiful. Whatever's happened now doesn't mean you can't still have a great life. Do your parents know where you are?'

'What do you think?' said Erin.

'I think they'd probably be worried sick if they knew, don't you?'

'I ran away from home over two years ago. I've not seen them since.'

'Where's home?' asked Southall. 'Are you a Llangwelli girl?'

'A village not far from Llangwelli.'

'If you've been missing for over two years and never been in touch, don't you think your parents have suffered enough?' asked Southall.

'It's not that simple,' said Erin. 'My parents are the problem.'

'So, talk to them. You can't solve a problem without talking about it.'

'That's why I came back, but it's complicated.'

'D'you know what I think?' said Southall. 'I think you came here hoping to see your family, but now you're here you're not sure. The thing is, these situations always seem complicated but once you get talking they're never as bad as you think they're going to be.'

Erin studied Southall's face for a few moments, seeming to turn this over in her mind.

'Did they know you were coming?' asked Southall, crossing her fingers. Had she planted a seed of doubt?

'My mum does.'

'I can't believe you care more about the feelings of a bus driver you've never met than about the feelings of your family,' Southall continued. 'You can't arrange to come back after two years and do this to them. How do you think they are going to feel? They'll never forgive themselves.'

'You have no idea how my parents will feel.'

'Actually, I do,' said Southall. 'I lost my own daughter in a traffic accident a few years ago.'

Erin's eyes widened. She was really looking at her now. 'Oh. Was it your fault? Were you driving?'

'I wasn't there. She was with my ex-husband and his girl-friend. They were on a day out when a lorry ploughed into their car.'

'That must have been hard. How did you get over it?'

'Ah, well, that's the thing. You never do get over something like that. It will always be there, just as it will be for your parents. I only managed because I got help and learned how to live with it.'

Erin considered this for a moment. 'Was it really bad?'

'It was so bad I can't describe it. No parent expects to outlive their children, but at least I know I lost my daughter to a freak accident. I'm sure your parents will feel much worse knowing you chose to die.'

Erin remained silent. The seconds ticked by.

'All right,' she said. 'If you were me, what would you do?'

'Well, I wouldn't jump for a start,' said Southall. 'We're only six floors up. I can tell you that's not necessarily high enough for certain death.'

'It isn't?'

'You'd definitely break a few bones, and probably mangle some of your internal organs, but there's no guarantee you'd die.'

'I don't think that's true,' said Erin. 'I think you're lying.'

'Maybe,' said Southall. 'But what if I'm right? Anyway, you asked me what I would do if I was you.'

'Yeah, go on then, what would you do?'

'When I thought I couldn't get any lower, I found a reason to go on. I wanted to make a difference so I lost myself in my job and studied for promotion.'

'Well, goody for you,' said Erin sarcastically. 'I don't happen to have a job.'

'There must be something you care about.'

'I care about the state of the planet. Our leaders are too scared to do anything, and none of the older generation seem to care.'

'You sound like an eco-warrior.'

'I've done a bit,' admitted Erin. 'I suppose you think people like me are too young to know what we're talking about, and we should keep quiet and stay at home.'

'No, I actually think you're right,' said Southall. 'Our leaders don't seem to have the stomach for it. Secretly, I actually admire those who try to get people to wake up and see what's happening.'

'Why secretly?' asked Erin.

'I'm a detective inspector in the police. It wouldn't look very good if I openly condoned law-breaking, would it?'

Erin smiled.

'Yeah, right. I see what you mean.'

'But there are ways you can support a cause without breaking the law,' said Southall.

'What? You mean like working for one of those official charities?'

'Why not?' asked Southall.

'The stuff they do never seems to have any impact, does it? You know, petitions and the like.'

'Okay, if you're not sure about that, why not do something for yourself? Do you have a bucket list?'

'Bucket list? What's that mean?'

'It's a list of all the things you really want to do. You make a list of them and work your way through it.'

'Yeah, but do things like what?'

'Well,' said Sarah, 'I've never told anyone this before, but I've always wanted to do a parachute jump.'

Erin broke into a smile. 'You're kidding.'

'No, seriously.'

'Aren't you too old for something like that?'

'Excuse me, young lady,' said Southall, indignantly. 'I'm not that old! Anyway, there's no age limit as long as you're fit enough.'

'Cool. I wouldn't mind having a go at that,' said Erin, and then her face fell. 'But I've got no money and, anyway, how is that going to help save the planet? It's not exactly eco-friendly, is it?'

'You could use it to raise some money and make a statement.'

Erin looked sceptical.

'I've a friend who's a journalist,' said Southall. 'She knows lots of people in all sorts of places. I bet if I asked her she would know someone who could help arrange it.'

'Are you for real?'

'We could even get someone to video the whole thing.' She glanced back at Morgan. 'Catren's a bit of a daredevil. I bet she'd be up for that. Wouldn't you, Catren?'

Morgan, who had only caught the occasional word, saw Southall glance at her and gave a thumbs-up.

'There you are,' Southall said. 'I told you she'd be up for it.'

'Oh, wow! A video would be really cool,' said Erin.

'What else would you like to do? Think of some other things that are just for you.'

'I've always wanted to go to a football match to see the big teams, and a real rock concert, like at the Millennium Stadium or somewhere. I've never been to anything like that.'

'My journalist friend might be able to arrange those things too,' said Southall.

'You're just saying all this to get me off this roof, aren't you?' said Erin, doubtfully. 'I bet if I come down now I'll never see you again.'

'I said I'd ask my friend to help arrange your parachute jump.'

'How do I know you mean it?'

'We've got a witness,' said Southall, nodding across at her colleague. 'Catren heard what I promised. Trust me, she wouldn't let me leave you stranded.'

Erin didn't look convinced.

'Nah,' she said. 'You're her boss. She'll just do whatever you say. You lot are all the same.'

Southall beckoned to Morgan.

'Believe me, Erin, we are definitely not all the same. Catren isn't. She'd make me keep a promise whether I'm her boss or not. Ask her if you don't believe me.'

Erin looked at Morgan.

'Sarah's promised to ask her friend to organise a parachute jump for me, and she's volunteered you to come along and video the whole thing,' Erin said.

Morgan looked at Southall in surprise. This was a side of her boss she hadn't seen before.

'Has she now? It's a good job I've done it before, then.'

'She also says you would make sure she kept her promise,' added Erin.

Morgan grinned at her. 'Oh, I certainly will. You can bet on it.'

Erin looked from Morgan to Southall. 'Yeah, but you're just saying it, aren't you?'

'All right, you tell me how I can prove we mean it,' said Southall.

Erin thought for a moment, and smiled.

'Here,' she said, fumbling in her pocket. 'Tell it to my phone.'

She took a mobile phone from her pocket and pressed a couple of keys.

'It's set to record your voice,' she said. 'You'll have to come here and speak into it.'

'I'm not going to sit on that wall,' said Southall. 'It's much too cold in this wind. You'll have to come back over this side.'

Erin tutted.

'I don't know. You old people.' She swung her other leg over the wall and slid down onto her haunches. She shuffled a little closer to Southall and handed her the phone.

'What do you want me to say?'

'Just tell me who you are, and how you promise to ask your friend to arrange a parachute jump for me. That way you can't pretend you never said it.'

Southall did as she was asked. She shuffled closer to Erin and, as she handed the phone back, slipped an arm around the girl's shoulder and gently pulled her close.

'Your battery is nearly dead.'

Erin looked down at the blank screen.

'Yeah, it's on its last legs,' she said, switching the phone off and slipping it into her pocket. 'There aren't many places you can charge a phone when you live rough, so you have to learn how to save power and eke it out as long as you can.'

'Anyway, as I was saying,' said Southall. 'You could use the parachute jump to make a statement and raise some money for your cause. With a bit of publicity, I bet we could raise a small fortune.'

'Seriously?' asked Erin, leaning into Southall.

'Cross my heart.' Southall drew the girl closer, while Morgan eased herself down on Erin's other side. Erin began to sob quietly.

'It's okay,' said Southall. 'You're safe now.'

They sat in silence until Erin stopped crying. Then Southall raised Erin's face towards her and wiped the tears from her cheeks.

'Are you okay?' she asked.

'I came here to meet my mum but she never turned up. She said she was going away for a week but it's been ten days now.'

'Have you asked your father about her?'

'I haven't spoken to him since I left home. Anyway, I don't think he would know. They're separated. Besides, I need to speak to her before I see him. Like I said, it's complicated.'

'How complicated?'

'It's not important.'

'It might be. Perhaps it's the reason your mum's missing.'

Erin rolled her eyes.

'If you must know, we did a project on DNA at school. I thought it would be cool to send off samples from me, Mum and Dad.'

Southall immediately realised the potential problems such an action could create.

'Ah. I see,' she said. 'Did you tell them what you were doing before you sent the samples away?'

Erin shook her head. 'No, I didn't. And when the results came back I found out my dad isn't my real dad.'

'And that's why you ran away?'

'Yeah. It sort of blew my mind and I couldn't deal with it. I mean, why didn't they tell me?'

'There could be any number of reasons,' said Southall. 'Didn't you ask?'

'I was too hurt at the fact they'd kept it a secret from me, so I packed a bag and left.'

'I think you should have asked the question first.'

'Yeah, well, that's why I've come back. I was supposed to be meeting Mum last night so she could explain, but she didn't turn up. I think she's ashamed of me and doesn't want to see me.'

'You do rush to conclusions, don't you?' said Southall. 'Why on earth would she think that?'

'Because it's my fault they split. Everything was great until I did that stupid DNA test.'

'Have you tried calling her?'

'She's not answering her phone,' said Erin. 'Can you do something for me, Sarah?'

'What's that?'

'Can you find her?'

'We can definitely make some enquiries. And if you give us her mobile phone number, we might be able to trace her that way,' said Southall. 'But only if you come down off this roof, so we can get you to a hospital.'

* * *

By the time Southall and Morgan had handed Erin over to two waiting paramedics, it was approaching midday. They waved goodbye as the paramedics closed up the ambulance and set off for the hospital. Southall and Morgan headed for their cars.

'I want you to follow her over to the hospital,' said Southall. 'Make sure she's okay, get her full name, and see what she can tell you about her mother. I'm going home to get changed, then I'll be back at the office.'

'Okay, boss.' Morgan turned to go, then turned back. 'This parachute jump you promised. You do know I'm not going to let you duck out of it, don't you?'

Smiling, Southall opened her car door and got in. 'Oh yes, Catren. I'm relying on it.'

'Good for you, boss!' she called out to the departing car.

CHAPTER FOUR

At the hospital, Morgan sat with Erin while she waited to be seen.

'You said you left home over two years ago. So, what have you been doing?' she asked.

'I've been travelling around with my boyfriend.'

'Does he have a name?'

'He's called Wozzy.'

'And how old is Wozzy?'

'Nineteen.'

'Did he ask you to run away with him?'

'What, like did he entice me away from home? No, he didn't. I met him in London.'

'And you've been travelling around together ever since?'

'More or less, yeah.'

'I'm guessing that means you've been living rough.'

'Mostly. But you have to accept a bit of hardship if you want to change things.'

'Change things?'

'The state of the planet. We're trying to get people to wake up and see what's happening.'

'Ah, yes, I remember, you told my boss. You're eco-warriors.'

'I suppose you think we're wasting our time,' said Erin.

'Not at all. I agree people need to be made to wake up to the reality, I'm just not sure you guys are going about it the right way.'

'How would you do it then?'

'Trust me, if I knew that, I'd be doing it, but I'm afraid I don't,' said Morgan. 'Are you intending to protest while you're in Llangwelli, or are you only here to see your mum?'

Erin smiled. 'Even eco-warriors need a break now and then. I'm just here to see my mum — if you can find her.'

'Well, I'm going to need some information if we're going to track her down,' said Morgan, producing her notebook.

'Like what?'

'Well, her name for a start.'

'Dilys. Dilys Watkins.'

'Address?'

'She moved out of our house to a flat, but I can't remember the address.'

'Will your father know it?'

'I suppose so.'

'What's his name?'

'Ross.'

'And his address?'

'What if he's moved too?'

'Give me the address you have. Even if he has moved, I'll be able to trace him easily enough.'

Erin reeled off the address.

'What's your mum's mobile number?' Morgan asked, and wrote that down too.

'Okay. Description. What does your mum look like?' asked Morgan.

'I've got some photos on my phone,' said Erin.

She switched on her phone, which had been charging while they waited, found the photos and handed the phone to Morgan. Morgan stared at them, barely suppressing a frown.

'I can see where you get your good looks,' she said. 'Can I share one? It's easier than trying to write a description.'

'Yeah, sure. Help yourself,' said Erin.

Morgan downloaded what she considered to be the best photograph, and handed the phone back to Erin.

'Can I have your father's phone number?'

'Why do you need that?'

'He might know where your mother is, and I should tell him you're here.'

'Why do you have to?'

'Because he's your father and you're only sixteen. That means he's entitled to know what's going on.'

Erin looked desperate.

'Is there any particular reason why you don't want to see him?' asked Morgan. 'Don't you like him?'

'It's not that. He's been a great dad, but what's he going to think of me now he knows I'm not his daughter?'

'I'm sure it would have been a shock for him to find out, but he'll still love you, whatever.'

'You don't understand. Everything sort of blew up after the DNA results came back. Mum and Dad did nothing but scream at each other, the constant arguing was doing my head in. They were never like that before. That's why I don't want to see him until I've spoken to Mum. Can't you put him off until I've spoken to her?'

'If you really don't want to see him you don't have to, but if you've been missing for over two years, he's bound to be worried sick about you. Now we've found you, we have to tell him, and that you're safe, but we don't have to say where you are.'

A nurse bustled into the waiting room and called out Erin's name.

She and Morgan stood up.

'Are you going to be okay?' asked Morgan.

'I think so,' said Erin.

'You've got my mobile number,' said Morgan. 'Let me know what's going on. I'll come back later. Promise me you won't do anything stupid in the meantime.'

'I promise.' Erin followed the nurse.

As soon as she'd gone, Catren Morgan ran back to her car and called Southall.

'Are you sure?' asked Southall.

'The photo was taken before Erin ran away two years ago, so I wouldn't stake my life on it, but there were enough similarities to make me look twice. I'll send the photo now, and you can see what you think.'

'What are you doing now?'

'I said I'd come back to see Erin later, meanwhile I'll be back at the office.'

* * *

Southall took Morgan's call just as she was driving into the Llangwelli police station car park. She sat in her car and studied the photograph Morgan had sent. No wonder her young colleague had sounded so worried.

Frowning, she made her way into the incident room. 'How are we doing?'

'The initial forensic reports don't help much,' said Norman. 'They have found some interesting fibres on the victim's clothes that they think may be from a carpet, but that's not confirmed yet.'

Southall turned to Lane. 'Have you managed to identify the victim?'

'Sorry, but we've got nothing so far,' said Lane. 'I tried widening my search to the national missing persons reports but there's still no one that comes close.'

'I think we're going to be relying on dental records to identify this one,' said Norman. 'Congratulations, by the way.'

'Pardon?'

'Your jumper. I hear you managed to talk her down.'

'Oh, Erin. Yes, poor kid. Another confused teenager who has fallen out with her parents.'

'We've all been there, haven't we?' said Norman.

'But this was over two years ago, Norm. She ran away when she was fourteen and she's been living rough with her boyfriend ever since, trying to save the planet.'

'So, why come back now?' he asked.

'To see her mother, who didn't show up, so now she thinks her mum doesn't really want to see her. Hence the suicidal thoughts. I said we'd see if we can find out what's happened. Catren's been with her at the hospital, hoping to learn a bit more.' Southall grimaced. 'She's just sent me a photograph I think you need to see.'

'What does that look mean?' Norman asked. 'Do you know something we don't?'

'Take a look for yourself,' said Southall, passing Norman her phone.

'Who's this?' he asked.

'Her name is Dilys Watkins. D'you think she could be our victim?'

Norman stared at the photo, and then across at the photos of their victim pinned up on the whiteboard.

'It's difficult to say. I mean it could be, but our victim is blonde, and she definitely isn't laughing in our photos.'

'That's what I thought when I saw it but this photo was taken more than two years ago and, let's face it, people change their hair colour all the time.'

Norman looked enquiringly at Southall.

'We don't know the whole story yet,' she said. 'But, basically, a young girl called Erin Watkins was about to jump from the roof of the Madoc Building, so we went up to talk her out of it. She told us that two years ago she ran away from home after she found out that the man she thought of as her dad isn't her birth father. She came back here having arranged to meet her mother on Sunday night, but Mum seems to have gone missing. Apparently, she told Erin she'd be away for a few days but she should have been back by now. She isn't, and she's not answering her phone.'

'I don't like the sound of this,' said Norman. 'It's too much of a coincidence.'

'That's exactly what I'm thinking,' said Southall. 'We need to get a more recent photograph of Dilys Watkins, but I don't want Erin to know anything about this until we know for sure.'

'Doesn't her father know where Dilys is?'

'They're separated, apparently,' said Southall. 'I haven't had a chance to speak to him yet, but if we're right, we'll have to ask him to identify the body.' She turned to address Winter. 'And, while I think of it, Frosty, can you run the name Erin Watkins through the database? I want to know if she was reported missing. It would have been around two years ago or thereabouts.'

'I'll do it now,' said Winter.

'I've got Dilys Watkins's mobile phone number, Judy,' said Southall, scribbling the number down and handing it to Lane. 'See what you can do with it.'

'Shall we go and see the girl's father now?' asked Norman.

'We'll have to leave it for a couple of hours,' said Southall. 'We have a post-mortem to attend.'

'Before I've had my lunch?' asked Norman. 'Jeez, you kept that quiet.'

'I'm sorry, Norm. I would have told you first thing but it must have slipped my mind while we were up on that roof.'

'I suppose, in the circumstances I'll forgive you,' he said. 'I guess saving a life is more important than my stomach.'

Southall smiled.

'I thought you'd be pleased it wasn't straight after your breakfast. And I thought you liked Bill Bridger.'

'You know I don't have a problem with Bill. It's what we're going to watch him do that turns my stomach.'

'Come on,' said Southall. 'I'll buy you a sandwich afterwards to make up for it.'

'I can't promise I'll be able to eat it,' said Norman.

As they left the building, big heavy drops of rain began to fall.

Norman sighed. 'Jeez, do we really need more rain?' he said. 'I swear I'm beginning to grow webs between my toes.'

* * *

'In deference to Norm's queasiness, I've already started,' said Bridger, as Southall and Norman were shown into the mortuary.

'I hope we haven't missed anything important,' said Southall.

'It's okay, Sarah,' said Norman. 'It's not watching the organs being removed that's important, it's what the organs reveal. Isn't that right, Bill?'

'Yes, I suppose it is,' said Bridger.

'And what do they reveal?' asked Southall.

'They were too badly damaged to be much use, to be honest,' said Bridger.

'What does that mean?' asked Southall.

'I'll get to that in a minute,' said Bridger. 'I can tell you her last meal was fish and chips, and she had that a couple of hours before she died. I can show you, if you like.'

'No, that's okay,' said Norman. 'I think we can trust your opinion on that one.'

'Obviously I haven't got a toxicology report for you yet, but I didn't find anything to suggest drink or drugs were involved. However, I have established a time of death, which was between eight and midnight on Friday night, and I can also tell you the cause of death.'

He led them to the autopsy table, where their victim lay, covered in a shroud.

'Jeez, I didn't realise she was so small,' said Norman.

'Five feet one inch tall, weighing in at barely fifty kilos,' confirmed Bridger.

'Can you convert that?' asked Norman. 'After all these years I still can't get my head around all this metric stuff.'

'For you, Norm, that's a couple of pounds short of eight stone.'

'You make that sound as if it has some particular relevance,' said Southall. 'Does it?'

'Yes, I think it might. Norm will remember, when I first examined her I said I didn't think she had died where she was found.'

'Yeah, that's right,' said Norman. 'And we subsequently found evidence at number nineteen that suggested she may have died there. I guess what you're saying is Forensics couldn't find any drag marks because she was light enough to carry, right?'

'Correct. You wouldn't need to be an Olympic weight-lifter to carry a woman this small,' said Bridger. 'A reasonably fit man, using a fireman's lift, would be able to carry her quite a distance without too much difficulty. In fact, a fit, strong woman could do it.'

'Well, if the murder scene was at number nineteen,' said Norman, 'why would the killer have bothered moving her?'

'Are you absolutely certain it was the murder scene?' asked Bridger doubtfully.

'Well, we can't say for sure, but what looks like blood was found on the floor. Are you saying it's not?'

'I won't be able to confirm that one way or the other until we get the results from the blood,' said Bridger.

'But you think it's unlikely, right?' said Southall. 'So, if she didn't die where we found her, or in number nineteen, where did she die?'

'I'm afraid it's up to you to find that out,' said Bridger. 'It'll be clearer when I tell you how she died. Then you'll understand why I have my doubts about number nineteen.'

He pulled back the covering shroud. Slight, pale, she had been laid out face down, the pallor of her skin serving to highlight the darkness of the bruises that covered large areas of her back and legs.

'It's undignified for her to be laid out like this, but I wanted you to see—'

'Holy shit!' said Norman. 'Whoever did this must be some sort of psycho.'

'In this case, not a "whoever" but a "whatever",' said Bridger. 'Her injuries are consistent with being hit by a vehicle travelling at speed.' He pointed to her legs. 'You can see from the impact wounds that both legs are broken above the knee which suggests it was a vehicle with plenty of ground clearance.'

'Well, that definitely didn't happen in the bedroom at number nineteen,' said Norman.

'What was it, some sort of four by four?' asked Southall.

'That's my guess,' said Bridger. 'Note the injuries higher up her back. They confirm she was hit from behind and was almost certainly thrown over the bonnet and into the windscreen.' He pointed to the back of her head. 'Which explains the trauma sustained to the back of her head.' Now he pointed to her left shoulder. 'You can see there a small tattoo of a bluebird. It doesn't tell us anything about how she died but it might help when it comes to identifying her.'

'Am I right in thinking the vehicle that did this would be damaged?' asked Southall.

Bridger nodded. 'Probably, but not necessarily. It would depend on what vehicle it was, but there could be damage to the front panels, the bonnet, and probably a bull's-eye on the windscreen.'

'So, it looks as if someone ran her down, then put her in the car and took her to where she was found,' said Norman.

'We have found some fibres that could be from a carpet in the back of a car, but she wasn't necessarily taken there straight away,' said Bridger. 'Lividity suggests she could have been laid out flat on her back for a while after death.'

'She could have been laid out at number nineteen,' said Norman. 'But why? Why take her there and then move her again? It makes no sense.'

'Fortunately, it's not in my remit, to work that out,' said Bridger. 'That's down to you guys.'

'So, we're looking for a damaged four by four and an accident scene that could be just about anywhere,' said Southall. 'Just what we need.'

'We may be able to help you narrow down the scene,' said Bridger. 'There was some plant material and mud on her clothes. I've sent it off to a friend who specialises in soil and flora. No guarantees, of course, and it won't happen overnight, but we might get lucky.'

'Any signs of sexual activity?' asked Southall.

'Not recently,' said Bridger.

'What about an ID? Have you got the dental records yet?'

'I've sent them off. If we're lucky and she's reasonably local we should get a hit, but I doubt if I will see any results until tomorrow.'

'Is her hair dyed?' asked Southall.

'Why, yes,' said Bridger, looking surprised. He pointed to the top of her head. 'If you look closely, you can see the dark roots.'

'Oh, crap,' muttered Norman.

Bridger glanced at Norman, then back to Southall.

'Why do you ask? D'you know her?'

Southall produced her mobile phone and showed him the photograph of Dilys Watkins.

'We think this is a photograph of our victim in happier times.'

Bridger studied the photograph.

'I think you're right,' he said. 'But I need to have DNA or dental records to officially confirm her identity.'

'I think Sarah was hoping you would tell us we were wrong,' said Norman.

Bridger looked enquiringly at Southall. Her chin quivered.

'If we're right this is the body of Dilys Watkins who was supposed to be meeting her daughter, Erin, two nights after she died but never showed up,' she said. 'It's a long story. I'll tell you later.'

'Are you okay, Sarah?' asked Bridger. 'Can I get you a cup of tea? Something stronger?'

She took out a tissue and blew her nose.

'No, I'm fine, thanks,' she said, 'and thank you for sharing your findings.'

'No problem,' said Bridger. 'It's what I'm here for. I'll send a full report later.'

'Come on, Norm, we'd better get going.'

* * *

'This job can be crappy sometimes, can't it?' said Norman when they were back in their car.

Southall sighed. 'With a fragile daughter involved, we need to think about the best way to approach this.'

'There's no shame in showing your emotions sometimes, you know,' said Norman.

'I don't do the poor weak woman bit, Norm. You should know that by now.'

'Trust me, Sarah, I think we all know.'

'Well, if you still want that sandwich, you'd better change the subject pronto,' warned Southall.

'Consider it done,' said Norman. He was used to Southall's evasiveness whenever he embarked on a conversation involving the emotions. He shook his head slightly and smiled to himself.

The radio was tuned into the local station and as it happened, they were just in time for the local news. Norman, concentrating on his driving, wasn't really listening, until Southall swore loudly.

'What?' he asked.

'Our murder. It's all over the bloody news,' she said. 'How the hell did they get hold of it?'

When Norman paid attention to what the newsreader was saying, he realised why she was so angry. 'From the way they're telling the story, I'd say it's that guy Harding who tipped them off. I bet he called them because he's pissed off with us. He probably sees this as an opportunity to get some publicity for his redevelopment scheme.'

'If it is him, I'll have his bloody balls for paperweights,' Southall growled.

'At least they didn't mention the victim,' said Norman.

'Only because they don't know who she is.'

'When I spoke to Harding, he said he was going to call Nathan Bain to complain about me,' said Norman.

'Yes, I know, but Superintendent Bain backed us to the hilt. And he certainly wouldn't have given him permission to tell the press, would he?'

'No way,' said Norman. 'Knowing Nathan, if Harding tried to interfere with our investigation, he would have told him where to go. Maybe that's what's happened and now Harding's trying to get his own back.'

'Let's see how he feels when I keep his site closed down for weeks!' Southall said.

'Why don't you ask Nathan to deal with this?' suggested Norman. 'According to Harding they're like bosom buddies, although I suspect he's kidding himself. Nathan can speak to Harding and tell him to keep away from the media.'

'This sort of thing makes me so bloody angry.'

'I suspect Harding makes most people angry,' said Norman.

Southall said nothing.

'I understand your anger, Sarah, I really do,' said Norman. 'But we need you focused on this investigation and, trust me, Nathan excels at dealing with people like Harding. I guarantee you he'll bring you those paperweights gift-wrapped, and what's more, he'll enjoy doing it.'

'I'm not sure I want someone else to do my dirty work for me,' Southall muttered.

'At least think about it,' said Norman. 'Personally, I think it would be better to focus your attention on the case — but you're the boss.'

Southall raised her eyebrows.

Norman fell silent. He'd made his point and knew not to push it any further.

CHAPTER FIVE

It was late afternoon by the time Southall and Norman returned to the office. Southall went across to speak to Winter.

'Any luck?'

'Just as you suggested, Erin Watkins was reported missing by her parents just over two years ago.'

'What was the outcome?'

'She was last seen getting on a train to London. She's listed as a runaway.'

'Thank you,' said Southall. 'At least we know she's telling the truth about that.' She turned to Lane. 'As soon as you get a chance, Judy, I want you to get in touch with every car windscreen repair business within twenty miles. I want to know if anyone has requested a replacement windscreen for a four by four vehicle.'

'No problem,' said Lane.

'And your searches?'

'I haven't had time to do anything with the mobile number yet, but I have tried searching the database for Dilys Watkins. She's definitely not been reported missing, but I did find something interesting. Thirteen months ago she made a complaint that someone was stalking her.'

'Was the stalker identified?'

'According to the case file, it was her husband, Ross Watkins.'

'Really?' said Southall. 'Now that is interesting. Where was the complaint made?'

'Here in Llangwelli,' said Lane.

'What was the outcome?'

'The file was closed after the investigating officer recommended that no further action was necessary,' said Lane.

'Does it say who the investigating officer was?' asked Southall.

'It's signed DS Marston,' said Lane.

'Marston? Why does that name ring a bell? Oh, yes, I know. Wasn't he the DS here before Norm arrived?'

'Yes, that's right,' said Lane. 'He was useless and you got rid of him.'

All innocence, Southall said, 'Come, now, Judy. Would I do such a thing? I seem to recall he had already applied for a transfer. I merely suggested that he wouldn't be missed and that his talents would be better utilised elsewhere.'

'I think he's at Region now,' said Lane.

'Well, there you are then. I rest my case,' said Southall. 'From what I've seen of Region it's the perfect place for him.'

'Do you want me to ask him if he can recall anything about it?' asked Norman.

'Hold fire on that for now, Norm. We all know our victim is Dilys Watkins, even if it's not yet confirmed by DNA. And now Dilys has been reported missing by Erin, I think we need to interview Ross Watkins and inform him that we've found a body.'

'Fair enough,' said Norman.

'We can always refer to Marston later,' said Southall.

'I've downloaded some more photographs from social media that confirm we're right about Dilys,' said Morgan, looking up from her computer. 'I've got one where she's not laughing, and another with her hair dyed blonde. There's no doubt in my mind that she's our victim.'

'Right,' said Southall. 'Now we're beginning to make some progress. Judy, do you have an address for Ross Watkins?'

'I'll write it down for you,' said Lane.

'I've got his mobile number,' said Morgan. 'I was going to call him and let him know about Erin, but first I wanted to go back to the hospital and see how she's doing. Is that okay with you?'

'Yes, get over to the hospital, but don't call Ross Watkins. We can tell him about Erin.'

'She says she doesn't want to see him,' said Morgan.

'Did she say why?' asked Southall.

'I don't think he's been abusing her or anything like that. She says he's been a great dad but she's worried he won't be the same now he knows he's not her real father. She thinks it would be better to speak to her mother first, and she'll let her know where she stands with him.'

'Ah. Now that's awkward,' said Norman.

'You're telling me,' said Morgan.

'The law says that as Erin was reported missing, he has a right to know she's been found alive,' said Southall. 'But at sixteen, she's not obliged to see him if she doesn't want to.'

'Yes, that's what I told her,' said Morgan. 'But what do I tell her when she asks about her mum? I don't like the idea of lying to her.'

'I understand what you mean,' said Southall. 'This is one of those difficult situations where we're going to be in the wrong whatever we do, but I think we need to bear in mind the fact that Erin was fragile enough to consider suicide this morning. See what her doctor says but, in my opinion, I don't think we should tell her we suspect that her mother's dead until we know beyond a shadow of a doubt that she's our victim. So, for now, just tell her we've started looking for her.'

Morgan looked glum.

'There's no easy way around it, Catren,' said Norman. 'Would you rather tell her we think her mum's dead but we don't actually know for sure?'

Morgan sighed. 'It's just that she's a nice kid, you know?'

'A nice kid, but fragile,' said Norman. 'Unfortunately, this job sometimes deals us a crap hand. It goes with the territory.'

'I know. I can deal with it,' said Morgan.

'Right, then if we're all set, let's go,' said Southall.

* * *

'How are we going to approach this?' asked Norman, as they drew up outside Ross Watkins's house. 'I'm assuming he is a suspect.'

'Of course he is, Norm, he's her estranged husband,' said Southall.

'Right. So, do you want to tell him about Dilys first, or about Erin?'

'Let's see how he reacts when we tell him Erin is here to meet Dilys. We'll play it by ear after that. Unless you've got a better idea.'

'What me? Challenge your strategy? I don't think so,' said Norman.

* * *

The door was opened by a short, stocky man with untidy, shoulder-length hair and a scruffy beard. Ross Watkins had only just turned forty, but life had aged him way beyond that. Dark shadows encircled his eyes, and heavy lines creased what Southall thought would otherwise have been quite a handsome face. She guessed he was a heavy drinker and wondered if the drinking had started after he and his wife separated.

'Ross Watkins?' asked Norman.

'Who wants to know?'

Norman produced his warrant card. 'I'm DS Norman, and this is DI Southall. We're with Llangwelli Police. We'd like to ask you a few questions.'

'What about? Don't tell me you've found my daughter? It's taken you bloody long enough.'

'Can we come in, Mr Watkins?' asked Southall.

'What?' he said. 'It is about Erin, isn't it? Don't tell me she's dead.'

'No, Mr Watkins,' said Southall. 'Erin isn't dead, but I think it would be better if we went inside.'

'But I'm just going to work,' he said. 'I work the late shift.'

'It's important,' said Southall.

'Let me make a phone call,' said Watkins. 'I'll get my mate to clock me in.'

Southall nodded. 'We'll come in and wait.'

Watkins showed them into the lounge, then went into the kitchen to make his phone call. A couple of minutes later, he was back.

'So,' he said. 'What's this all about?'

'Can I call you Ross?' asked Southall.

'It's my name, so yeah, why not?'

'Right then, Ross. I can tell you that Erin has been found, and she's alive and well,' said Southall.

Watkins's face lit up with a huge, beaming smile. 'Oh, that's fantastic. Where is she? When can I bring her home?'

'It's not quite that simple,' said Southall. 'I'm afraid Erin doesn't want to see you at the moment.'

'But that's crazy. Why wouldn't she want to see me? What have I done?'

'I don't think she's blaming you for anything, it's just that she wanted to speak to her mother first.'

Watkins's smile was instantly replaced with a scowl.

'This isn't fair,' he said. 'Erin's my daughter too, you know.'

'Do you know why Erin ran away?' asked Southall.

Watkins looked devastated, he seemed almost to shrink before their eyes.

'Yeah,' he said. 'I didn't know when I first reported her missing, but I found out after.'

'Erin told us about the DNA test,' said Southall. 'It was the shock of finding out. She couldn't deal with it.'

'Shock? Yeah, tell me about it,' said Watkins. 'If it was a shock for her, how do you think I felt?'

'And the police didn't find any trace of her, is that right?'

'All they ever found out was that she'd got on a train to London, but the trail went cold after that. The Met say they did their best, but they drew a blank. I even spent a month up there looking for her myself. Day and night, going to the homeless shelters, the places homeless people gather, anywhere I thought I might find her.'

'That must have been difficult for you,' said Southall.

'It still is,' said Watkins. 'I've never given up hope, but as time went on it seemed obvious she didn't want to be found and wasn't coming back. I couldn't keep looking forever, so after that first month I came back home. And that's when my wife told me she'd known all along why Erin had gone. But then, of course, she knew long before Erin was even born.'

'Is that why you split up?'

Watkins nodded. 'We brought our wedding forward because she was pregnant. We were living together but we hadn't planned on getting married until we could afford our own house. Maybe it was naïve of me, but when she told me she was pregnant, I assumed I must be the father. I thought getting married before Erin was born was the right thing to do.'

'And you never suspected?' asked Norman.

'We were living together when she got pregnant, so why would I?' asked Watkins. 'Are you suggesting that if the person you loved and lived with told you she was pregnant, the first thing you would do was ask her who the father was?'

'Well, no, when you put it like that, I guess not,' said Norman. 'But I can imagine finding out something like that could change your feelings towards your family.'

'I loved Erin the moment she was born, and I still do,' said Watkins. 'Whatever happened before that wasn't her fault.'

'I take it that means your feelings towards Dilys have changed?' asked Southall.

'Before I knew about it, I would have trusted Dilys with my life. I've been trying to come to terms with it ever since. I still love her, and I want to trust her, but since she betrayed me I just can't, no matter how hard I try.'

'Do you know who Erin's biological father is?' asked Southall.

'I have no idea,' said Watkins. 'And Dilys won't tell me.'

There was an awkward silence.

'You said you'd spoken to Erin,' Watkins said. 'Does that mean she's here in Llangwelli?'

'She's in the area but, as I said, she wanted to speak to her mother first. I think she's looking for an explanation before she speaks to you.'

'So I've just got to sit here doing nothing, knowing Erin's nearby, and wait for Dilys to speak to her first? I've been at my wits' end for over two years, and now I have to wait for Dilys? Can't you tell her to get a move on?'

'They were supposed to be meeting on Sunday evening,' said Southall, 'but Dilys didn't show up. Can you think of any reason why?'

'Me?' said Watkins. 'We're separated now. I have my life and she has hers. How should I know why she didn't show up?'

'So, you and Dilys don't speak?'

'We keep in touch. I still care about her even though we're separated, but I try not to interfere.'

'So, you haven't seen Dilys, or spoken to her recently?'

'The last time I spoke to her was the Friday before last.'

'And she didn't mention meeting with Erin?' asked Southall.

'No, she didn't.'

'Can you tell us what you did talk about?' asked Norman.

Watkins sighed. 'She called me to say she was taking a week off to go and see a friend up in Scotland but her car was giving her trouble and she didn't trust it to get her there and back. She asked if she could borrow mine while hers is being fixed.'

'And you let her?' asked Norman.

'Why not? I can manage without it for a while. I can walk to work from here.'

'What about living separate lives?' asked Southall.

'Look, I admit I was bitterly disappointed when I found out what had happened,' said Watkins. 'It's the reason we separated, but I don't hate Dilys. I might not be able to trust her anymore but, as I said, I still care about her and we're still friends. I'll always help her out if I can.'

'And she went for a week?' asked Norman. 'Does that mean you have your car back?'

'Not yet. I told her to keep it until hers is back on the road.'

'Have you heard from Dilys since then?' asked Southall.

'No. I did try calling her mobile but it must have been switched off.'

'When was that?'

'Monday morning.'

'And it was switched off, you say?'

'Or the battery had run down. She's always forgetting to charge the damned thing.'

'Why did you call her?' asked Norman.

'I just wanted to know if she had finished with the car, but it wasn't important. Like I say, I can walk to work from here. If I'm honest it was just an excuse to speak to her, to make sure she was okay. Is there a reason you're asking me all these questions about Dilys?'

Southall and Norman exchanged a look.

'Is there something wrong?' asked Watkins. 'Has something happened to her?'

'There's no easy way to say this, but we think we know why Dilys didn't meet Erin as arranged,' said Southall. 'A woman's body has been found and we think it's Dilys.'

Watkins stared at Southall uncomprehendingly, his face drained of all colour.

'No way. It can't be her,' he said finally. 'There must be some mistake.'

'I'm sorry, Ross,' said Southall.

'Are you sure it's my Dilys?'

'We can't be one-hundred-per cent certain because she was carrying no identification when we found her,' said Southall. 'Did Dilys have a tattoo of a bluebird on her left shoulder?'

Watkins gasped and nodded slowly, tears beginning to glisten in his eyes.

'But it's a common tattoo, isn't it?' he asked desperately. 'Lots of women must have one like that.'

'We need your help, Ross. Would you be prepared to come to the mortuary and identify her?' asked Southall.

'It won't be her,' he said, wringing his hands. 'It can't be. Not my Dilys.'

'There's only one way to be sure, Ross. Please?'

Helplessly he looked up at Southall and nodded.

'Okay. I'll do it.'

CHAPTER SIX

After tramping endless miles of hospital corridor, Morgan finally managed to track down Erin's doctor.

Dr Caroline Brenner was probably of a similar age to Morgan but clearly considered herself superior to a mere detective. She swished her long dark hair back over her shoulder and looked down her nose at Morgan.

'Are you the one who talked Erin down from that roof?'

'Actually, it's my boss who deserves the credit for that, but I was there. I came here to the hospital with her.'

'I suppose I should say well done,' purred the doctor.

'I wouldn't want you to put yourself out,' said Morgan. 'We were just doing our job. Anyway, how is Erin?'

'Physically she's fine, but we won't be able to do a full psychological evaluation until the morning. For now she needs to rest and get some sleep, so if you're hoping to question her you're going to be disappointed. The last thing she needs right now is an interrogation.'

Morgan smiled. 'Actually, that's not why I'm here. When I left Erin earlier, I promised I'd come back to make sure she was okay. I like to keep my promises.'

'Oh, I see. I'm sorry. I assumed—'

'Yeah, well, you assumed wrong,' said Morgan. 'Look, Dr Brenner, I didn't come here to field thinly veiled criticisms from you. I came because I promised Erin I would, and because there are a couple of things you should know before you start poking around inside her head.'

Morgan could see her barbs had the desired effect.

'I don't "poke around" in people's heads,' snapped Brenner, her eyes narrowing to slits.

'And I don't go around interrogating people,' said Morgan. 'Now, do you want to hear what I have to say, or not?'

'What do you think I need to know?'

'Well, for a start, Erin ran away from home over two years ago.'

'Yes, I know that already. She told me.'

'Did she tell you why she ran away?'

'We didn't get that far.'

'Right,' said Morgan. 'I'll let Erin fill you in on the details, but basically, she sent samples of her family's DNA away without telling them, and the results showed that her father isn't her biological father. She ran away after the resulting family meltdown. Her parents are now separated.'

'I suppose that's useful to know,' conceded Brenner.

'Erin came back after contacting her mother. They were supposed to be meeting so her mother could provide some answers. But Mum didn't show up, which is why Erin ended up on the roof of the Madoc Building.'

'I see,' said Brenner. 'So, you're saying she has a mother who doesn't care about her.'

'No, I don't believe that's the case,' said Morgan.

'But you just said—'

'The thing is, Erin thinks her mother has gone missing, but we believe we have Erin's mother's body lying on a slab in the mortuary. She didn't show up because she's dead.'

'You *believe* it's her mother. Don't you know?'

'We only found her yesterday afternoon, and there's no ID on the body. As we speak, my boss has gone to see Erin's father. We're hoping he will be willing to identify the body.'

'My God, this sounds a bit of a mess,' said Brenner. 'Is it always like this?'

'You really don't want to know,' said Morgan. 'But I hope now you understand why I thought you should have some background before you start any treatment.'

'In cases like this we lean towards counselling as the best form of treatment, and I have to say what you've just told me will be very helpful,' said Dr Brenner.

'I don't know if we're doing the right thing, and I really don't like lying to Erin, but we thought it would be best if we let her believe we're looking for her mother until you think she's ready to learn the truth. What do you think?'

'I think that's probably for the best, at least until we've assessed her,' said Dr Brenner. 'I think I probably owe you an apology. You're in such a complicated situation, almost impossible really, and here I am giving you a hard time.'

'Don't worry about it,' said Morgan. 'I'm used to it. We get it all the time.'

'It must be very frustrating. How do you cope?'

'We just have to develop a thick skin,' said Morgan. 'It seems we're fair game, but we can't answer back in case we offend someone. It's okay for them to offend us, of course.'

Morgan was pleased to see that Dr Brenner looked suitably uncomfortable.

'Anyway,' she said. 'I came here to see Erin. Is it okay if I have a couple of minutes with her?'

'Yes, of course,' said Dr Brenner. 'We've put her on her own in room five for tonight.' She pointed down the corridor. 'You'll find her down there on the left.'

It seemed to Morgan that no sooner had she settled in a chair next to Erin than a nurse arrived with a glass of water and a couple of tablets.

'Time for you to sleep, Erin,' she said.

'I'd better get out of the way,' said Morgan. 'You've had quite a day, and now you need a good night's sleep. I'll speak to you tomorrow.'

'Before you go, can I ask another favour, Catren?'

'Of course,' said Morgan.

'Can you get a message to my boyfriend?'

Morgan grinned. 'You mean Wozzy, the eco-warrior?'

'He'll be expecting me back.'

'He doesn't know you're here?'

'He knows I'm in Llangwelli, but he thinks I'm with my mum. He doesn't know about me wanting to jump off a roof.'

'Can't you call him?' suggested Morgan.

'We've only got the one phone between us,' said Erin.

'Oh, I see,' said Morgan. 'Where is he?'

'There's an old deserted mining village a few miles from here. It's called Cartrefi i lowyr.'

For a split second Morgan's face almost gave her away. 'Yeah, I know it,' she said, forcing a smile. 'Where will I find him?'

'We've been dossing down in house number nineteen. I can't remember the name of the road, but it's the very last house on the left. It's next to a big wooden fence.'

'How will I know it's him?'

'He's probably the only person there, but just in case, he's wearing jeans, a blue T-shirt and an ancient parka, and he's got tattoos all over his arms and his body.'

'It's dark now,' said Morgan. 'I'll go over there first thing in the morning. Is that okay?'

'He's got a double sleeping bag to wrap himself up in so he should be fine until the morning,' said Erin.

'Have you got a photo of him?'

Erin found a photograph, which Morgan downloaded to her phone. She said goodbye and made her way through the hospital as quickly as she could, her phone to her ear.

He answered her call a few seconds later. 'Yo. This is Norm.'

'Is the boss with you?' she asked.

'Yeah. We're just taking Ross Watkins to the mortuary.'

'Am I on loudspeaker?'

'We're in the car, so yeah, you are. Why? What's up?'

'It'll keep,' said Morgan.

'Are you sure?' said Norman. 'Do you want me to call you back?'

'When it's convenient.'

Norman glanced at Southall.

'Sounds urgent,' she said. 'You'd better call her back when we get to the mortuary. I can escort Mr Watkins to the viewing room.'

'Give me ten minutes, and I'll call you back,' Norman told Morgan.

Although it was getting late when they reached the mortuary, pathologist Bill Bridger, looking solemn, was there to greet them at the door. Having made the introductions, Southall led Watkins to the viewing room while Bridger peeled off towards the mortuary.

* * *

As Bridger led Southall and Watkins to the viewing room, Norman stepped into Bridger's office to make his call.

'Okay, Catren, I know it must be important, so what's up?' he asked.

'You and Frosty went through the houses at the mining village, right?'

'Yeah,' said Norman, 'but we only searched the houses in the same street.'

'And one of them was number nineteen?'

'Didn't you see I marked it on the map at the office?'

'And is there a wooden fence nearby?' asked Morgan.

Norman sighed.

'Yes, that's right. It's the end house on the terrace, and the fence crosses the street right next to it. It's where we found what looks like blood on the floor. You should know all this if you've been paying attention.'

'I do know it, but I wanted to make sure I remembered right,' said Morgan. 'Did you see any sign of a young guy hanging around?'

'We didn't see anyone who wasn't a builder, a cop, or a scene of crime officer,' said Norman. 'Come on, Catren, I can hear it in your voice. What's going on?'

'I've just come from the hospital. As I was leaving, Erin asked me if I could find her boyfriend and let him know where she is. Guess where he's staying?'

'Number nineteen? Are you sure?'

'Did you find a double sleeping bag?'

'There was a sleeping bag, but I didn't see if it was a double. Thinking about it, there were two mats on the floor, so it probably was a double.'

'Is it still there?'

'Forensics took everything away to test for DNA.'

'According to Erin, she left her boyfriend waiting at number nineteen when she set off to see her mother,' explained Morgan. 'The plan was for him to wait for her to come back.'

'Does this guy have a name?'

'Wozzy,' said Morgan.

'Wozzy? What sort of name is that?' asked Norman. 'No, don't tell me, it doesn't really matter. I don't suppose they have mobile phones if they live rough?'

'They share one, but Erin's got it.'

'Didn't you say something about them being eco-warriors?' asked Norman.

'Yeah, that's right.'

'So there's a good chance he's been in trouble with the law somewhere along the line,' said Norman. 'Maybe he ran off when all the uniforms started arriving. Or, maybe the builders scared him off. Whatever, we definitely didn't see him.'

'I told Erin I'd go and look for him in the morning, but now I'm wondering if I should go out there now,' said Morgan. 'What do you think I should do?'

'One thing's for sure,' said Norman. 'Going out there at night, on your own, is not a good idea. You don't even know if he'll be there.'

'I can't just do nothing. I promised Erin.'

'Listen, Catren. This is a murder investigation. How do you know you can trust this Wozzy guy?'

Morgan said nothing.

'Your silence suggests you hadn't considered the possibility,' said Norman. 'I understand that you think Erin's a nice kid and you made her a promise, but think about it for a minute. We know nothing about this guy or what he's capable of. You go rushing over there on your own, and who knows what might happen. Besides, you said you told Erin you'd go and find him in the morning, didn't you?'

'Yeah, but—'

'So, if you go home now, you won't be breaking your promise, will you?'

'No. I suppose not,' conceded Morgan.

'Take my advice and reel in your enthusiasm, Catren. In the morning, we can send someone over there with you to search for Wozzy. I'll even come with you myself if you want but, for now, I need you to promise me you'll go home and get some sleep. Will you do that, please?'

'Okay, Norm. You're right. I'll head for home, and I'll see you in the morning.'

'Eight on the dot,' said Norman.

* * *

While Norman was talking to Morgan, Southall explained to Ross Watkins what was about to happen.

'I know it's difficult, but if it's Dilys, you need to say it out loud,' she told him.

'Okay,' said Watkins.

Southall reached forward and pulled a cord. The curtain across the viewing window slid open to reveal Bill Bridger standing alongside a shroud-covered body laid out on a table. Southall gave him a nod and Bridger slowly drew the shroud back to reveal the face of Dilys Watkins.

Ross Watkins stared at her. For a moment Southall thought he was going to faint as he slowly leaned forward

66

until his forehead was almost touching the glass. He let out a desperate, agonised howl, sank to his knees and began to sob uncontrollably.

Southall exchanged a worried look with Bridger, who hastily covered the body and ran to help.

She placed a gentle hand on Watkins's shoulder.

'I'm sorry, Ross, but I have to be sure. Is it Dilys?'

'Yes, it is,' he gasped between sobs. 'My beautiful Dilys. Who did this to her?'

'I don't know,' said Southall. 'But I promise we'll do everything we can to find out.'

Bridger had arrived now and between them, he and Southall got Watkins to his feet.

'Let's sit him down,' said Bridger.

'Can I get you a drink?' Southall asked Watkins.

He shook his head. 'No, thank you.'

'There is one other thing,' said Southall. 'You said Dilys was driving your car, but there was no car where she was found. Do you think you could give me the registration number?'

'My registration number?' said Watkins, confused.

'If you could write it down for me,' explained Southall, 'it'll help us search for it.'

'Oh, right. Yes, of course. Look, do you think I could have a few minutes to myself?'

'Of course,' said Southall. 'Is there anyone we can call, a family member perhaps?'

'Dilys was my only family. Well, her and my daughter, Erin.'

'A friend, then?'

'I can call my best mate. I've known him since we were kids.'

'Would you like me to call him?' asked Southall.

'It's okay, I'll call him in a bit. I'd like it to be me who tells him what's happened.'

'Of course,' said Southall. 'We'll be through that door. Just call us when you're ready to go home.'

Southall and Bridger made their way into Bridger's office, where Norman had just finished his call.

'We have a complication,' he said.

'What's the problem?' asked Southall.

'It seems Erin came to town with her boyfriend. She's asked Catren to let him know where she is and what's happened.'

'Why is that so complicated?'

'Because they were staying just a couple of houses from where Dilys's body was found. In fact, they were in number nineteen.'

'Isn't that where you found the bloodstain on the floor?' asked Bridger.

'Exactly,' said Norman.

'That is a complication,' said Southall.

'Catren's talking about going to look for him,' said Norman. 'I don't think she realises what this could mean.'

'Where is she now?'

'I told her I didn't think it was a good idea to go looking for the guy on her own now it's getting dark, and that she should go home and get some sleep,' said Norman.

'Do you think she will?'

Norman shrugged.

'I said it would be better to wait until the morning and we can send someone with her. I can't guarantee it, but I think I got through to her. What about Watkins? Do you want to question him now?'

'I don't think he's in a fit state to answer questions tonight,' said Southall, 'but we'll have to take him home.'

'I can take him,' suggested Bridger.

'Are you sure?' asked Southall. 'It's a bit irregular.'

'Yes, but it's getting late, he's not under arrest, and I was leaving anyway. I can give you a lift home too, if you like. Norm can take your car. It'll save him hanging about when I know he'd much rather be at home with Faye.'

'That works for me,' said Norman. 'I can pick you up in the morning, Sarah.'

'That won't be necessary, Norm,' said Bridger. 'I'll drop Sarah off on my way to work.' He turned to Southall. 'Is that okay with you?'

Southall looked a little startled. Norman would obviously guess the implications of what Bridger had said but she could hardly object.

'Er, yes, I suppose that's okay.'

'Great,' said Norman. 'I'll get away then, and leave you to it.'

* * *

No sooner had Norman climbed into Southall's car and started the engine than his mobile phone began to ring.

'Hi, Judy. What's the problem?'

'An old man has just come into reception claiming he murdered the woman found at number nine.'

'You're kidding me,' said Norman.

'That's what he says. I didn't want to call you this late, but I don't feel I'm qualified to interview a man who insists he's committed a murder. Should I call the boss?'

Norman smiled. 'I wouldn't like to disturb her, not tonight. I get the feeling she has something a bit more fun in mind. Let me come in and speak to the guy first. We can always call Sarah later if we need to. I'll be there in fifteen minutes.'

* * *

It was just coming up to seven thirty p.m. when Norman got back to the office.

'Where is he?' he asked.

'We weren't sure what to do with him so we've put him in the interview room,' said Lane. 'Frosty is sitting with him to make sure he doesn't do anything stupid.'

'Stupid? What do you mean?'

'Well, he's drunk,' said Lane.

'It's a bit early for that, isn't it?' said Norman.

'Then if he's not drunk, he's on something,' said Lane. 'Is he violent?'

'Oh no, he seems harmless enough, but it's difficult to understand what he's rambling on about.'

'And he definitely said he knows something about Dilys Watkins's murder?'

'Not exactly. He says he knows who we found in that house, and that he murdered her. That's why Frosty thought he should bring him in. But the thing is, he's referred to her as Cariad, as well as Dilys.'

Norman frowned. '*Cariad?*'

'That's what he told Frosty,' said Lane.

'*Cariad* means "love" in Welsh, doesn't it?' asked Norman.

Lane looked suitably impressed. 'Someone's been doing their homework.'

'I pick bits up from Faye,' said Norman.

'And that's what she calls you at home, is it?' asked Lane.

Norman blushed. 'Let's leave my private life out of this, shall we?'

'Oh, I'm sorry,' said Lane. 'I didn't mean to—'

'It's okay, Judy, honestly.'

'Right. Of course,' said Lane, embarrassed. 'Anyway, the thing is it's not uncommon for Welsh people to use *cariad* as a pet name. So, maybe that's what this was.'

'So, what do you think?' asked Norman. 'Is this guy for real?'

'To be honest, I'm not sure what he is,' said Lane. 'I should mention he also thinks I'm called Bronwyn.'

'Bronwyn?' said Norman. 'Jeez, listen to me, I'm starting to sound like an echo. Why does he think that?'

'We didn't get that far,' said Lane. 'As soon as Frosty brought him in here and he set eyes on me he fell to his knees and started crying. When he tried to reach for my hands Frosty stepped in and took him to the interview room.'

'Jeez, no wonder you think he's on something. How old is he?'

'I'd say he's in his late seventies or early eighties.'

Norman scratched his head.

'So he's old, he's drunk or, at least, off his head on something, he thinks you're called Bronwyn, and he thinks Dilys Watkins is called Cariad. Is that right?'

'Now you know as much as we do,' said Lane.

'What's his name?'

'He wouldn't say.'

'You don't look right, Judy. Are you sure you're okay?' asked Norman.

'Yes, I'm fine. I admit having a man fall at my feet is not something that happens every day, and it was really embarrassing, but there's no harm done. I suppose I should be flattered, even if he is old enough to be my grandfather.'

'Okay. I'd better go and see how Frosty's coping.'

Norman made his way to the interview room, opened the door a crack and peered inside. The man, who was sitting at the table with his back to Norman, appeared to have fallen asleep with his head resting on his arms. Winter was sitting opposite, and as Norman looked in, he got to his feet and made his way over to the door.

'Is he behaving?' asked Norman.

Winter nodded.

'Yeah, he's fine. He's not an aggressive drunk, he's the type that gets more amiable, like everybody's his friend. It's a pity all drunks aren't like him.'

'Are you sure he is drunk? I mean, he doesn't reek of booze.'

'Yeah, I thought that,' said Winter, 'but then I don't think he's on drugs either.'

'And you're okay?' asked Norman.

'No problem. He worried me a bit when he saw Judy and almost threw himself at her, but he backed off easily enough when I told him to.'

'Any idea why he did that?'

'I'm not sure, it's not easy to understand what he's saying. All I can tell you is that as soon as he saw her he burst into tears and started gabbling on about Bronwyn and how he hadn't seen her for all these years, but she was still as beautiful as ever. Poor Judy didn't know what to do.'

Norman smiled. 'She was a bit embarrassed about having the guy fall at her feet. What else can you tell me about the old guy? Has he told you his name yet?'

'He won't say, but I had a look in his pockets once he fell asleep. He's not carrying any ID, but there's an envelope in his jacket pocket with the name Dafydd Thomas written on it.'

'No address?'

'Just the name, like it had been hand-delivered.'

'Okay, let's go with Dafydd Thomas for now,' said Norman.

There was a snort from the table. Dafydd Thomas was waking up.

'Let's see if he's ready for a chat,' said Norman.

He led Winter back to the table and settled into the chair opposite their supposed murderer.

'Are you awake, Mr Thomas?' he asked.

Thomas looked around, seemingly bewildered to find himself in a strange room.

'Hi, Mr Thomas,' said Norman. 'My name's DS Norman. I understand you have something you want to tell us.'

The man's face lit up as he suddenly seemed to remember why he was there. When he began to speak Norman found it took considerable concentration to understand what he was saying at first, but he seemed to become more lucid as he went on.

'It's about the body you found,' he said. 'I heard it on the radio.'

'What was it you wanted to tell us about the body?' asked Norman.

'It's my daughter, Dilys. I killed her.'

Winter was visibly startled by this admission even though he'd heard it before, but Norman had been around the block enough times to not even bat an eyelid.

'Your daughter's name was Dilys?' asked Norman. 'I thought it was Cariad.'

'Cariad, and Dilys.'

'I'm guessing Cariad was like a pet name, but Dilys was her real name, is that right?' asked Norman.

'Did you know that *cariad* means "love" in English?' said Thomas, dreamily.

'Yeah, so I understand,' said Norman.

'And she was a lovely little girl for sure. I loved her, you know, I really did, but she changed when she became a teenager. She turned against me. Now, I couldn't have that, could I?'

'Can I ask how old Dilys was when you killed her?' asked Norman.

'Let me think now. She must have been sixteen. Or was it seventeen? I can't remember for sure.'

Winter was struggling to follow the conversation. Norman, on the other hand, thanks to his years of experience, was able to let Mr Thomas ramble on. He was gradually coming to see that whatever this man might have done, it had nothing to do with Dilys Watkins.

'When exactly did you murder your daughter, Mr Thomas?' asked Norman patiently.

'During the strikes. Cariad should have been supporting me, but she wanted me to accept the pit closure. I couldn't do that. What would people think?'

'Just to be clear, you're talking about the miners' strikes which, if I recall, would have been in the early eighties, right?'

Thomas eyed him as if he were a fool. 'Of course it was in the eighties. There's been nothing to strike for since they closed the pit, has there?'

'No, I guess not,' said Norman.

Thomas looked at Norman thoughtfully. 'You look like a reasonable sort of fellow for a policeman.'

Norman smiled. 'We do our best to be fair.'

Thomas leaned forward conspiratorially. 'Could I ask a favour?'

'What's that, Mr Thomas?'

'Do you think you could arrange for me to have a few words with Bronwyn?'

'Who is Bronwyn, Mr Thomas?'

'My wife. I saw her earlier.'

Norman exchanged a glance with Winter.

'You mean when you first came into the police station?' asked Norman.

'That's right,' said Thomas. 'I know she's angry with me, but if I could just explain—'

'I think you must have been mistaken, Mr Thomas,' said Norman. 'That wasn't Bronwyn. That was Detective Constable Lane, she's one of our detectives.'

Thomas looked confused.

'It must have been Bronwyn. I'd know her anywhere.'

'I promise you there's no one working here called Bronwyn,' said Norman.

'But she was beautiful, just like my Bronwyn.'

'She is beautiful for sure,' agreed Norman. 'But I'm afraid she's not your wife.'

Thomas suddenly looked crestfallen and his bottom lip began to tremble.

'Can I get you a cup of tea, Mr Thomas?' suggested Norman. 'You've been here a couple of hours now. You must be parched.'

'That's very good of you. Milk and two sugars, please.'

'Will you be okay here on your own while we get it for you?' asked Norman.

'What's that?' asked Thomas.

'Can you wait here while we get you a cup of tea?'

'Tea? Oh, yes please. Milk and two sugars.'

Norman led Winter from the room.

'I'm sorry, if we've ruined your evening,' said Winter. 'It looks as if we called you in to speak to a time-waster.'

'There's no need to apologise,' said Norman.

'I'll make his cup of tea,' said Winter.

'Actually, you were going to,' said Norman. 'Anyway, who's to say he's a time-waster? For all we know he may well have murdered his daughter back in the eighties. But if he did, it was forty years ago, so it's got nothing to do with our current investigation.'

'So, why come forward now?'

'I'm no doctor, but if I had to guess, I'd say the poor old guy's got Alzheimer's or something similar. Maybe he heard about our investigation on the radio and it triggered a distant memory. Or perhaps he wanted to clear his conscience. He might not even have done it but, for whatever reason, he believes he did. The only thing I know for sure is that he's probably gone missing from somewhere.'

'You think he's escaped from a home?'

Norman smiled. 'I'm not sure I'd put it quite like that. And I think you should understand he can't help being a time-waster. Remember, we could all end up like that, or even worse.'

'You're right, it's not very respectful of me, is it?'

'Anything but,' said Norman.

'So, what happens to him now?'

'You head for the kitchen and make him a cup of tea, and I'll see if he's been reported missing.'

* * *

'I think I've got a name for our visitor,' said Judy Lane, when Norman reached the office.

'Dafydd Thomas?' asked Norman.

'Oh, how did you know?'

'Envelope in his pocket,' said Norman. 'How did you find out?'

'He's been reported missing. His nursing home organised an outing to Llangwelli, and he went AWOL from the bus.'

Norman smiled. 'Yeah, I had a feeling it might be something like that. Do they want us to take him back?'

'Someone is on their way to collect him. They should be here in about ten minutes.'

'Perfect,' said Norman. 'That's just long enough for him to drink his cup of tea before they get here.'

'Did he kill Dilys?'

'He claims he killed someone called Dilys but, even if he did, it wasn't Dilys Watkins. It could be he killed his daughter who would have been called Dilys Thomas, and who he also called Cariad, but that was back in the eighties when the miners' strikes were raging.'

'Are you going to take him seriously?'

'For the murder of Dilys Watkins? No way. You've seen him, do you think he looks as if he's capable of using a car to murder Dilys and then carrying her body to that house? And, if he's living in a nursing home, how could he be out half the night committing the crime? Now, if our dead body had been lying in that house for forty years I might consider it, but right now? I don't think so.'

'I'm sorry, Norm.'

'What is it with you and Frosty that you feel you have to keep apologising to me for doing your jobs?'

'But we don't want you to feel we're wasting your time.'

'Making sure is never a waste of anyone's time,' said Norman. 'If anyone walks in here and confesses to a murder we're investigating, we have a duty to check them out sufficiently to be sure one way or the other, no matter how unlikely a suspect they appear to be. And, anyway, why were you still both here after seven o'clock? Why haven't you gone home?'

'We were just trying to keep up to date with everything,' said Lane. 'We don't want to let the boss down and have her think we can't cope.'

'That's all very commendable,' said Norman. 'But I can assure you the boss doesn't think that at all. She is actually in awe of the way you all cope when we're so severely undermanned. I can also assure you that if she was here now, she would have told you to go home.'

'Yes, but—'

'Judy, listen to me. For your own good, close up shop for tonight, go home and get some sleep.'

'I've just got to—'

'Look, Dilys won't be any less dead even if you stay all night, will she?'

'I suppose not,' said Lane, reluctantly.

'And is there anything that can't wait until tomorrow?'

'Not really.'

Norman winked.

'Well, there we are then,' he said.

Lane grinned. 'Spoken like a true Welshman.'

'Yeah,' said Norman. 'I may not be able to get my head around the language, but I am picking up one or two colloquialisms.'

'But if I go home, who is going to wait for Mr Thomas to be collected?'

'I'll do it,' said Norman. 'I'd like to see if they can shed any light on this story of his.'

CHAPTER SEVEN

Wednesday, 15 March

At eight a.m. the next morning, the small team gathered for a briefing.

'Just so we're all on the same page,' said Southall. 'All we know so far is that Dilys Watkins was run down by a car. Her body was possibly laid out somewhere before it was taken and dumped at number nine. It's possible that somewhere along the line she was left at number nineteen, as blood was found there, but at this stage we can't say anything for sure.

'Just to complicate matters further, we also now know that Erin and her boyfriend, Wozzy, were sleeping at number nineteen, so it's possible the blood found there belongs to one of those two. I'm hoping the results from forensic samples taken at number nine and number nineteen will clarify this. Meanwhile, I want to revisit our "possible suspects" list and consider their motives.'

She turned to the whiteboard and used a marker pen to point to the two names, Joe Harding and Ross Watkins. 'Now I'm going to add two more: Erin Watkins and her boyfriend, Wozzy.'

'The daughter? Wow, I didn't see that one coming,' said Winter. 'Why her?'

'Remember that sleeping bag we found at number nineteen?' said Norman.

'Yeah,' said Winter. 'And—'

'The fact they were sleeping so close to where the body was found opens up the possibility that either Erin, Wozzy, or both of them, could have killed Dilys,' said Southall.

'And if she was full of remorse afterwards, it could explain why she wanted to jump off that roof,' added Norman.

'But wasn't Dilys run down by a car?' said Winter. 'Would they even have a car if they were living rough?'

'They could have stolen one,' suggested Norman.

'What, just to murder her mum? I know I'm the new boy here, but that's a bit of a stretch, isn't it?' said Winter.

'Yeah, maybe,' agreed Norman. 'But it would be clear evidence of premeditation if that's what they did.'

'And why kill her?' asked Winter. 'I thought Erin had come back to see her mum and clear the air.'

'That's what she told us up on the roof,' said Southall. 'But what if that's not the real reason? You've heard about what happened after the DNA result came through. If Erin blames Dilys for breaking up the family, wouldn't that be a powerful motive for murder?'

'Another possibility is that they stole a car not with the intention of killing Dilys, but ran her down accidentally,' said Norman. 'Then they panicked and dumped the body.'

Southall glanced at Morgan, who hadn't said a word so far. 'You're very quiet this morning, Catren. What do you think?'

'I can't believe Erin could kill anyone,' she said. 'And if I'm wrong and she did kill Dilys on Friday night, why would she come into Llangwelli to meet her on Sunday? It makes no sense.'

'Do we have any proof she came into town to meet Dilys?' asked Norman.

'What do you mean, proof?' asked Morgan.

'What I mean is we only have her word for it,' said Norman. 'What if she's lying? What if she wasn't in Llangwelli at all on Sunday and she didn't come into town until Monday morning?'

'Are you saying you think she's playing us along?'

'She wouldn't be the first murderer to play the innocent,' said Norman. 'Can you say for sure that she's not?'

'If she did kill Dilys, why would she hang around?' asked Morgan. 'Her and Wozzy could have cleared their stuff from number nineteen and been back in London by Sunday night, and the chances are we would have had no idea they'd been anywhere near the murder scene.'

'Unless, of course, she was filled with remorse and wanted to kill herself,' said Norman. 'Anyway, talking of this boyfriend, Wozzy, what do we actually know about him? Perhaps he thinks he's done Erin a favour by killing her mother.'

'I haven't met him yet,' said Morgan, 'but I did a search for him online when I got home last night. He's quite famous for his exploits in trying to save the planet. He's even been arrested a few times, but there's never been so much as a hint that he's capable of violence.'

'Well, we can't interview Erin at the moment, so the only way we can really learn anything about Wozzy is to find him and ask him,' said Southall. 'So, why don't you and Frosty go and see if he's still in the old village somewhere?'

'Do you want us to bring him in, or take him to see Erin in hospital?' asked Morgan.

'We don't have sufficient grounds to arrest him at the moment,' said Southall, 'so I'll leave that one up to you.'

'Yes, boss,' said Winter, getting to his feet.

'Not so fast, Frosty,' said Southall. 'Did you manage to check out Joe Harding as I asked?'

'I've printed it all out for you,' he said. 'It's here, on my desk.'

He handed a folder to Southall.

'Thank you,' she said. 'Now you two can go.'

Norman waited until they had left the room, then turned to Southall.

'So Catren doesn't believe Erin killed her mother,' he said.

'And she may well be right,' said Southall. 'But until we know different, everyone's a suspect, so we have to explore all possibilities. It doesn't hurt any of us to have someone make us question our beliefs now and then.'

'Do you want me to go through that report on Joe Harding?' asked Norman.

'It'll keep until later,' said Southall.

'I'm doing the same thing for Ross Watkins,' said Judy Lane. 'But I'm not quite finished.'

'Do you think you can finish it this morning?' asked Southall.

'I only need an hour or so,' said Lane.

'Excellent,' said Southall. 'Perhaps you'd like to run through it for me and Norm when we get back.'

'Shouldn't we hear Judy's report before we interview Ross?' asked Norman.

'We will,' said Southall. 'But there's something else I want to do first. I asked Ross for Dilys's address when we dropped him at home last night. I thought it might be useful to take a look around her flat before we speak to him again.'

'Oh, right. Did he have a key?'

'No, but there's a caretaker with keys for all the flats.'

* * *

'I hear you had someone come forward with a confession last night,' said Southall, once they were in the car.

'Yeah, poor old guy. His name's Dafydd Thomas, but even if he has murdered someone, it was forty years ago so it definitely wasn't Dilys Watkins.'

'D'you think he's for real?'

'I spoke to the nurse who looks after him. She says he has dementia and he often comes out with rambling stories that don't add up. She also says that as far as they know, he doesn't have any family. In all the time he's been there no one has ever come to visit him, or called to see how he is.'

'There's no need to open another murder investigation then?'

'Without any evidence?' said Norman. 'Unless the reason he gets no visitors is because he murdered his entire family, I reckon it's just a figment of a bewildered imagination.'

'So, you're discounting his confession?'

'Come on, Sarah. You know as well as me that, even if it is true, any half decent defence lawyer would argue that the guy's seriously ill and has no idea what he's talking about.'

'I agree,' said Southall. 'And besides, can you imagine how popular we'd be with the bean counters if we spent a big slice of our budget on a forty-year-old case we're never going to win?'

* * *

Forest House was a long, low building built just five years ago on the outskirts of Llangwelli. Dilys Watkins's flat was on the second floor.

They found the caretaker in flat number one on the ground floor.

'Mr Evans? I'm DS Norman and this is DI Southall. We're from Llangwelli Police,' said Norman showing his warrant card. 'I understand you have spare keys for all the flats here.'

'That's right,' said Evans, eyeing them suspiciously.

'Do you have a Mrs Dilys Watkins living at flat eighteen?'

'Yes, that's right. You won't find her there, though. She's gone away.'

'Yes, we know,' said Norman. 'But we need to get into her flat.'

'Why?'

'Do you know Mrs Watkins well?' asked Southall.

Evans sucked on his teeth thoughtfully.

'She's all right, she is. One of those people who always has time for a chat, you know?'

'Well, I'm afraid Mrs Watkins has been found dead,' said Southall.

Evans's mouth dropped open. 'Dead? Bloody hell. Really?'

'I'm afraid so,' said Norman. 'That's why we want to get into her flat.'

'Yeah, of course. Hang on, I'll get the key for you.'

A few seconds later, muttering under his breath all the way, he was leading them to flat eighteen. He unlocked the door and stepped back to let them in. Southall stepped into a narrow hallway, Norman behind her. Evans seemed to think he was coming in too.

'Thank you, Mr Evans, we can take it from here,' said Norman turning to block his way.

Evans held his hand out. 'I'm not supposed to let that key out of my sight.'

'I think you can trust us with it,' said Norman. 'We're the police. And we're probably going to need to come back at some stage.'

'It doesn't matter who you are, or how often you intend to come back, I'm still responsible for that key. What if you lose it?'

'Will it make you happy if I give you a receipt for it?' asked Norman.

'Well, yeah, I suppose so. I'll have to let my boss know you've got it, though.'

'Who is your boss?' asked Norman.

'Mr Joe Harding,' said Evans.

'Really?' said Norman, unable to hide his surprise.

'You know him?' asked Evans.

'Oh, yes, we've met,' said Norman. 'Is he a good boss?'

'He's not someone you want to mess with. He won't be happy about you lot being here.'

Norman smiled. 'Just tell him DI Southall and DS Norman are here. He knows who we are. I'll give you a receipt for the key when we've finished here, okay?'

Norman closed the door, glad to be rid of Evans. As he fumbled in his pocket for a pair of latex gloves, Southall emerged from a door to the left.

'Nothing to see in the kitchen,' she said. 'It looks clean and empty, just as I would expect if the owner had gone away over a week ago.'

Norman grinned. 'You're gonna love the little snippet of information I just gleaned from our friendly caretaker.'

'Go on then, let's hear it,' said Southall.

'Guess who owns this building?'

'I have no idea.'

'It's only our favourite property developer,' said Norman.

'Not Harding?'

'Yep.'

'So, he owns the place where she lived, as well as the site where she was found dead,' she said. 'Interesting.'

'I know he's already on our suspect list, but that sort of coincidence is kinda hard to ignore, right?' said Norman.

'You can say that again,' said Southall.

Norman followed Southall into a sparsely furnished lounge containing a two-seater settee, a small, square dining table and three chairs, the fourth chair obviously missing.

'She doesn't seem to have gone in for luxury furnishings,' said Norman.

'What were you expecting?' asked Southall. 'Don't forget, she's separated from her husband and he seems to have kept their house. Unless she has a seriously well-paying job, she probably can't afford much. This flat won't be cheap to rent.'

'Yeah, you're right,' said Norman. 'It's been so long since my marriage broke up I tend to forget that side of it. But, even so, there's no cupboards or drawers to search in here.'

Southall pointed to a door opposite them.

'The bedrooms and the bathroom must be through there,' she said. 'Maybe they'll have more.'

Norman followed her into a second short hallway with three doors leading off. Southall opened the door to the right.

'I'll take this one,' she said.

Norman opened the door to the left and stepped into the second, smaller bedroom, which was obviously being used as a makeshift office.

'Aha,' he muttered to himself. 'What do we have here?'

A laptop sat on a cheap workstation set against one wall, with a coffee table alongside it to hold a printer. The fourth dining chair was being used as the office chair. On the opposite side of the room, a board on two trestles was serving as a makeshift table.

The laptop was obviously of interest, but Norman guessed he would need a password to gain access to it. Furthermore, he was first to admit that anything even remotely technical was way beyond his capabilities.

Instead, he turned his attention to the two folders sitting invitingly on the table. Flipping open the first one and sliding its contents onto the table, he picked up the top sheet of paper and began to read.

He had been reading for a few minutes when Southall joined him.

'It looks a bit more interesting in here,' she said.

'Have you drawn a blank?' he asked.

'She has a distinctive patchwork handbag in her wardrobe. It's the sort of thing someone might notice, so I've taken a photo with my phone in case we need to trace her movements before she went away. Otherwise there doesn't seem to be anything to get excited about.'

'Well, you might be interested in this stuff then,' said Norman.

'What have we got?'

'Two things,' said Norman. 'First, it seems our Dilys has been taking notes from county council planning committee meetings for the last couple of years.'

'Bringing work home? That's unusual, isn't it?'

'This isn't work as such,' said Norman. 'It's more what you might call homework. She's been corresponding with the planning department, too, and guess what she's interested in?'

'The mining village development?'

'Right first time,' said Norman. 'She thinks Harding's not averse to bending the planning rules.'

'Are you saying Dilys was conducting her own investigation into Harding for bribing people on the planning committee?' asked Southall.

'I'm not sure if you'd call it an investigation,' said Norman. 'I'd say it's a collection of suspicions, rumours and suggestions, some of which go back several years but, as far as I can see, there isn't actually any proof to back up the accusations. Just read some of this stuff and see what you think.'

He handed Southall a few of the sheets he had already read and waited for her reaction.

'But even if just one or two of those rumours are correct, and Harding knew she was on to him, he would have a very good motive for murdering her,' said Southall.

'Even if the rumours aren't true, simply finding out she was digging for dirt would be sufficient motive, if he has something to hide,' said Norman.

'You said there were two things,' said Southall.

Norman grinned.

'Take a look at this,' he said handing Southall another sheet of paper.

Southall skimmed the page. 'She's a member of the History Group?'

'It looks that way,' said Norman. 'And isn't that what's been holding up Harding's development all these years?'

'We have to take this stuff back to the office and look into it, Norm. Harding was already a person of interest, and now I've seen this, I think he's even more interesting.'

'I'd love it to be him, too, Sarah,' said Norman. 'But let's not get carried away. I've yet to see any proof that he's done anything wrong. There again, I haven't read all of it yet, and I've no idea what might be on the laptop.'

* * *

Over at the demolition site, Winter parked up at the end of the short street that had been cordoned off. As he climbed from the car, he noticed Joe Harding's Rolls Royce parked outside his portacabin.

'Is old whatshisname supposed to be here?' he asked Morgan.

'Who?'

'The developer guy, Harding. That's his Roller.'

'His office is outside the cordon,' said Morgan, turning to look. 'So, as long as he's not going to start demolishing the houses, I don't think we have reason to stop him. Who does the other car belong to?'

'The blue Mercedes? I've no idea. I don't recall seeing it yesterday. Should we go and ask?'

'Maybe later,' said Morgan. 'We don't want to give Harding a reason to accuse us of harassing him before we've even started.'

'Good point,' said Winter. 'After the way he behaved yesterday, that's probably just what he would do.' He looked around the site, rubbing his hands together enthusiastically. 'Right then, where shall we start?'

'If Wozzy came back to number nineteen and found we'd taken his sleeping bag, I can't imagine he would have stayed, but we'd better check it out first, just in case,' said Morgan. 'Then we'll do a quick sweep of the other houses in this street. If we haven't found him after that, we'll just have to work our way through the entire village.'

Twenty minutes later, they were back by their car.

'That's twenty minutes of my life I'm never going to get back,' said Morgan. 'Come on, we'd better try the houses in the other streets.'

'Did you really think he'd be here?' Winter asked as they started walking. 'I mean, if he came here to help Erin kill Dilys, he's not going to be hanging around here waiting for us to catch him, is he?'

'Erin didn't kill Dilys,' said Morgan, dismissively.

'How can you be so sure?'

'I've spent time with her, Frosty. I just don't think she's got it in her,' said Morgan. 'I believe she came back to bring her family together, not to tear it apart.'

'All right, so Erin's an angel, but what about this Wozzy bloke? What if he decided to take the law into his own hands?'

Morgan stopped dead in her tracks. 'Are you seriously suggesting he stole a car, used it to run Dilys down, and then hid her body in number nine without Erin knowing?' She marched on, leaving Winter behind.

'Yeah, I see what you mean,' he said guiltily, running to catch up with her. 'But she could have found out after he killed Dilys, then decided to commit suicide rather than tell us what he'd done.'

'You think knowing her mum was dead, and that her boyfriend had betrayed her, disturbed Erin enough to make her want to commit suicide. That's your theory, is it?' asked Morgan.

'Exactly.'

'Okay, so why didn't she jump as soon as she got up onto the roof?'

'Sorry?'

'There was no one to stop her when she first got up there, so why didn't she jump straight away? Why wait for someone to talk her down, knowing the truth might eventually come out?'

Winter looked blank. 'I dunno.'

'Because she didn't know Dilys was dead, that's why,' said Morgan. 'All she knows is that Dilys didn't show up on Sunday night. Going up to that roof was a cry for help, not an admission of guilt.'

Winter offered her a wry smile. 'If I ever get in trouble, will you defend me?'

'Only if we find Wozzy in one of these houses,' she said, indicating the street now in front of them.

'How will we know it's him?' asked Winter.

'How many young guys do you think we're going to find hiding out here?' Morgan said.

'I was only asking,' said Winter. 'Anyway, how do you know we're not going to find more than one?'

Morgan sighed in exasperation. 'Erin told me he's wearing jeans, a blue T-shirt and an old parka, and he's covered in tattoos. All right?' She pulled her mobile phone from her pocket. 'And I have his photograph on here.' She brandished her phone like a weapon.

'Look, there's no need to get like that,' said Winter. 'I'm only trying to do my job. Don't they always tell us there's no such thing as too much information?'

'I'm sorry,' said Morgan, contrite. 'It's just that—'

'You think Erin can't possibly be guilty,' finished Winter. 'Yeah, I get that, but whatever happened to being objective and not letting your emotions cloud your judgement, eh?'

'I'm not wrong about Erin,' said Morgan flatly.

'Okay, fine,' said Winter. 'And I hope you're right, but I'm keeping an open mind.'

An hour later, after a fruitless search, they were making their way back to their car when the blue Mercedes estate car that had been parked outside Harding's office approached from the opposite direction and pulled up alongside them. The driver's window glided silently down.

Morgan thought her mother would probably have described the man looking out at them as dishy, whereas to her eyes he looked like every other forty-something smoothie, all of whom assumed they were God's gift to women. The way he looked her up and down only served to prove her point.

'Can I ask what you're doing wandering around this site?' he asked.

Morgan produced her warrant card. 'I'm DC Morgan and this is DC Winter. We believe there may be a person of interest hiding out on the site.'

The oh-so-smooth smile widened further.

'A person of interest? That sounds exciting. Has it got something to do with this body that was found?'

'Can I ask who you are, sir?' said Winter.

The man reached down and produced a business card.

'Name's on the card,' he said, as Winter took it. 'I'm the environmental project manager for this development.'

Winter glanced at the card and then looked at the driver.

'I don't recall seeing you on Monday,' he said.

'No. I was away for the weekend. I only got back on Tuesday evening, so I missed all the fun.'

'Fun?' asked Morgan. 'I would hardly call a murder fun, sir.'

The smile disappeared. 'Well, no, of course not. I'm sorry. It's just a manner of speaking.'

'A manner of speaking. Is that right?' said Morgan.

'I can assure you I intended no offence.'

'Oh, well, that's all right, then,' said Morgan, deadpan. 'As long as you intended no offence.'

He stared at Morgan but she held his gaze until he looked away.

'Will there be anything else, sir?' she asked.

'What? Oh, no, of course not. Don't let me keep you from your work.'

Morgan watched as the window glided back up and the car pulled away.

'You know, you can be quite intimidating at times,' said Winter admiringly.

She smiled. 'I find it's often the best way to deal with idiots like him.'

'And did you see the way he was looking you up and down?' said Winter. 'I'd say he fancied you.'

'Wanker,' said Morgan. 'Only in his dreams.'

Winter looked down at the card. 'Graham Watkins, project manager. Now, how's that for a coincidence?'

'Norm's always suspicious of coincidences,' said Morgan. 'He's not local, is he?'

Winter shook his head. 'Not unless they moved Yorkshire down into West Wales while we weren't looking.'

'We can check him out later,' said Morgan. 'Right now our priority is an eco-warrior called Wozzy.'

'Who seems to be long gone,' added Winter.

'Yes, all right, there's no need to rub it in,' said Morgan. 'We had to check, even though we knew it was a long shot.'

'Where do we look now?' asked Winter.

'We don't,' said Morgan. 'It would almost certainly be a waste of time. It will be much better to circulate his details and let Uniform locate him.'

'To my mind, the fact that this guy has gone missing is suspicious,' Winter said. 'It suggests he has something to hide.'

'How are you defining "gone missing"?' asked Morgan.

Winter stared at her blankly. 'What do you mean? He's not around, is he?'

'No, but has it occurred to you he would probably have been expecting Erin to come back on Sunday night or Monday morning?'

'So why wasn't he here when we searched the houses on Monday morning?'

'He probably hid when the builders were searching the place, and then legged it when he heard sirens and saw blue lights everywhere.'

'But why run if he's done nothing wrong?'

'Come on, Frosty, keep up. He's an activist who's been in trouble with the police on several occasions. What do you think he's going to do, stick around and welcome us with a cup of tea?'

'I suppose that's a fair point,' conceded Winter.

'Erin's got their only mobile phone, so there's no way she can call him and let him know what's happened, and he'll be worried about her. I wouldn't be at all surprised if he's gone into Llangwelli to see if he can find her there.'

'Why don't we drive around town before we go back to the station?' suggested Winter.

'It wouldn't hurt, would it?' said Morgan.

CHAPTER EIGHT

'Here we are, Judy, this'll be right up your street,' said Norman.

'What is it?' asked Lane, eyeing the two folders Norman was carrying suspiciously.

'It looks as if Dilys Watkins suspected Joe Harding of bribing people on the planning committee. We need to know if she was right, because if she is, and Harding knew she was on to him—'

'Then he's got motive,' finished Lane. 'Okay, give it here.'

'There's a laptop, too,' said Norman, 'but it's asking for a password.'

'What have you tried?' asked Lane.

'What? You mean I should take a guess?' said Norman.

Southall had been printing the photograph of the handbag she had taken at the flat.

'He hasn't tried anything, Judy,' she said. 'You know how terrified Norm gets when he's faced with anything vaguely technical.'

'I just know that if anyone's going to get us locked out, it'll be me,' said Norman. 'I did it once before, and even the tech guys couldn't fix it. These days I take the pragmatic approach and get someone else to take the risk.'

'Frosty's quite good at stuff like that,' suggested Lane.

'Talking of Frosty, where have those two got to?' asked Southall.

'Catren called in about half an hour ago,' said Lane. 'They should be back any minute.'

As if on cue, Morgan pushed her way through the doors.

'Well, that was a waste of time,' she said. 'There's no sign of him anywhere on that site. We even had a quick drive around town in case he's come looking for Erin. Do you want me to circulate his details and see if Uniform can find him?'

'Yes, I think you'd better do that,' said Southall. 'There aren't enough of us to waste time looking for someone who's probably got a lot of experience in hiding from the police.'

Southall pinned her photo of the handbag to the whiteboard.

'That's an expensive bag,' said Morgan. 'Did you find it at the flat?'

'Have you seen it before?' asked Southall.

'No, but I used to go to school with the woman who makes them,' said Morgan. 'Each one is handmade, and although they're all of a similar style, each one has a little variation in the patchwork, making them all unique. That's why they're so expensive.'

'I'm hoping it might help us trace her movements before she went away, if we need to,' said Southall.

'I can call the maker if you like,' said Morgan. 'She might be able to tell us something useful.'

'Yes, why not,' said Southall. 'It can't hurt, can it?'

Winter barged in through the doors.

'Ah, Frosty,' said Southall. 'We have Dilys Watkins's laptop here. D'you think you can help us get into it?'

'I can try,' he said. 'But I can't promise anything.'

'Just don't get us locked out,' said Norman.

'I can't promise that, either,' said Winter. 'But it should warn us before that happens.'

He took the laptop to his desk, sat down and opened it up. Like a grand piano master about to perform, he flexed his fingers. Intrigued, Norman sidled across the room and peered over his shoulder.

'Try Erin,' suggested Lane.

'That's not long enough on its own,' said Winter. 'What year was Erin born in?'

'She's sixteen,' said Lane, 'so that would be 2007.'

Winter thought for a few seconds, typed Erin07, added an exclamation mark, then pressed decisively on the return key. *Password incorrect* said the laptop.

'Why did you add the exclamation mark?' asked Norman.

'Usually it needs to be a combination of numbers and letters, with at least one capital letter, and at least one special character. People often use names and dates, despite the obvious risk, so the special character was introduced to make it a little harder for hackers.'

Winter thought for a minute. 'What month was Erin born in, Judy?'

'November,' said Lane.

Winter typed in Erin11! Then, holding his breath, he pressed the return key.

The laptop whirred into life. Winter let out his breath and grinned at his audience.

'Holy crap, will you look at that!' said Norman. 'He's only gone and done it!'

'It was the month, not the year,' said Winter, writing the password on a piece of paper. 'I take it you're going to need this,' he said, handing laptop and password to Judy Lane.

'Well done, Frosty,' said Southall.

While the others crowded around Winter, Morgan had been quietly speaking on the phone.

'Was there just one handbag at the flat, boss?'

'Yes, why?'

'Cassie keeps a record of all her buyers, complete with a photograph of the handbag. She says Dilys liked the first one so much she bought another.'

'Maybe she lost one,' said Norman.

'Not according to Cassie. She says Dilys loved her hand-bags and was really careful with them. She was even talking about possibly buying a third.'

'So, if she owned two, and there was only one at her flat, and there wasn't one with her body, where is the second one?' said Southall.

'You think whoever killed her took the handbag?' asked Norman.

'Since she was wearing Jimmy Choos and a Chanel jacket, it figures she would probably have had an equally nice bag with her,' said Southall. 'And now we know she had two of these bags, it's fair to assume she had the missing one with her.' She turned to Morgan. 'Is there any chance your friend could send us a photograph?'

'I've already asked her. She's going to email it to us,' said Morgan.

'Right, Catren. When that photograph comes in, com-pare it with the one I found, then get copies of the miss-ing handbag distributed everywhere you can think of,' said Southall. 'Get it on local TV if you can. Maybe we'll get lucky and someone can tell us where it is.'

Having ticked off everything on her mental checklist, Southall turned to Norman. 'Come on, Norm. Let's go.'

'Where do we start?' said Norman.

'Harding first, then we'll pay the history group a visit.'

* * *

'I don't mind saying that Dilys Watkins was a pain in the arse,' said Harding, 'but why would I kill her?'

'She was trying to stop your development going ahead,' Norman said.

'But I knew all along that she wouldn't get anywhere, and I've been proved right, haven't I? As you well know, the planning committee gave me their blessing on Monday morning, which is why we were starting to demolish the old houses. Or at least that was the plan until you lot came along and stopped us.'

'It's a bit of a coincidence, though, wouldn't you say?' said Norman. 'One of the main objectors to your plans is murdered over the weekend, and the very next working day, your plans get the go-ahead. I mean what are the chances?'

'All I can say is that I agree with you — it's an unfortunate and very sad coincidence. But I can assure you the plans were going to be given the go-ahead anyway.'

'How come? After all these years?' asked Norman.

'There was nothing sudden about it,' said Harding. 'It's been getting closer and closer all the time. Right from the start, I promised to ensure the project wouldn't have a massive environmental impact. The latest environmental report finally convinced the committee that we really were doing everything possible to minimise the impact, and that it would even improve the local environment. If you people had done your homework instead of listening to the ramblings of that crazy woman, you'd know all this.'

'Do I need to remind you that Mrs Watkins is dead, Mr Harding?'

'If you mean do I need reminding that my development project is being delayed, of course I don't. Look, I'm sorry Dilys is dead but I had nothing to do with it. Anyway, did it ever occur to you to find out what she was really up to?'

'We know what she was up to,' said Norman. 'She was trying to stop your development.'

Harding sighed. 'That's what she made out.'

'Dilys was part of the history group,' said Norman. 'She was going to supply them with proof of your corrupt dealings so they could challenge you in court.'

'And did she provide any proof?' Harding said.

'She told them she had the proof but she died before she could give it to them,' said Norman. 'Which is another unfortunate and very sad coincidence.'

Southall studied Harding's face. She had assumed it wouldn't take long for Norman's questions to provoke a reaction, but he remained calm and unflustered.

'Here's the question you should be considering,' said Harding. 'This redevelopment has been at the planning stage for over ten years, yet Dilys Watkins only got involved two years ago. Now, why is that?'

'Maybe that's when she became suspicious that members of the planning committee were being bribed,' said Norman.

Harding laughed. 'You mean being bribed by me? Good God, man, if that was how I did business, my plans would have been approved years ago.'

'Perhaps you didn't use bribery from the start, but it was taking so long you got tired of waiting and felt it was time to oil the wheels,' suggested Norman. 'Dilys obviously thought that's what was happening.'

'I can see you've taken everything she claimed to know at face value, and haven't looked beneath the surface. This is exactly what she would have wanted,' said Harding. 'Now, would you like me to tell you what Dilys Watkins was really trying to do?'

'It's easy to spout accusations about someone who can no longer defend themselves,' said Norman.

'Yes, I realise that,' said Harding, 'But I'm not the one spouting accusations. What I'm about to tell you is fact, and it shouldn't take you too long to check what I'm saying. Then perhaps you'll stop wasting your time trying to prove I committed a murder which I know nothing about.'

Norman stared at Harding for a few seconds, but he maintained his implacable gaze.

'Okay,' said Norman finally. 'I'm listening.'

'The truth is, Dilys didn't really give a damn about the redevelopment or the history of the village. She joined the history group offering the promise of evidence that would provide them with grounds to stop me because that way she would achieve her hidden agenda.'

'What hidden agenda?'

'She was trying to smear my good name because I sacked her husband after he spent a month away from work without permission.'

'That's Ross Watkins, right?' asked Norman.

'That's correct,' said Harding.

'When was this?'

'It was about two years ago, and Dilys has hated me ever since.'

'That would have been around the time their daughter went missing,' said Norman.

'Yes, I believe that had something to do with it.'

'But his fourteen-year-old daughter had gone missing and he was up in London trying to find her. Didn't you think the guy deserved some compassion?'

'Compassion? I don't have time for namby-pamby stuff like that,' said Harding. 'It's one of the reasons why I'm so successful.'

Norman couldn't hide his distaste. 'Jeez, listen to yourself. How do you sleep at night?'

'I sleep very well, thank you,' said Harding. 'You might find the way I do business offensive, Sergeant, but it doesn't make me a murderer.'

'Are you telling us that you knew all along that Dilys was trying to prove you were corrupt?' asked Southall.

'Of course I knew. If you want to succeed in business, you have to know who your enemies are, what they're up to, and why they're doing it.'

'You admit you regarded Dilys as an enemy?' asked Southall.

'That wasn't my intention, but when it became obvious that she wasn't going to let up, I decided I had to make her an offer she couldn't refuse.'

'What sort of offer?' Southall said.

'Dilys and Ross were already in disarray because their daughter had gone missing, and as I had also sacked Ross I knew they would be short of money. Then, as luck would have it, they separated. Ross had got himself another job by then, but I knew it wouldn't be paying anything close to what I'd been paying him. So, with things being so tight, how could Dilys afford to keep paying part of the mortgage on the house, and rent a flat?'

'Why would Dilys still be paying the mortgage?' asked Southall. 'I thought they were separated, pending a divorce. Weren't they going to sell the house?'

'Although they had separated, as far as I know they had never actually taken any steps towards getting divorced. I believe they shared this vague, unspoken hope that one day their daughter would come back and they'd all live happily ever after. Anyone with half a brain would know it was never going to happen, of course but, for whatever reason, Dilys and Ross couldn't, or wouldn't, see it. I suppose they were both in denial.'

'You seem to know a lot about their affairs,' said Norman.

'I make it my business to know as much as I can about people who are trying to make life difficult for me,' said Harding.

'So, how did you take advantage of this situation that Dilys was in?' asked Southall. 'That is what you're saying, isn't it?'

Harding smiled. 'I told her I felt guilty about sacking Ross and offered her a flat, rent-free.'

'And she took it?' asked Norman.

'Nearly bit my hand off,' said Harding. 'I think she was motivated by spite, so she didn't put much thought into it. It was more a case of taking something from me as part compensation for me sacking her husband.'

'And what did you expect in return?' asked Southall.

'Nothing,' said Harding.

'You seriously expect us to believe there was nothing in it for you?' asked Norman.

Again, Harding gave them his self-satisfied smile. 'Come now, you must have heard the expression, "keep your friends close, and your enemies even closer"?'

'And exactly how did you keep Dilys close?' asked Southall.

'Not the way you're thinking, Inspector. Despite everything I actually liked Dilys. I know most men would have called her physically attractive, but she wasn't my type, and I don't do affairs. But even if she had been my type, I don't believe she was that sort of woman, and in any case, I was the last man she would have been interested in.'

'I'm not sure I understand how you think Dilys was in your pocket, if you never asked anything of her,' said Southall.

'In her rush to take what she could from me, Dilys accepted my offer without thinking it through,' said Harding. 'But once she took the bait, I knew that if she ever tried to smear me, I could damage her credibility by pointing out that she had accepted rent-free accommodation from me. It wouldn't look very good, would it? At the very least it would be enough to make her an unreliable witness.'

'You admit you've got something to hide, then,' said Norman.

'I don't admit I've got something to hide because I haven't,' said Harding. 'Believe me, if I was the sort to cut corners, I wouldn't have paid a small fortune for three different environmental surveys. Nor would I be paying for a specialist environmental expert to ensure I meet the requirements put forward by the planning committee as a result of those surveys. And, furthermore, as I have already said, if I was the sort to pay bribes to get things done, I wouldn't have had to wait this long for my planning permission to be passed. It would have gone through years ago without any environmental considerations.'

'You understand we're going to have to check all this,' said Norman.

'I sincerely hope you will,' said Harding. 'And then you'll see you've been wasting your time hassling me when you could have been finding out who really murdered Dilys Watkins.'

* * *

'Good morning, Mr Roberts,' said Southall. 'I understand you run a history group, is that correct?'

Roberts's eyes flickered nervously from Southall to Norman and back.

'Yes, I do. Why? Is there a problem?'

'We're investigating the death of Dilys Watkins,' said Southall. 'I believe she was a member of your group.'

'What a terrible thing that was,' said Roberts. 'Why would anyone want to do that to such a lovely person?'

'That's what we're trying to find out,' said Southall.

Roberts looked horrified. 'Surely you can't think it was anyone in the history group!'

'You're probably right,' said Southall. 'But as part of our investigation we have to explore every avenue so we can get to know more about Dilys and her life.'

'You should try looking at Joe Harding,' said Roberts. 'He's the one you want to be arresting.'

'I can assure you we're looking into every possibility,' said Southall. 'But we don't go around arresting people unless we have evidence to suggest they're guilty of something.'

'He's been bribing people on the planning committee,' said Roberts.

'And you possess evidence that proves this, do you?' asked Norman.

'Well, no, I don't,' said Roberts, 'but you can ask anyone, and—'

'Yes, we've heard the rumours,' said Southall, 'but rumours without evidence don't prove anything, I'm afraid.'

'Tell us about your group,' said Norman. 'When did it start?'

'My father started it back in the eighties when the pits were forced to close. He felt it would be wrong to just forget the mines ever existed, and it turned out he wasn't the only one who thought that way. Then, when the group started, they decided there was more to the area than just coal mines, so it has a much broader focus these days.'

'Do you have many members?' Southall asked.

'There are about a dozen full members and a couple of hundred associate members,' said Roberts.

Norman raised an eyebrow. 'I'm not sure I understand what you mean by "associate members",' he said.

'Full members are people like me who are genuinely interested in local history,' explained Roberts. 'We introduced associate membership when we needed a way to raise money to fight Joe Harding and his redevelopment plans. It's surprising how many local people agreed with us and were willing to put their hands in their pockets to try and help.'

'What can you tell us about Dilys?' asked Southall, not wishing to let Roberts get started about the redevelopment.

'She seemed a nice enough person, but I didn't really know her that well on a personal level,' said Roberts.

'When did she join?' asked Southall.

'It must have been a couple of years ago,' said Roberts.

'Did she say why she joined?'

'Oh, there was only one reason,' said Roberts. 'She believed passionately that Harding should be stopped. She was convinced he was bribing people in the planning department, and she offered to bring us the evidence to prove it.'

'And were you aware of this alleged bribery before Dilys brought it to your attention?' asked Southall.

'I'm not quite sure what you mean,' said Roberts.

'What I mean, Mr Roberts, is this: did anyone ever suggest Joe Harding was bribing people on the planning committee before Dilys brought it up?'

'Well, no, not exactly,' conceded Roberts.

'But Dilys was convinced she was right, and she was going to provide the proof, is that right?' asked Southall.

'That's what she told us, yes.'

'How was she going to get this evidence?' asked Norman.

'She didn't say,' said Roberts. 'She told us she had access to the planning committee, so I assumed that's how she was getting her proof.'

'And did she?' asked Norman.

'She called me a couple of weeks ago to say she had sufficient evidence, but before she gave it to us she was going to
see someone who could verify that it would stand up in court.
Then, when she came back, she would hand it to us so we
could make a proper legal challenge. That was supposed to be
this week, but it's not going to happen now, is it?'

'So, you're saying that last week Dilys took her evidence
somewhere to get it verified?' said Southall.

Roberts nodded. 'That's what she told me.'

'Did she say where?' asked Norman.

'She didn't, only that she would be away for the week.'

* * *

Even as Norman started the engine, Southall's brain was tick-
ing over.

'What do you think about these bribery allegations, Norm?'

'He wouldn't be the first developer to grease a few palms,
would he?' said Norman.

'Yes, but this development has been at the planning
stage for years. If you were prepared to pay people to grant
permission, why would you wait until now when you could
have done it years ago?'

'I dunno,' said Norman. 'Maybe he couldn't afford it
until now.'

'No. Harding doesn't give me the impression he's ever
been short of money.'

'Are you saying you think Dilys was making it up?' asked
Norman.

'I'm not sure what I'm saying,' said Southall. 'But there's
no denying it's just like you said — one minute Dilys seems
to be about to reveal the evidence about Harding, then suddenly she's dead, and almost immediately he gets his planning permission.'

'It's certainly a coincidence we can't ignore,' said Norman.

'When we get back to the station I'm going to see if I
can find out who Dilys went to see in Scotland.'

'You think that's the key?' asked Norman.

'I believe it could be,' said Southall. 'Think about it for a minute. If you had spent months gathering the dirt on Harding and were ready to go public, wouldn't you want to get it out there as soon as possible? Why go on vacation for a week just at that critical moment?'

'Maybe the trip had been planned and she couldn't put it off.'

'Yes, fair enough, but if what she knew about Harding was so important, why not spill the beans as soon as she had the evidence and before she went away?'

'I see what you mean,' said Norman. 'You're thinking she needed to see this person who was going to verify it before she released it.'

'Either that or she went to see someone who had the final, missing piece of her jigsaw.'

Norman nodded. 'Yeah, I reckon you could be right. What do you want me to do?'

'See if you can get hold of someone in the local planning department who can tell us about Harding's redevelopment plans and how they suddenly got passed. I particularly want to know if he's—'

'They're not going to be falling over themselves to tell me how much he's paid out in bribes,' said Norman.

'Of course they're not, that's not what I was going to say. I want to know if he really has paid for three environmental surveys.' She thought for a minute. 'Anyway, you can recognise a liar when you hear one, can't you, even over the phone?'

'I like to think I can,' said Norman.

'Then you'll know if the person speaking to you is trying to pull the wool over your eyes. There again, Harding's adamant he doesn't pay bribes.'

'Do you think he's telling the truth?' asked Norman.

'I don't like to admit it, but he's very confident that he's in the right.'

'Guys like him are always confident they're in the right,' said Norman. 'But half the time they're using all that confidence bullshit as a shield to hide behind.'

'Are you telling me you're convinced he's lying?' asked Southall.

'I'm undecided right now,' said Norman.

'You mean you're keeping an open mind?' said Southall. 'That's very commendable, considering you dislike the man so much.'

'Yeah, I'm sorry about that. I do try not to let it show but right from the start he pissed me off. He's got under my skin, I suppose. It's not showing too much, is it?'

'No, you're okay,' said Southall. 'You certainly shouldn't lose sleep over it. Guys like Harding must be used to people disliking them. I wouldn't be surprised to find that he's got such a thick skin he doesn't even notice.'

'I've been trying not to let my dislike of him influence my opinion, but now I'm thinking maybe that's actually clouding my judgement. Do you think I should take a step back?'

'Good heavens, no, Norm. I trust you to do the right thing. You usually do, even when it involves people you don't like.'

CHAPTER NINE

'Have we got anything back from Dilys's mobile service provider yet?' asked Southall.

Lane held up a sheaf of printed papers. 'It came in while you were out, but I haven't had time to look at it yet.'

'That's okay, I can do that,' said Southall, taking the papers from Lane and heading for her office. 'I'm hoping there's going to be a phone number in Scotland there somewhere.'

As she settled at her desk and began searching through Dilys's call history, Norman found a number for the County Council planning office.

* * *

Half an hour later, Southall had just ended her call to Scotland when she looked up to see Norman leaning against the doorpost at the entrance to her office.

'How did you get on?' he asked.

'Her name is Gaynor McGowan. She and Dilys met many years ago at uni and they've kept in touch ever since. So, the first thing I had to do was tell her what has happened and why I needed to speak to her.'

'That's not the best way to start a conversation, is it?' said Norman. 'I hope she wasn't too upset.'

'I got the impression they'd drifted apart over the years so they weren't exactly best mates, but even so, it was a shock for her to hear that Dilys was dead.'

'And did she know anything useful?'

'It turns out Gaynor is a solicitor working for a law firm that specialises in corporate law. She says Dilys had contacted her about ways to stop Harding. Gaynor's a smart cookie, and she refused to offer Dilys any sort of opinion or advice without first seeing concrete evidence.'

'And that's why Dilys went up to Scotland,' said Norman.

'Apparently, she went laden with a couple of files of evidence, which I assume are the two files we now have. She was convinced these contained all the necessary evidence to bring Harding down.'

'And what did Gaynor think?' asked Norman.

'When you first saw it, you said that it seemed to be all rumour and no proof, right?' said Southall.

'That's right. I couldn't see anything that showed proof of any wrongdoing,' said Norman.

'Well, Gaynor goes a step further. The way she saw it, what Dilys actually had was evidence to show Harding went way over his obligations when it came to due diligence on environmental matters. Dilys claims Harding only paid for three different surveys because the first two didn't say what he wanted to hear. The way Gaynor sees it, Harding paid for three different surveys because he wanted to be sure he'd covered every eventuality and that the first two hadn't missed anything.'

'So Harding's straight?' asked Norman.

'Gaynor believes he's been totally honest in all his dealings with the planning committee, and she told Dilys she was wasting her time and that she had no case against him.'

'So why was Dilys so sure he was up to no good?'

'Gaynor thinks Dilys blamed Harding for destroying her marriage, and because she was so obsessed with getting even, she more or less convinced herself that everything he did must be corrupt,' Southall said.

'She didn't think the marriage might have broken up because her husband found out he'd spent fourteen years raising another man's child?' said Norman.

'She told Gaynor they would have got over that if Harding hadn't fired Ross.'

'So Gaynor already knew Ross isn't Erin's biological father?' asked Norman.

'Oh, yes, she's known since it all came out in Erin's DNA test results. She says she tried, on more than one occasion, to point out to Dilys that most men would probably find that sort of news difficult to deal with, but Dilys always refused to accept it.'

'Jeez, that's what you call being in serious denial,' said Norman.

'Anyway, when that argument failed yet again last week, Gaynor tried to convince Dilys that, while it was true Harding wasn't very sympathetic, it wasn't actually his fault that Ross wasn't Erin's father. But Dilys remained adamant that everything was Harding's fault. Finally, when Gaynor refused to agree with her, she packed her bags and left in a huff.'

'So, she wasn't in Scotland all week as we thought,' said Norman.

'She got to Gaynor's on Monday evening, and was on her way back home on Wednesday evening,' said Southall. 'I'm guessing she wouldn't have driven all night, so I think we can assume she would have stayed in a hotel Wednesday night, then headed for home on Thursday morning.'

'So, it's quite possible she could have been back here late afternoon or early evening on Thursday,' said Norman. 'I'll run the registration number through the ANPR database and see if we can trace her as she drove back.'

'How did you get on with the planners?' asked Southall.

'If you accept the rumours about Harding being crooked, you would think that, while he might have paid for three surveys, he would only have submitted the one that best suited his purposes, right?'

'So, Gaynor was right?' asked Southall.

Norman nodded. 'The planners confirmed exactly that. Far from being the bad guy, Harding paid for three environmental surveys just to make sure nothing had been missed.'

'That's unusual, isn't it?' said Southall.

'For most people, yes, it is, but according to the lady I spoke with, Harding might be a five-star arsehole as a person, but as a developer he always goes above and beyond when it comes to the environment.'

'What about bribes?' asked Southall.

'Honestly? I think your new friend Gaynor McGowan is right. Dilys was misguidedly obsessed with the idea. Obviously, these planning guys wouldn't admit to it if it was happening, but I was told we can have access to the minutes of every meeting, letter, email, text, even handwritten notes. You name it, if it relates to that site, we can examine it. Now, they wouldn't offer that sort of access if they had something to hide, right?'

'Did they know anything about Dilys?'

'Apparently, she was a regular correspondent, and she always attended the open planning meetings.'

'What was the nature of her correspondence?' said Southall. 'Though I don't really need to ask, do I?'

'There was only ever one subject. They even sent a cease and desist letter because she made so many false accusations about people on the planning committee.'

'Oh, wow, so she really was obsessed,' said Southall.

'Yeah, that's for sure,' said Norman. 'But it makes me wonder how Harding must have felt about all these false accusations she was making about him. It's all very well for him to say he knew she couldn't stop his development, but she could still have ruined his reputation.'

'You're right,' said Southall. 'I think we should probably broaden our suspect list, but Harding isn't off the hook yet.'

* * *

'I've got the forensic results from number nineteen,' said Norman, his eyes on his computer screen.

'Let's hear it then,' said Southall.

'It was definitely blood on the floor, but it's not a match for Dilys.'

'Do we know whose blood it is?'

'No idea. They can't match it to anyone on the database,' said Norman.

'What about the sleeping bag?' asked Southall. 'Was there any DNA evidence to suggest Dilys had used it?'

'No exact match to Dilys, but they did find one familial match, and one unknown.'

'Erin says she was sleeping there with her boyfriend,' said Southall.

'I can't imagine we're going to find another familial match, so that would explain it,' said Norman.

'It backs up her story about her and Wozzy sleeping there, too,' said Southall. 'Did they find anything to link Dilys to the house?'

'Nada,' said Norman.

'In that case I think we can safely rule it out as our murder scene,' said Southall. 'And if they found no evidence to suggest that Dilys's body was ever there, we can also forget any ideas about her body having been kept there.'

'I agree,' said Norman. 'But it leaves us with the question of whose blood we found on the floor.'

'It could have been one of the builders,' said Southall. 'We know they were checking all the houses.'

'Yeah, but did they check any more houses after they found the body?' said Norman thoughtfully. 'If you think about it, there were two guys checking out the houses, right? Logic says they would have started from the lower end of the street same as we did. Now, even if one guy found the body and called the second guy in, or they were working the houses together, we know they both saw the body in number nine. And we know what can happen when someone comes across a dead body, right?'

'You think they didn't search the other houses in that street?'

'After the shock of finding the body I reckon the odds are pretty high that they didn't search the remaining houses. If they had, they would have found the sleeping bag, but they didn't mention it when Frosty interviewed them.'

'When we were with Erin on the roof there was definitely nothing to suggest she had been injured. And Catren was with her at the hospital. She would have noticed a wound or a bandage,' Southall said.

'That just leaves us with Wozzy the eco-warrior then,' said Norman.

'Why would you think something's happened to him?' asked Southall.

'You mean apart from the blood we found on the floor, and the fact Catren and Frosty couldn't find him?' asked Norman. 'Well, what if Catren's wrong about Erin being an angel? Suppose she told Wozzy she was coming to make her peace with her mum, but the real reason was to kill her. Then, when she comes back and tells Wozzy what she's done, he's not happy. Murder wasn't part of the deal as far as he's concerned, so he freaks out. They get into a fight, she smacks him over the head with something, thinks he's dead and does a runner.'

'You said she "thinks he's dead and does a runner",' said Southall. 'Why "thinks"?'

'Because, if he really had been dead, Frosty and me would have found his body. But if she only knocked him out, he could have woken up later. Maybe he did, and decided he didn't want to be involved with Erin any longer. So he fled the scene, leaving her to face up to whatever she'd done on her own.'

'That's all very well, Norm, but we know Dilys was run down by a car.'

'Okay, so maybe Erin pushed her out in front of the car.'

'I really think you're barking up the wrong tree here, Norm,' said Southall. 'If Erin pushed Dilys into the path of the car that killed her, why didn't the driver come forward?'

'Possibly because he'd been drinking and was way over the limit,' said Norman.

'It's a theory, Norm, but I'm not sure it works for me. There's also the question of how the body got to number nine if she was run down in Llangwelli.'

'But we don't know she was run down in Llangwelli, do we?' said Norman. 'What if Erin met her mum in Llangwelli but then persuaded her to drive them back out to the village. Dilys isn't sure where she's going, so she follows Erin's directions. But Erin directs her to stop on the road outside the perimeter fence, and comes up with some excuse for them to have to wait by the side of the road. While they're waiting, a car comes along, Erin gives Dilys a shove, and bang, job done.'

'But why would Dilys drive Erin back to the village?'

'I dunno. Maybe Erin told her about Wozzy, and Dilys wanted to meet him.'

'I'll say one thing,' said Southall. 'You have a great imagination, Norm.'

'You might think it's far-fetched,' said Norman, 'but it could explain why Erin was up on the roof, thinking about jumping.'

'Are you saying she was up on the roof because she was feeling remorse after killing her mother?' asked Southall.

'Yeah, it's a possibility,' said Norman doubtfully.

'I can tell from the sound of your voice you're unconvinced,' said Southall.

'I just wonder, would she be feeling remorse about murdering her mother if she'd been planning it for months?' said Norman. 'Maybe, but I don't think so.'

'I take it you have an alternative theory?' asked Southall.

'What if Erin ran off believing she had killed Wozzy,' said Norman, 'but when she calmed down she realised she might be wrong and he could have just been knocked out, so she comes back to see.

'But when she arrives she finds builders on site, and the next thing she knows, the place is full of sirens and blue lights.

At first she thinks maybe there's a raid and Wozzy is about to be arrested, but then she slowly begins to realise there are way too many different vehicles for that. Now she starts to think she must have killed him after all and someone has found his body.'

'But Erin would have known it was Dilys's body that had been found,' Southall said.

'How would she know?'

'If you're saying she killed Dilys, she would have known where the body was.'

'Yeah, but remember she's seriously stressed by now and she's also trying to keep out of sight, so she can't see exactly where it's all happening. But perhaps she does manage to get close enough to hear what's being said. She hears someone mention something about a body being found, but is it her mother's body, or is it Wozzy? Perhaps it's both. Whatever, she's now beginning to panic as she realises the full extent of what she's done. Even if she hated her mother and doesn't regret killing her, Wozzy was the one person who seemed to care about her and she's killed him. Now the remorse kicks in, and that's why she heads for the Madoc Building where you found her.'

'I'm sure her mother cared for her before she died, and her dad cares for her now,' said Southall.

'Yeah, we know that,' said Norman. 'But remember, Erin has been out of their lives for over two years, they've been replaced in her affections by Wozzy, so maybe she doesn't realise they still care about her.'

Southall rested her gaze on Norman while she thought about it.

'Sorry, Norm, but as theories go, I think it ignores too many of the established facts.'

'You mean the bit about Dilys being pushed under the car?'

'If Erin is as devious as you say, wouldn't she simply have blamed the driver?' Southall said.

'He could have denied it and said she pushed Dilys in front of his car,' argued Norman.

'But he would say that, wouldn't he?' said Southall. 'If she denied it, it would be his word against hers, and who would a jury be more likely to believe? A driver who ran someone down, or a traumatised kid who watched her mother being killed by a car?'

'Good point,' conceded Norman, 'but that would mean taking a chance that we might find out the truth when we questioned her.'

'You haven't met her, have you?' asked Southall.

'Not yet.'

'Well, perhaps you should,' said Southall. 'I might not be quite as convinced as Catren, but I don't think this kid is capable of being that devious, and I can't believe we've both got her so totally wrong.'

'It's part of my job to offer alternative scenarios,' said Norman, looking hurt.

'I know that, Norm, and I've told you before that I do appreciate your input. But I'm the one who has to decide what direction the investigation should take, and I just think that on this occasion you're wrong.'

* * *

'Hallo. Is that DC Morgan?'

'Speaking,' said Morgan.

'This is PC Karen Alloway calling from Region.'

'What can I do for you, PC Alloway?'

'You sent out a photograph of a missing handbag?'

'That's right, I did,' said Morgan.

'Well, I've got it here in lost property.'

'Really? Wow, well done, Karen, that's fantastic news. How come you've got it?'

'A lady brought it in this morning.'

'Where did she find it?' asked Morgan.

'She didn't say exactly, just that she was walking her dog when she came across it. She comes past here on her way home so she handed it in in case someone had reported it lost or stolen.'

'Is there anything inside it?'

'Not a thing,' said Alloway. 'The lady said it was open when she found it, and empty.'

'What condition is it in?'

'It's a bit wet from having been out in the rain, but otherwise it's a really nice bag. Is it important? Only I quite fancy it for myself if the owner doesn't claim it.'

'Well, I've got two bits of news on that score. The good news is that the owner won't be claiming it. The bad news is that you can't have it because it's evidence in a murder investigation. I'm afraid if you want one you'll have to buy it, but I can put you in touch with the maker if you like.'

'I don't think I could afford to buy one on my wages, that's why I was . . . well, what I mean is . . . What do you want me to do with the handbag now?' asked Alloway.

'I'll come and collect it,' said Morgan. 'And can you give me the phone number of the lady who found it?'

'Yes, of course.'

Morgan hung up and swung her chair around. 'We've got a hit on the handbag.'

'Already?' said Norman. 'Jeez that was quick!'

'It's in the lost property office at Region. Apparently, it was handed in by a dog walker. I'll go over there to collect it, but first I'm going to call the lady who found it and ask her where it was.'

* * *

'Mrs Regan? My name's DC Morgan from Llangwelli Police. I understand you found a handbag and handed it in to our regional office.'

'Yes, that's right. It looked expensive, not the sort of bag you'd take for a walk in the countryside, so I thought it might have been stolen. I know if it was mine I'd want it back, so

115

I picked it up. I pass that station every day, so it seemed the right thing to do. Did I do something wrong?'

Morgan would have much preferred it if the handbag had been left where it had been found, but Mrs Regan couldn't possibly have known that it was connected to a murder investigation.

'Not at all, Mrs Regan,' she said. 'You did exactly the right thing. I just wanted to know if you could tell me where you found the bag.'

'Rather than try and explain it, I can go one better if it helps,' said Mrs Regan. 'I'll be taking my dog for a walk a bit later. If you want to come and meet me, I can show you the exact spot.'

'That would be fabulous, Mrs Regan,' said Morgan. 'Are you sure you don't mind?'

'Of course not. I'm going there anyway. And, please, call me Jan. Mrs Regan makes me feel old.'

'Okay, Jan. Where shall I meet you?'

Jan Regan explained where she would be parking her car, and they agreed to meet at three. 'And bring your wellies,' added Jan. 'It's a bit muddy out there.'

* * *

Jan Regan regularly walked her dog in an area of two hundred and fifty acres of mixed woodland which had been planted in stages over the last ten years. Several small car parks had been built around the periphery, allowing both ramblers and dog walkers to make use of the various paths which criss-crossed the plantation.

Morgan drove her car into the small car park Jan had indicated and parked opposite the only other car there, a small red hatchback. As she did, a woman climbed from the other car, walked around to the boot and opened the hatch to release a springer spaniel which began to run around in circles like a mad thing.

The woman smiled, waved at Morgan and pointed at the dog. 'It's okay, he doesn't bite,' she said. 'He might even calm down in a minute.'

'Don't worry,' said Morgan. 'I'm used to crazy spaniels. My father has one.'

The woman approached Morgan and offered her hand. 'I'm Jan Regan.' she said.

Morgan shook her hand, and produced her warrant card. 'I'm DC Morgan. It's really good of you to help out like this. I can't tell you how grateful I am.'

'Not at all. If my handbag had been pinched, I'd like to think someone would do the same for me. I take it it was stolen and then dumped out here?'

'Something like that,' said Morgan.

'Don't you know? Hasn't the owner reported it missing?'

'Not exactly,' said Morgan. 'The handbag is part of an ongoing investigation, so I can't really say.'

Jan Regan was evidently no fool, and she soon put two and two together. 'Is it anything to do with that poor woman who was found dead the other day?'

'I'm sorry, Jan, but I really can't discuss it,' said Morgan. 'Oh God. It is, isn't it?'

'If you could just show me where you found the bag,' said Morgan.

'Yes, of course.' She pointed along one of the paths and the dog zoomed off ahead. 'It's this way.'

'Is it far?' asked Morgan.

'Only about five minutes.'

Though smart, Jan Regan apparently couldn't deal with silence. 'Of course, I understand why you can't talk about it,' she said. 'I really didn't mean to pry.' She suddenly stopped dead in her tracks, a horrified expression on her face. 'I haven't destroyed forensic evidence, have I?'

'Sorry?' said Morgan.

'Where I found the handbag. Was it where she was murdered? Oh, God, I'm so sorry.'

'It's okay, Jan, there's really no need to apologise,' said Morgan.

'I didn't realize the significance of the bag.'

'Of course you didn't,' said Morgan. 'There's no reason why you should.'

The dog kept a short distance ahead of them, zig-zagging across the path, nose to the ground, tail wagging furiously as he carried out high-speed investigations of everything in his path.

'The bag was under a tree just up here on the left,' said Jan. 'I probably wouldn't have noticed it if my dog hadn't been so excited. I suppose it was a different smell to the usual stuff he comes across out here.'

A few yards further on, she stopped at a small group of birch trees.

'This one here,' she said, pointing to a tree that stood about fifteen feet high. 'I assume someone must have thrown it in there thinking it would never be noticed.'

Morgan looked up and down the path. 'Do you come here every day?'

Jan nodded towards the dog. 'He'd go mad if I didn't walk him twice a day. I need the exercise too, and I swear being out in a peaceful place like this is good for the soul.'

'Do many people walk here?' asked Morgan.

'I can't say for sure,' said Jan. 'All I can tell you is that I come here most mornings, and again in the afternoons, but I don't often see anyone else.'

'Do you always come at the same times?'

'I'm retired, so I have the luxury of being able to walk whenever I choose, but generally I tend to come anytime between nine and eleven in the mornings, and again between three and five in the afternoons.'

'Do you know if many people come at other times, like in the early morning before work, or later in the afternoons, after work?'

'I'm afraid I can't answer that. There is a warden who keeps an eye on the place occasionally. He might be able to tell you, but I don't know how you would find him.'

'Well, I won't hold you up any longer,' said Morgan, who was itching to start looking around. 'Thank you so much for your help.' She fished a card from her wallet. 'If you think of anything else, just give me a call.'

Jan took the card, glanced at it and slipped it into her pocket. Her disappointed expression indicated that she had been hoping to be a little more involved.

'Yes, right. If you're sure I can't be of any more help . . .'

Morgan smiled. 'Enjoy the rest of your walk. And, thank you again.'

Slowly, reluctantly, Jan went on her way.

Waiting for Jan to finally disappear, Morgan studied the area around the tree. Then she called Norman.

'Yo, Catren, how did you get on with your bag-finding lady?' said Norman.

'I think she fancied playing Miss Marple until I moved her on, but to be fair, she was very helpful.'

'Why, what did you find?'

'Nothing in the way of evidence. I'm sure this can't be the murder scene.'

'Why not?' Norman asked.

'It makes no sense. I'm in the middle of nowhere, and the nearest place to park a car is nearly ten minutes' walk from here. No one would come out here unless they were walking a dog, and Dilys didn't have a dog.'

'Okay,' said Norman. 'But you have a theory, right?'

'I think whoever killed Dilys possibly took the handbag to make it look like a mugging, and to make it harder for us to identify her body.'

'Yeah, I think we've all agreed that much,' said Norman. 'But how did the handbag end up out there?'

'What if the murderer has a dog?'

'Go on,' encouraged Norman.

'Jan, the lady who found the bag, says she doesn't think many people come here, especially during the day,' explained Morgan. 'To my mind that makes it the perfect place for a dog walker to get rid of something without being noticed.'

'Why does it have to be a dog walker?' Norman asked. 'Why not just go there on their own?'

'It doesn't have to be,' said Morgan. 'But I think you'd be much more conspicuous out here if you were seen without one.'

'Was the bag well hidden?' asked Norman.

'I wouldn't say so. It was behind some small trees, but my guess is that it was thrown in there from the path rather than deliberately hidden.'

'Is there any other access to those trees?' asked Norman. 'Like from the other side?'

'No way,' said Morgan. 'There's a big patch of dense thicket behind them. It would have to have been thrown from the path, more or less from where I'm standing now. Jan Regan says she probably wouldn't have noticed it if her dog hadn't found it, and I don't think anyone else would have noticed it either, unless they were searching for it.'

'What about SOCOs?' asked Norman. 'Do you want me to call them out?'

'Seriously?' said Morgan. 'The bag was dumped days ago, and we've had a lot of rain since. It was sniffed out by a mad spaniel whose owner climbed all over the site to reach it, and I don't know how many other people have walked their dogs along this path in the meantime. I think it would be a waste of their time.'

'It sounds like you're probably right,' said Norman.

'What do you want me to do?'

'It sounds like you've got it covered, Catren. Unless you want me to come out there and check for myself, I think you should head back here.'

'D'you think I've missed something?' Morgan asked.

'Not from what you've just told me,' said Norman. 'I've said this before, Catren, if we didn't trust you, we wouldn't let you loose on your own. I'll say goodbye now, and we'll see you when you get back.'

CHAPTER TEN

DS Marston reluctantly agreed to meet up with Norman, but not at Region. Instead, he suggested they meet halfway. He gave Norman directions to a roadside cafe and snack bar.

Norman had been around the block enough times to realise it was unlikely that Marston was being considerate. More probably it was a case of having something to hide from his colleagues. Whatever, Norman decided he would play it by ear and see what happened.

As he got out of his car, he could see Marston sitting outside at a picnic table warming his hands on a cup of coffee. Norman got one for himself and went across to Marston's table.

'Well, this is nice,' he said, surveying their surroundings. 'Very salubrious I don't think.'

Marston looked up at him, frowning. 'Salubri-what? What's that mean?'

'Salubrious,' repeated Norman, putting one leg over the bench seat opposite Marston. 'It's actually a fancy way of describing something that's good for you. But I think you'll agree this place definitely isn't good for anyone, what with the smell of exhaust fumes and the constant racket of heavy lorries rumbling past. D'you come here often?'

'It might not suit a poncy Londoner like you, with your fancy words,' said Marston, 'but I happen to like it and yes, I do come here often. In fact, I have my lunch here almost every day.'

'Wow! You sure know how to live,' said Norman. 'And, just so we're clear, I'm not here because I'm hoping to become your regular bosom buddy lunch date.'

'Don't worry, mate, there's no chance of that,' said Marston. 'I wasn't planning to add you to my Christmas card list either.'

'That's fine by me,' said Norman. 'And, as we now both know where we stand, I can get straight down to business.'

'What's this about?' Marston said.

'About two years ago, you investigated the disappearance of a girl called Erin Watkins.'

'Did I?' said Marston.

'It's got your name on the case file,' said Norman.

'I suppose I must have then.'

'Don't you remember?'

'Can you recall the details of every case you've been on?' asked Marston.

'No way,' said Norman. 'But I don't think I would forget a case from a couple of years ago of a girl of fourteen who went missing and was never found.'

Marston fidgeted awkwardly on his bench seat and took a sip of his coffee. 'Oh yeah. Now you've jogged my memory, I think I do recall that one. She got on a train to London and was never seen again. That the one, is it?'

'Are you asking me, or telling me?' asked Norman.

'I'm telling you. I remember now. Once we knew she'd gone to London we handed it over to the Met. I don't know how much effort they put into looking for her but I remember them drawing a blank. After six months, when we still hadn't found her, or her body, I was directed to mark her down as a runaway, and leave it as an open case. You didn't need to drag me all the way out here to learn that. It's in the notes, if you'd only taken the trouble to read them.'

'Well, I've obviously read the case notes,' Norman said, 'or I wouldn't know what I was talking about, would I? And before you start complaining, I didn't drag you anywhere. It sounded to me like you couldn't wait for an excuse to get out of the office for an hour.'

'Yeah, well,' said Marston, 'we all need a break from our colleagues sometimes, don't we? You should know that, working at Llangwelli station.'

He directed a conspiratorial smile across the table which Norman failed to reciprocate.

'I hate to disappoint you, Marston, but I actually like my colleagues. They make a great team. You'd have found that out if you'd given them some encouragement when you were working there.'

Norman couldn't tell if Marston's grunted response was one of dissent, but he thought it probably was. On another occasion he would willingly have argued the case for his team, but he didn't want to antagonise Marston just yet.

'So, are you going to tell me why we're here?' asked Marston.

'As it was your case, I thought you'd like to know the girl has come back,' said Norman.

'You could have told me that over the phone,' said Marston.

'You're right, I could,' said Norman. 'But I want to ask you some questions, and if we're face to face like this, you can't hang up on me.'

Marston's eyes narrowed. 'Questions? You mean questions about the case? Look, mate, I did everything as directed by the DI running the case from Region. If you've got a problem you need to take—'

'Relax,' said Norman. 'I'm not here to pass judgement on how the case was run.'

'Oh, right. Well, then, what do you want?'

'What can you tell me about Erin's parents?' asked Norman.

'Her parents? Why do you want to know about them?'

'Because Dilys Watkins was found murdered on Monday morning.'

Marston had raised his coffee halfway to his lips. Slowly, he lowered it, his hand shaking slightly. 'Bloody hell! Really?' said Marston. 'I heard a body had been found but I had no idea who it was.'

'Are you okay?' asked Norman, indicating Marston's hands.

'What?' Marston looked down at his hands. 'Oh, that. It's nothing, just a bit of arthritis. I'm supposed to wear special gloves for it but I left them in the car. So, tell me about this murder.'

'If you're suggesting I share information about my murder case in exchange for what you know about the family, you should understand that's never going to happen,' said Norman.

Marston rolled his eyes. 'You really do go by the book, don't you?'

'You mean compared with you?' said Norman. 'Yeah, I guess I do, mostly.'

Marston sighed. 'Okay, so what do you want to know?'

'What do you recall about Dilys?'

'How d'you mean?'

'We've been led to believe she was a good mother. Was that your impression?'

'She seemed genuinely distraught that her daughter had gone missing, if that's what you mean.'

'I detect a "but",' said Norman. 'Care to share?'

'Did you know that the name Dilys means genuine, steadfast, valid, true or perfect in English?'

'No, I didn't,' said Norman. 'Why? Does it matter?'

'It matters because it's totally ironic, that's why,' said Marston, with a lascivious smile. 'That Dilys Watkins was hot stuff, man.'

'I'm sorry?' said Norman.

'You know the sort. Sexy, and she knows it — sorry, knew it.'

Norman frowned. 'I think we may be on different wave-lengths here. Or perhaps you're mixing her up with someone else. I'm asking you about Dilys Watkins, mother of Erin Watkins. And you could show a little respect, as she is so recently deceased.'

'Yes, I know who you meant,' said Marston. 'You asked me what Dilys Watkins was like, and I'm telling you. She was giving me the come-on every time I saw her.'

Norman studied Marston's face. He appeared to be per-fectly serious.

'Let me get this straight,' said Norman. 'Are you seri-ously telling me that, despite the fact that she was distraught because her daughter had gone missing, Dilys Watkins couldn't resist flirting with you?'

'That's right.'

'Are you sure about this? You couldn't have misunder-stood her intentions?'

'Of course I'm sure. I'm a man of the world, me. I know when a woman's coming on to me.'

'I see,' said Norman. 'And did you take advantage of the, er, situation?'

'You're kidding, right?' Marston made a vain attempt to look shocked. 'I'd have lost my job.'

Norman shrugged. 'Only if you got caught. You wouldn't be the first detective to get involved wi—'

'Well, I didn't, all right?' snarled Marston, glaring at Norman.

Norman raised his hands. 'Okay, okay. I was only asking.'

Marston took a sip from his coffee. 'Look, if you've come here to make accusations—'

'What about Ross Watkins?' said Norman quickly. 'What did you make of him?'

'He was okay, I suppose. I felt a bit sorry for him really, what with his daughter running away, and then learning he wasn't actually her father.'

'You knew about that then.'

'That was the reason the kid ran away, wasn't it?' said Marston.

'Was Ross angry about it?' asked Norman.

'He was hardly going to be pleased, was he?' said Marston.

'Angry enough to murder his wife?'

'Really? Is that what you think? Well, I dunno about that.'

'Didn't Dilys report him for stalking her after they separated?' asked Norman.

'Sorry?' said Marston.

'She made a complaint that Ross was stalking her,' said Norman.

'Oh, yeah, that's right. I remember now,' said Marston. 'The poor bloke was convinced she was seeing someone. He thought if he followed her he'd find out who it was. I think he was hoping it might be the girl's father.'

'You opened the case and then closed it within days, stating, "no further action required".'

'If you say so,' said Marston.

'It's not what I say,' said Norman. 'It's what the note you put in the file says. So, how come you decided no further action was required?'

Marston cleared his throat. 'I realised the poor bloke's world had been shattered, what with finding out his daughter wasn't really his daughter, and then with her running away. So, I had a quiet word with him like, explained that now him and Dilys were separated he couldn't keep interfering in her life. I told him that if he promised to behave I'd close the file, but if she complained again I'd have to arrest him.'

'And he got the message, just like that?'

'She never complained again, so I guess he must have,' said Marston.

'Did either of them ever say who Erin's biological father was?' asked Norman.

'Dilys never mentioned a name,' said Marston, 'and I'm sure Ross didn't have a clue. Or, if he did, he certainly never told me. Personally, I always had my doubts about the brother.'

Norman sat bolt upright. 'Brother? Whose brother?'

'Ross's brother,' said Marston.

'Ross has a brother?' asked Norman.

'Yep,' said Marston. 'Now, what was his name . . . Graham? Yeah, I think that's it. I seem to recall he lives in England, somewhere up north. Yorkshire, perhaps.'

'Shit,' muttered Norman.

'Problem?' asked Marston.

'Ross told my boss he had no family.'

'Yeah, well he would say that, wouldn't he? As far as he's concerned his brother doesn't exist.'

'Why is that?'

Marston shrugged. 'He never said. But if you think about it, it all adds up, doesn't it?'

There was a silence, while Norman absorbed this piece of news.

'So, Ross told your boss he had no family? The amazing super-detective DI Sarah Bloody Know-it-all.' Marston chortled. 'Surely she would have asked someone to check? Or perhaps she's not so clever after all.'

'Shut up, Marston,' said Norman. 'You know damned well we're only a small team. There's only so much we can cover between us. Anyway, I don't remember seeing this brother mentioned in your report. How come?'

Marston shrugged again. 'He wasn't relevant to the investigation.'

'How could a close family member not be relevant?' Norman said.

'He'd been off the scene for years,' said Marston. 'And neither Dilys nor Ross were in touch with him.'

'What about Erin? Was she in touch with him?'

'I can't remember,' Marston said.

'You can't remember, or you didn't bother to find out?'

'What's that supposed to mean?' snapped Marston.

'Well, you obviously think it's no coincidence that Ross had a brother he'd fallen out with,' said Norman.

'That's what I meant when I said I had my doubts about him.'

'But when Erin disappeared and you suspected he could have been her father, didn't you think to explore the possibility that he could have been in touch with her?'

'Why would he?' asked Marston.

'Why would he?' repeated Norman. 'Because, if he was her father, maybe he was trying to entice her away. Jeez, he might even have kidnapped her. Perhaps the reason the Met Police couldn't find her in London was because she was two hundred odd miles away in Yorkshire!' He banged his fist on the table. 'I can't believe you had your doubts about the guy but didn't make him part of your investigation. I mean, it's basic procedure to check out the family, isn't it? Was it incompetence on your part? Or, perhaps you were so busy flirting with Dilys you just couldn't be arsed to do your job properly.'

'Tone it down a bit,' said Marston. 'What does it matter now? You said the girl had come back home, so there's no harm done, right?'

'No harm done?' roared Norman. 'Of course there's been harm done. A family has been torn apart, and Dilys Watkins is dead, for God's sake!'

'Well, I hope you're not trying to suggest any of that's my fault,' said Marston angrily. 'Anyway, who do you think you are, telling me how I should do my job? You're the same rank as me. You've got no right to speak to me like that.'

'I have every right to point out your incompetence, especially when you've ignored basic procedure,' snapped Norman. 'It's morons like you who get the rest of us a bad name.'

'And I suppose you're perfect,' sneered Marston.

'No, I'm not perfect, and I'm not afraid to admit it. I make mistakes like anyone else. But no one can ever accuse me of being too bloody idle to do my job properly,' said Norman, slamming his fist down on the table again.

Marston glared at Norman, then stood up.

'This meeting is over,' he said. 'I didn't come here for the likes of you to start accusing me of not doing my job.'

'Yeah, I think that's probably a good idea,' said Norman. 'You'd better clear off before I get really angry.'

CHAPTER ELEVEN

When Morgan got back to the office, Southall called the team to come and stand at the large map. She had something to show them.

'Where's Norm?' asked Morgan.

'He's meeting DS Marston,' said Southall. 'He wants to see if Marston can offer any insight about Erin's family from when he was investigating her disappearance.'

'Catren, please can you put a cross on the map where this handbag was found.'

'Any particular colour?' Morgan asked.

'How about blue?' said Southall, stepping aside.

Morgan took a blue marker pen and made a cross on the map.

'So, what have we got?' said Southall. 'Dilys lived in a flat, here.' She pointed at the flat. 'Her body was found here.' She moved her finger to the old mining village. 'And her handbag was found here.' She pointed out the woodland, and then stepped back. 'Anyone have any observations?'

'It doesn't flow from one site to the next, does it?' said Lane.

'What does that mean?' asked Winter.

'The logical thing would be to collect Dilys from her flat, murder her somewhere between the flat and the village, dump the body at the village, and then dump the handbag on the way home, wherever that is. Whoever killed Dilys must have spent half the night driving back and forth if they did it in sequence.'

'Doesn't that suggest it wasn't planned then?' asked Winter.

'That's one possibility,' said Southall. She turned to Morgan. 'Norm tells me you have a theory.'

Morgan looked startled. 'Didn't he explain it to you? I suppose he thought it was rubbish.'

'Not at all,' said Southall. 'He said it had been well thought out, and that it's very plausible. But as it's all your own work, he thought you should be the one to share it.'

Now Morgan looked slightly embarrassed. 'Oh, right, I see.'

'Come on then, Catren, let's hear it.' Southall stepped back, conceding her place to Morgan. 'The stage is all yours.'

Morgan took Southall's place by the board and faced her colleagues.

'As you know, someone found the missing handbag and handed it in at Region. I picked it up from there this afternoon and arranged to meet up with the lady who found it, so she could show me exactly where it was.'

She pointed to the forest on the map. 'The bag was found in this woodland area, which is open to dog walkers. In fact, it was the woman's dog who discovered the handbag.

'Now, according to Jan — that's the woman — she doesn't think many people walk their dogs there during the day which, to my way of thinking, makes it the perfect place to dump something if you have a dog. I mean, who is going to question someone walking their dog, especially if they're the only people who ever go there?'

'But who walks their dog in a forest in the middle of the night?' asked Winter.

'No one,' said Morgan. 'People walk their dog during the day. What I'm saying is that the killer picked up Dilys, murdered her, took her body to the village, took her handbag and went home. Then, next day he, or she, dumped the bag when they were out walking their dog. Of course, at this stage, this is just a wild guess. I have no evidence to back it up.'

'It may be a guess, but it makes sense,' said Southall. 'Anyone else have any ideas?'

'Can I ask a question?' said Winter.

'Of course you can, Frosty, that's part of the job,' said Southall.

'I might be stating the obvious, but why are we assuming the killer collected Dilys from her flat? Didn't Ross Watkins tell us she was using his car while hers was off the road?'

Southall smiled. She had been hoping someone would spot that.

'Well done, Frosty. You're right, Ross Watkins did tell us that and, as far as we know, he didn't get the car back, meaning Dilys could have driven to her rendezvous with death.'

'That's what I was thinking,' said Winter.

'So, we need to find that car urgently,' said Southall.

'And then some,' added Morgan.

'I can ask Traffic to set up a search through the APNR cameras and see if it appears anywhere,' said Lane.

'I think we need to request a search of the records,' said Southall. 'Starting from the Monday she went up to Scotland and ending today. If someone else has been driving around in that car after her murder, I'd love to hear them explain why.'

* * *

Southall and Lane were discussing the ANPR search when the doors banged open. Norman was back from his meeting with Marston.

'You don't look very happy, Norm,' said Southall. 'What's the problem? Wouldn't Marston cooperate?'

'Depends on how you look at it,' said Norman.

'Come on then,' said Southall. 'Don't keep us in suspense.'

'We all know Marston's a slippery sod,' said Norman. 'And, sure enough, he's definitely hiding something.'

'Hiding what?' asked Southall.

'The way he was talking about Dilys, I think there may have been something between them,' said Norman.

'Really?' asked Southall.

'According to Marston, Dilys couldn't stop flirting with him.'

'Yet Joe Harding said she wasn't like that,' said Southall.

'Don't forget we're talking about Marston here,' said Morgan. 'He firmly believes every woman he comes across fancies him.' She turned to Lane. 'Isn't that right, Judy?'

'Oh, yes,' agreed Lane. 'You could see it whenever a woman walked through those doors. And the way he always looked us up and down gave me the creeps.'

'We need to check that out then,' said Southall. 'Fantasy or not, we need to know the truth. And until we have, his name goes on our list of suspects.'

'It's not just that,' said Norman. 'I got the feeling I couldn't trust much of anything he said.'

'So, apart from becoming a new suspect, he wasn't much help then,' said Southall.

Norman pulled a face. 'Not exactly. He did tell me something that opens a whole new can of worms.'

'Oh?' asked Southall.

'Ross Watkins has a brother.'

'What?' Southall's normally soft voice rose by at least an octave.

'Ross Watkins has a brother. Marston thinks his name is Graham, and he lives somewhere in the north of England, possibly Yorkshire.'

Winter clapped a hand over his mouth. 'Excuse me a second.' Cursing under his breath, he went over to his jacket, which was hanging on the back of his chair, and began fumbling in the pockets.

'But Ross told me he had no family,' said Southall.

'According to Marston, they fell out a few years ago and as far as Ross is concerned, his brother doesn't exist.'

'How many years ago was this?'

'Marston doesn't know.'

'Did Marston say why they fell out?' asked Southall.

'He says he doesn't know for sure because neither Dilys nor Ross would talk about it, but he thinks Graham might be Erin's father.'

'So that's another suspect to add to our list,' said Southall.

'It all adds up, doesn't it?' said Norman.

'Right,' said Southall. 'I want Graham Watkins found, and I want to know where he lives and what he's been doing, especially over the last week or two, even if it means we have to go up to Yorkshire to question him.'

Winter walked up to them stiffly, holding out a business card. 'Er, I think I can tell you where Graham Watkins lives. And we won't need to go to Yorkshire to speak to him.'

Southall looked suitably stunned. 'I'm sorry, Frosty. What did you say?'

'He's the environmental project manager on Joe Harding's redevelopment,' said Winter, handing her the card. 'We saw him the other day when we were looking for Wozzy.'

'And you didn't think to mention this?' Southall asked, her voice like steel.

'I'm sorry, boss. I should have realised, but—'

'It's my fault, boss,' said Morgan. 'I told Frosty to check him out when we got back. But then, as soon as we walked in the door, you asked him to crack the password on Dilys's laptop, and I got distracted by the handbag, and we both sort of forgot it.'

Southall thought for a second, and then her expression softened.

'I remember now,' she said. 'You're right. As soon as you walked in the door, I hardly gave you time to draw breath before I started handing out tasks. If anyone's to blame, it's me, not you two.'

'If I can just butt in here a minute,' said Norman. 'I don't think it's anyone's fault. It's inevitable when you have such a small team to work big cases. As a matter of fact, I'm amazed it doesn't happen more often.'

Southall smiled at him. *Good old Norm. Trust him to put in a word of reason when things were in danger of getting too tense.*

'Norm's right,' she said. 'I think you all do fantastic work considering what a ridiculously small team we are, and I apologise for sometimes expecting too much of you. My only excuse is that you do so well I sometimes forget how stretched we are.' She looked at the clock. 'I think we could all do with some rest, so why don't we all stop work now and go home? We can start again in the morning.' She turned to Norman. 'Norm, I need a quick word before you go.'

Norman followed Southall to her office.

'Do you want to go and speak to Ross Watkins now?' he said.

'He'll be at work tonight so he'll keep until the morning,' said Southall, sliding into the chair behind her desk and indicating the one opposite.

Norman sat down. 'Give him a hard time when he's tired, right?'

'He's been keeping us in the dark, so he doesn't deserve any favours from us,' said Southall. 'And what about Marston? You said you thought he's hiding something.'

'No doubt about it,' said Norman.

'Anything in particular?'

'I reckon he had a real thing for Dilys,' said Norman. 'I'm not sure if it amounted to anything, or if it was just in his head, but something's not right about it. He knows all the different meanings of her name. I mean, that's not normal, is it? I don't even know what my own name means, never mind someone I met in an investigation two years ago.'

'It definitely sounds a bit creepy when you put it like that,' agreed Southall.

'And I'd like to ask Ross Watkins why Marston let him off with a lecture after Dilys had reported him for stalking her.'

'Do you think Marston will be willing to meet you again?'

Norman smiled. 'You mean for another informal chat, only with you as a surprise guest?'

'You think he'd refuse to come?'

'I was surprised he came last time to be honest, and he knows we're on to him now. We didn't exactly part on the best of terms either, so I wouldn't get your hopes up,' said Norman.

'We could always ambush him,' suggested Southall.

'That would be fun,' said Norman. 'But why don't we see what Ross has to say first? You never know, he might give us a reason to speak to Marston officially.'

'Right, that's a plan, then,' said Southall. 'Ross Watkins first thing, and then, hopefully, Marston later.'

'I think we need to have a closer look at Dilys's mobile phone record before we speak to Marston again,' said Norman.

'Good idea,' said Southall. 'I was only looking for a number in Scotland.'

'And about the guys,' said Norman. 'I hope I wasn't speaking out of turn back there, but I really think we sometimes expect too much.'

'You're quite right,' said Southall. 'It's a miracle we don't have many more cock-ups. The fact is we're much too small a team to be handling murder cases.'

'Yet here we are, doing exactly that.'

'But probably not for much longer,' said Southall.

'Oh? Don't tell me the bean counters have finally realised we can't go on running on a shoestring and we're going to get some additional funding.'

'Funnily enough what I'm about to tell you has come from the financial team,' said Southall. 'But giving us more money isn't quite what they have in mind.'

'Please don't say we're going to have to hand our bigger cases over to Region,' said Norman. 'That would be like taking a step backward. No, worse than that — more like ten steps.'

'If you'll just stop trying to second-guess me, Norm,' said Southall, 'I'll tell you what head office are proposing.'

'Okay. Sorry. I'm listening.'

'They've been looking at ways to improve efficiency and reduce costs.'

'Cutting costs has never improved efficiency,' said Norman. 'It just means asking overworked police officers to do even more work.'

'Norm . . .'

Realising what he'd just done, he passed a finger across his lips and sat back.

'Good move,' said Southall. 'Now, as I was saying, the proposal they've come up with — and I should stress that this idea is still in its infancy — is that they close Llangwelli station and move our team over to Region, where we absorb some of their more capable detectives and establish a brand-new murder squad.'

Norman stared at her. He had been around long enough to know that Llangwelli, being so small, was a likely candidate for closure but it still felt like a personal betrayal.

'Are you all right, Norm? It's not like you to have no opinion. Say something, please.'

'I honestly don't know what to say, Sarah.'

'I thought you'd be pleased.'

'Pleased? Why would I be pleased? I mean, where does this leave me?' he said.

'Alongside me, I hope,' she said. 'This is our chance to give everyone at Region the finger. Finally, we can show them just how good our team has become.'

'Yeah, I get that you would enjoy doing that,' said Norman, 'but I'm not sure it's what I want. I was recruited specifically to work with the small team of detectives here, not to compete with idiots like Marston at Region. Don't you remember how those arseholes tried to make life difficult for us when we first started here?'

'Of course I do,' said Southall.

'Right. So what do you think it'll be like if we're in the same building?' asked Norman.

'Half of them are going to be kicked out,' said Southall.

'Which means the half that's left will feel it's our fault their friends have been given the boot. That'll just make the hassle even worse.'

'I can deal with a bit of hassle,' said Southall. 'I'm always ready for a fight if that's what they want.'

'Well, if that's what you want, Sarah, then I'm pleased for you,' said Norman. 'But I'm not sure it's what I want. I didn't come out of retirement to spend my time fighting with people who are supposed to be working alongside me.'

'I'm sure it won't be that bad,' said Southall.

'Look, Sarah, the reason I love it so much here in Llangwelli is because we all get on, we're all on the same side. That means we don't have to deal with the sort of back-stabbing crap that goes on at Region. I really don't want to go back to a situation where I have to keep looking over my shoulder because morons like Marston might feel their pride has been hurt.'

Now Southall wasn't sure what to say. She had assumed Norman would be up for this as much as she was. It had never occurred to her that he might not feel the same way.

'You won over DS Hickstead, didn't you?' she said.

'Yeah, but from what I've seen Hickstead's probably the only adult working there, and even then, it took months to get through to him, didn't it?' replied Norman. 'I take it this was what your meeting was about the other day.'

Southall nodded.

'Am I right in assuming it's top secret and the guys aren't supposed to know?'

'They shouldn't be told anything about it until it becomes official,' said Southall.

'What does Nathan say?' asked Norman.

'If it happens, Superintendent Bain will oversee the change for the first year, and then he'll retire,' said Southall.

'That means the first year will be bad enough, but the shit will really hit the fan once Nathan has gone and there's no one to watch our backs,' said Norman.

'I think you're making it sound much worse than it actually will be,' said Southall. 'It might have been the accountants who came up with the idea of closing Llangwelli, but it was the chief constable who suggested we should become the new murder squad, meaning he'll be watching our backs.'

'Oh, come on, Sarah, get real. How is he going to do that when he's miles away in his ivory tower?' said Norman. 'And, anyway, if we're going to be the chief constable's pet project, that'll make us an even bigger target for the backstabbers. They'll be trying to bring us down every day. When, exactly, is this supposed to be happening?'

'It's still on the drawing board at the moment,' said Southall. 'It may not happen at all, but if it does, we're looking at several more months as we are.'

'Sarah, I can promise you they wouldn't have told you they were closing Llangwelli if it wasn't going to happen.'

'I'm told no firm decision has been made,' she said.

'Yeah, right,' said Norman. 'Anyway, who is going to be the boss? A team like that is normally led by a chief inspector. Are they going to offer it to you?'

'No chance. I've not been an inspector long enough to qualify.'

'You could always ask to be fast-tracked, or to be mentored,' said Norman. 'You may not have the years behind you but you've already shown them you can do the job as well as anyone.'

Southall felt emotions creeping up on her that she hadn't prepared for. It was only now, as she realised she might have to face the future without Norman, that she began to understand just how much she relied on him, and how much she would miss him if he wasn't there. He may have started out as a colleague, but he had quickly become a trusted friend.

'But what about you, Norm?' she said, trying to keep her voice steady. 'I was rather hoping you'd be part of the new team.'

'I dunno, Sarah. I need to think about it,' said Norman.

Southall swallowed, hard. 'Of course. It's a big decision. No one expects you to make up your mind at a moment's notice.'

'In that case no one will be disappointed when you tell them I'm undecided, will they?' said Norman. 'Can I go home, now?'

'Yes, of course,' said Southall. She watched him jump from his chair and head for the door. 'You're not going to let this come between us, are you, Norm?'

Norman turned in the doorway and smiled.

'Come on, Sarah, give me some credit. I think it's great you're going to get the chance to work in a proper murder squad. If anyone deserves to be in a top team, you do, and I am genuinely pleased for you. But you have to see it from my point of view. I'm no spring chicken, am I? So, while it's a great opportunity for you, it's come a little too late for me. But that's just how life is sometimes, right?'

Southall nodded sadly. 'Yes, I suppose it is.'

'I honestly don't know what I'm going to do, Sarah, but I can guarantee one thing. Whatever I decide to do work-wise won't change anything between you and me. Okay?'

Southall, who was already struggling with her conflicting emotions, suddenly felt herself welling up.

'I think you should go home before I embarrass myself,' she said.

'You don't have to be embarrassed in front of me,' said Norman.

'I know, but I will be,' she mumbled. 'That's just how I am. You should know that by now.'

Norman smiled. Of course he knew.

'Goodnight, Sarah,' he said quietly.

Southall made sure he was gone before she reached for a tissue and dabbed at her eyes. 'Come on, Sarah, pull yourself together,' she muttered. 'You've been here before. Colleagues come, and colleagues go. It's just part of the job.'

CHAPTER TWELVE

Faye Delaney had been together with Norman long enough to know when something was wrong. And it wasn't just that he came in through their front door, threw his car keys down, marched straight up to her and asked for a hug. This was serious.

He held her tight and buried his face in her hair, inhaling her delicate scent.

'Bad day, huh?' she asked him softly. 'Want to tell me about it?'

With his arms still around her, he leaned back and looked into her face.

'You know how they say all good things have to come to an end?'

Instantly, her smile was replaced by a frown of concern.

'What are you saying?' she asked, alarmed. 'Are you telling me we're finished?'

'What? Are you crazy?' he said. 'You're the best thing that ever happened to me. Why would I ever want us to end?'

'But you just said—'

He kissed her lips and hugged her tight again.

'Oh, Faye. Of course that's not what I meant. It's work, not you. Jeez, I don't ever want to lose you.'

'Well, I should hope not.' She giggled. 'I'd hate to think I've cooked dinner for nothing.'

She finally escaped Norman's hug. 'Now then, what's the matter at work?'

'They're going to close Llangwelli station.'

'Oh no,' she said. 'What's going to happen to everyone?'

'They're going to transfer us all to Region and create a new murder squad.'

'Well, that's exciting. Er . . . isn't it?'

'That rather depends on who you are and what you want,' said Norman. 'I mean, it's great for ambitious people like Sarah, and for the youngsters.'

'And what about you?' asked Faye.

'When Nathan first approached me about this job, I was a bit of a lost soul, stuck in the most enormous rut and going absolutely nowhere. So the idea of making a new start, in a new town, training young detectives, sounded perfect. And, from the minute I started I have loved just about every single minute of it — my job, the people I work with, the area, the slower pace of life . . . Jeez, I even bought a house I like it here so much! And then, to add the icing to my particular cake, I met the most wonderful woman.'

Faye smiled and took his hand.

'Do I know her?' she asked.

Norman grinned. 'You might have come across her. She shares my bed most nights.'

'Oh, her,' said Faye, squeezing his hand. 'Yes, I know who you mean. I've heard she's thinking about sharing it again tonight.'

'I do hope so,' said Norman, 'because there's nowhere else for her to sleep.'

'Then I suppose she'll just have to sleep with you then,' said Faye saucily, and Norman had to struggle to clear his head of the thoughts her words had conjured up.

He cleared his throat. 'Anyway, the only downside in my fabulous new life is occasionally having to deal with the backstabbing idiots at Region, and now it seems the chief constable wants to make it an everyday occurrence.'

'But that sort of thing is water off a duck's back to you, isn't it?' asked Faye.

'Yeah, maybe it was once, but I'm tired of all that, Faye. I came here to teach, not fight. I'm getting too old for all that "mine is bigger than yours" crap. And Llangwelli station is five minutes from here. Going to Region will take at least an hour each way. I want to be here with you, not sitting in traffic.'

'I'm not always here, Norm. I work too.'

'Yeah, I know. But I can work in the garden when you're not here.'

'Only if you like working in the rain,' said Faye. 'You know, that wet stuff you're always complaining about?'

'I also thought we might get a dog,' said Norman. 'I've always wanted one, but it wouldn't have been practical when I was living alone and never knew what time I was going to be home.'

'It rains on dogs too, you know,' said Faye.

'That's okay,' said Norman. 'I'll buy proper waterproofs so I can deal with it. It's different when you choose to go out and you're dressed for it.'

'I used to have a dog, years ago,' said Faye, wistfully. 'It would be fun to get another one.'

'Maybe we could get one anyway,' said Norman. 'We could rescue one from a dogs' home. We have a big enough garden, and the beach isn't far. We could take him for walks along the beach.'

'Or her,' said Faye.

'What? Oh, right, yeah. Boy or girl, I have no preference,' said Norman.

'Dog or bitch, Norm. They're not people,' said Faye.

'Yeah, whatever,' said Norman. 'So, what do you think?'

'If you mean about getting a dog, I don't see why not. I only work part-time so it wouldn't be home alone for long.'

'What about moving to Region?' asked Norman.

'Honestly? I think you need to take some time to think before you make a decision,' said Faye. 'What you're suggesting about retiring sounds great, and believe me I'd love to spend more time with you, but your job has been your life for so long I think you'd miss it much more than you realise. And I'd hate for you to become resentful towards me as a result.'

'I would never do that,' said Norman.

'You say that now,' said Faye, 'and I'm sure you mean it, but if you got bored . . .'

'How could I possibly get bored with you when I love you so much?' said Norman. 'It couldn't happen.'

'It's very sweet of you to say that,' said Faye, 'but I've seen it happen.'

'Not with me you haven't.'

'Do you have to decide today?' asked Faye.

'I haven't been asked to decide anything, I've just been given a heads up about what's going to happen.'

'Is it definite?'

'They've told Sarah no decision has been taken yet, but I can't believe they'd tell her about it if it wasn't going ahead.'

'So, you don't know for sure that it will happen, and if it does happen you have plenty of time to think about it,' said Faye. 'Is that right?'

'Yeah, I suppose that's about right,' said Norman.

'Look, Norm, I'm on your side whatever you decide. I'm just asking you to make sure it's what you really want. Perhaps you should talk it over with Nathan, or with Sarah.'

'Okay, maybe I'll speak with Nathan,' said Norman, unconvinced. 'I definitely can't ask Sarah for impartial advice. She's already made it clear she thought it was a done deal and that I was going.'

'That's because she sees you as an integral part of the team,' said Faye.

'Or is it because she takes me for granted?' said Norman.

'That's not true, Norm,' said Faye. 'I know Sarah. I've shared any number of bottles of wine with her. Yes, she's come to rely on you as a friend as well as a colleague, rather like a big brother but, believe me, she knows how lucky she is.'

'Really?'

'Yes, but don't tell her I told you.'

'I wouldn't dream of it,' said Norman.

* * *

At around the time Norman was sharing his concerns over the future of Llangwelli station with Faye, Southall was discussing the same thing with Bill Bridger, in his capacity of boyfriend and confidant, not as pathologist.

'I can see where Norm's coming from,' said Bridger. 'I think I'd be tired of it all if I'd had to put up with some of the shite he's had to deal with over the years. Did you know he was once sent to work in the wilds of Northumberland for three years?'

'Why?' asked Southall.

'Because some big-shot team were looking for a scapegoat, and he just happened to be seconded to them at the wrong time. I don't think he was even involved in the operation that went wrong, but when it happened they needed someone to carry the can and one of the senior officers had taken a dislike to him. Can you even begin to imagine what that must have been like for a guy who'd never been outside London before? His wife wouldn't move up there to be with him, and it was while he was stuck up there that his marriage went pear-shaped.'

'How do you know all this stuff?' asked Southall. 'He rarely mentions his past to us.'

'That's because he always tries to look forward, and he's not the sort to look for sympathy. But I can assure you he's got plenty of reason to have the most enormous chip on his shoulder where his employers are concerned. And the reason I know this is because I worked a few cases with him when he was in Hampshire. We had a few beers on more than one occasion.'

'But what am I going to do if he digs his heels in?' asked Southall. 'How can I persuade him he's got to come?'

'What you have to remember with a guy like Norm is that he doesn't have your ambition. Your ambition motivates you to show everyone how good you are. Norm's ends at doing his job well. What motivates him has always been solving the case in front of him, but I think you'll probably find his priorities are a little different now anyway.'

'In what way?' asked Southall.

'I think you have to take into account the changes to his life situation.'

'What do you mean "his life situation"?' asked Southall.

'Nathan Bain rescued Norm from dead-end street. He wasn't destitute or anything like that, but left where he was, lonely and bored, he could easily have gone on a downward spiral. But within a matter of weeks after Nathan's call it's like he's in heaven. He's doing the best job he's ever had, working with an enthusiastic and united team, alongside a boss he admires, respects and adores.'

'Does he?'

'I don't mean he fancies you, Sarah, he just thinks you're amazing. A bit like I do but without the added lust.'

'He never says as much.'

'Maybe not, but does he have to? I mean it's obvious to everyone else. Besides, do you tell him how much you appreciate him?'

'Well, yes, sometimes, but probably not often enough.'

'There you are then. Anyone on the outside looking in can see it's a mutual respect and admiration thing you share, even if you never tell each other so.'

'I suppose you're right,' she said. 'But I don't see how that stops him coming to Region.'

'It's not how he feels about you, or your team, that's affecting his decision,' said Bridger. 'My guess is that the major factor in Norm's case is that fabulous little cottage he's bought, and the woman he lives with. I mean, what more could a guy his age ask for?'

'Do you really think that will be the deciding factor?' asked Southall.

'As I said, it's all down to ambition and motivation. At his age, Norm doesn't find the idea of battling against the odds at Region remotely motivating, whereas the idea of settling down and spending his days with the woman he loves must be really appealing. He'll have his pension, so he doesn't need the money. If it was me, I know what I'd want to do and, believe me, Region wouldn't get a look in.'

'I really hope you're wrong,' said Southall.

'You can't put pressure on him, Sarah. You have to step back and let him make his own decision, or you could risk losing a very, very good friend.'

CHAPTER THIRTEEN

Thursday, 16 March

The morning after their discussion, the usual easy familiarity between Southall and Norman was gone. It was as if neither quite knew how to set aside the issue of the potential move to Region. The journey to interview Ross Watkins passed in an awkward silence, until Norman suddenly pulled over to the side of the road and switched off the engine.

'Please, Sarah, let's not do this,' said Norman.

'Let's not do what?' asked Southall.

'This uncomfortable silence thing,' said Norman. 'I get that you're upset with me, but I also think you ought to be able to understand my position. But if this is how it's going to be from now on, I might as well quit now.'

'I'm not upset with you,' said Southall.

'It sure seemed like it yesterday,' said Norman.

'I admit I didn't exactly handle the situation very well but, honestly, it's not you. I'm upset to think you might not be working with me anymore.'

Norman sighed. 'I feel like that, too, Sarah, and if I was twenty years younger I'd be there like a shot, but I'm not twenty years younger, am I? And, of course, I now know there's more to life than catching crooks.'

'Ah, yes,' said Southall. 'And how is Faye?'

Norman's face lit up. 'She's amazing. Everything I could have hoped for and then some.'

'I'm really pleased to hear that,' said Southall. 'We've all been able to see it in you from the moment you met her, but it's good to hear you say it. So many men don't appreciate what they've got until it's gone.'

'Oh, trust me, I know how lucky I am,' said Norman. 'It's like she opened a door to a world I had only dreamed of. Mind you, it also scares the hell out of me. I can't help thinking that I'm going to wake up one day and find these last few months were all a dream. If that happens I'll still be stuck where I was with nothing to do, nowhere to go, nothing to look forward to and no one to give a damn about what happens to me.'

'Was it really that bad?'

'I didn't think so at the time, but coming here made me realise how lonely I was, and how depressed. I honestly believe I was about to go under when Nathan Bain threw me that lifeline. Choosing to be alone is no bad thing when you're happy with your own company. But being alone isn't the same as being lonely. No one chooses to be lonely.'

'I had a long chat with Bill last night. I didn't realise you two went back such a long way.'

'It's not actually been that long,' said Norman. 'He used to work for an experimental mobile pathology lab. About ten years ago, we had two or three cases within a short period of time on which we had to ask for his help. He used to stay in a hotel, and I had nowhere to go, so we shared a few heavy nights. The trouble is I'm not a heavy drinker, so it doesn't take much to loosen my tongue. I'm sure I must have bored the arse off him, but I suppose I needed to get it all off my chest and, as I'm sure you know, Bill's a great guy and a surprisingly good listener.'

'I don't think you need to be concerned that you ever bored him, Norm. He's a definite fan. He was telling me how you once got shunted up to the middle of nowhere because your face didn't fit.'

'Jeez, yeah, that's right. Northumberland. If you think it's rural down here, you should see it up there.' Norman laughed. 'And trying to interview people! I mean, I struggle with Welsh, but at least I have the excuse that it's a different language. You should try understanding Geordie.'

He smiled briefly at the memory. 'It certainly wasn't fun. Not a single bugger up there made me welcome.'

'The way Bill tells it, you've had to put up with a lot more shit than fun in your career.'

'Yeah, but you can't dwell on it,' said Norman. 'It is what it is. Maybe after all that crap, my life now is down to karma.'

'Perhaps you're right about that,' said Southall. 'Maybe it's payback for the way you've not allowed yourself to be brought down by it all. Anyway, I want you to know that talking to Bill last night has opened my eyes, and I understand now why you're not so keen on moving to Region.'

'You do? So why did I get the silent treatment this morning?'

'I'm sorry about that. It wasn't that I didn't want to talk to you. It's just that I couldn't figure out if you were still annoyed, and I didn't want to say the wrong thing in case, well, you know . . .'

'And there I am thinking I'd better not say anything in case you're still pissed off with me,' said Norman. 'Jeez, it's a good job we're not a married couple. We'd never resolve a thing.'

'I hate to say it, Norm, but you're a bit too old for me,' said Southall with a mischievous smile.

'Hey,' said Norman with good-natured indignation. 'Faye doesn't mind me being older.'

'Yes, but Faye is ten years closer to your age than I am,' said Southall.

'I guess I'm gonna have to concede defeat on that one,' said Norman. 'But I concede with good grace because at least now we're both smiling.'

'So really that's a win-win,' said Southall. 'Who says we can't resolve anything!'

'We won't resolve this murder if we sit here talking any longer,' said Norman, switching on the ignition. 'Let's go and see Ross Watkins.'

* * *

The man who answered the door wasn't Ross Watkins, but Norman managed to hide his surprise rather well.

'Good morning,' he said. 'I'm Detective Sergeant Norman and this is Detective Inspector Southall. We were looking for Ross Watkins.'

'This isn't exactly a good time to call,' said the man. 'Have you no consideration?'

'And you are?' asked Norman.

'My name is Glen Matthews. I'm looking out for Ross. We've been mates for years.'

Norman wasn't one to miss the opportunity to launch a charm offensive.

'You're the friend Ross called to clock him in after we told him about Dilys, right?'

'That's right. And he called me after you made him identify her body. I've been keeping an eye on him ever since.'

'Well, we're pleased to meet you,' said Norman. 'Ross is lucky to have someone to look out for him at a time like this.'

'It's what mates are for, isn't it?'

'How's he doing?' asked Norman.

'How do you think he's doing? Having you people stopping him from sleeping isn't going to help either, is it? We've been at work all night, and the poor guy needs his sleep.'

'Do you really think he should be at work?'

'Ross said he'd go mad if he just sat here thinking about what had happened to Dilys.'

'I see,' said Norman. 'Well, we appreciate you feel it's inconvenient and inconsiderate of us, but I'm afraid convenience isn't always our highest priority when we're investigating a murder. Right now we have some questions that Ross needs to answer.'

'Why?' demanded Matthews.

'Why what?' asked Norman.

'Why do you have to ask him now? Why can't it wait?'

Southall's good mood was rapidly evaporating and her patience was wearing thin.

'We don't have to explain ourselves to you, Mr Matthews,' she said. 'And we don't have time to waste. The longer you keep us standing here, the more inconvenient this becomes for all of us.'

'What's going on?' asked a weary voice from behind Matthews. Ross Watkins peered over his shoulder.

'They want to ask you some questions,' said Matthews. 'I told them they should let you sleep and come back later.'

'But I'm not sleeping, am I? I just can't at the moment,' said Watkins. 'Of course they can come in and ask their questions if it's going to help them find out who killed Dilys.'

He headed back into the house, leaving the crestfallen Matthews to step aside and hold the door open for Southall and Norman.

'I was just trying to help him,' he mumbled as they filed past.

'Don't worry about it,' said Norman. 'But next time, try to remember we're not your enemy. We're the good guys trying to find out who did this.'

Looking disconsolate, Matthews followed them into the lounge.

'We'd like to speak to Ross alone,' said Southall. Matthews looked expectantly at Watkins.

'You should get off home and get some sleep, Glen,' said Watkins. 'I'll see you later.'

Reluctantly, his friend left the room. They listened as he collected his car keys from the kitchen and made his way out of the house, closing the door firmly behind him.

'Sorry about that,' said Watkins. 'Glen's a good bloke, and he means well, but he's a bit overprotective sometimes.'

'So, you two work together?' asked Southall.

'Glen put in a word for me and got me the job,' said Watkins. 'Working nights in a factory isn't what I would have chosen to do, but it pays the bills and no one else wanted to employ me.'

'He's not always so aggressive then?' asked Norman.

'He's a softie really. He's got an old Land Rover he likes to strip down and rebuild. He even wears gloves when he's working on it so he doesn't get his hands dirty. I ask you, whoever heard of a mechanic with soft hands?'

'I'm sure we asked you this before,' said Norman, 'but just for the record, can you tell me where you were from Friday morning to Monday morning on the weekend Dilys died?'

'That's easy,' said Watkins. 'Friday, I was here all day sleeping, until six p.m. when I went to work. I did a twelve-hour shift, then came back here. I did the same again on Saturday, and on Sunday.'

'You were working all weekend?'

'We got behind schedule a few weeks ago and we've been working weekends ever since to try and catch up.'

'And this can all be verified?'

'Glen was there all weekend, too. We have to clock in and out, and there's CCTV on the door.'

'That should be easy enough to verify then,' said Norman.

'Do I need an alibi?' asked Watkins.

'It's just a question of formalities,' said Southall. 'If we don't dot the i's and cross the t's where everyone's concerned, we make it easy for the culprit's defence lawyer to contest our case.'

'Are you any nearer to catching someone?' asked Watkins.

'I'm afraid I can't share much,' said Southall. 'All I can tell you is that we have one or two leads we're following. But, as you can imagine, these things take time.'

'And you're not going to tell me what these leads are because I'm a suspect,' said Watkins.

'We didn't say that,' said Norman.

'You don't have to,' said Watkins. 'I read somewhere that the family are always the primary suspects in a murder case.'

'Statistics tend to show that's often the case,' said Norman, 'and if we ignored the statistics we wouldn't be doing our jobs.'

'It's okay,' said Watkins. 'I understand that you have to ask me questions I might not like. I want you to catch whoever did this to Dilys.'

'Why didn't you tell us you had a brother?' asked Southall.

'Sorry?'

'You have a brother — Graham, I believe. You didn't mention him when we spoke before.'

'That's because, as far as I'm concerned, my brother doesn't exist. We used to be close but we fell out about ten years ago and we haven't spoken since.'

'Why did you fall out?' asked Norman.

'He kept pestering Dilys.'

'Pestering how?' asked Southall.

'He was always hanging around, watching her, and he would often turn up unannounced, expecting her to make him welcome. I didn't like it, and I told him so.'

'And how did Dilys feel about the attention he was paying her?' asked Southall.

'She told him she didn't like it and that he should leave her alone,' said Watkins.

'And did he?'

'I had to break his nose to convince him,' said Watkins. 'After that, we never saw him again. Last I heard he was living somewhere in Yorkshire.'

'What does he do for a living?' asked Norman.

'I don't know if he's still doing it, but he used to call himself an environmental engineer, whatever that means,' said Watkins.

'And you haven't had any contact with him recently?' asked Southall.

'Not in years.'

'How about Dilys?' said Southall. 'Would she have seen him?'

'Of course she wouldn't,' said Watkins. 'Hang on a minute. Are you suggesting she was seeing my brother when she was supposed to be in Scotland?'

'We're not suggesting anything, Ross,' said Norman. 'As far as we know, Dilys was in Scotland when she said she was. But did you know your brother is in this area at the moment?'

'What? He wouldn't dare come down here. If I find out he's been anywhere near Dilys, I'll—'

'You don't need to do anything, Ross,' said Norman. 'Now we know he exists and he's here, I can assure you we'll be speaking to him.'

'But why has he come back?' asked Watkins.

'We understand he's working for Joe Harding,' said Southall. 'He's overseeing the environmental aspects of the redevelopment at the old mining village.'

'I had no idea,' said Watkins. 'I swear I haven't spoken to him since I broke his nose. You don't think he'd been stalking Dilys again, do you?'

'That's what we'll be asking him,' said Southall. 'And, talking of stalking, we understand you're not averse to a bit of stalking yourself.'

Watkins couldn't have looked more surprised if he had tried.

'Stalking?' he said. 'What on earth are you talking about?'

'I had a chat with DS Marston the other day,' said Norman. 'You know Marston, right?'

'Yes, I know him,' said Watkins. 'He was our family liaison officer when Erin disappeared.'

'Well, since he knew you guys, I thought he might be worth talking to, could fill in some blanks, give us some background — you know the sort of thing.'

'And did he?' asked Watkins.

'He couldn't add much to what we already knew,' said Norman, 'but he did tell me about the time Dilys made a complaint that you were stalking her.'

'Me? Stalking Dilys? No, that's not right. It was a misunderstanding.'

'In what way?' asked Southall.

'A couple of months after we split up, Dilys told me she thought someone was following her but she didn't know who

154

it was. Then, a week or so later, I went to a gig with Glen, and Dilys was there with a bloke. So, yes, I did bump into them. I admit I was upset to see her with another bloke, but I swear I had no idea she was going to be there.'

'And why were you there?' asked Southall.

'I was there because Glen had a couple of tickets. His girlfriend was ill and she didn't want him to waste a perfectly good ticket, so she said why didn't I take her place. You can ask them, and they'll tell you the same thing. It was just a case of me being in the wrong place at the wrong time. Dilys dropped the charges after Glen and his girlfriend explained how I came to be there.'

'That's not what Marston says,' said Norman. 'He says he persuaded Dilys to drop the charges, and that he only let you off with a verbal warning because he knew what you'd been through after Erin disappeared.'

'That's complete bollocks,' said Watkins, angry for the first time since their arrival. 'That's just what that tosser Marston would say. Do you know, when Erin disappeared he didn't give a rat's arse about finding her. All he wanted to do was fuss around Dilys. Right from the start, he couldn't keep his eyes off her, and it wasn't long before he started to get familiar with her.'

Southall and Norman exchanged a look.

'Familiar in what way?' asked Southall.

'Any excuse and he'd be putting his arm around her, "comforting" her. I mean, what bloody police officer does that? It wouldn't surprise me if it was him stalking Dilys.'

'So, you weren't impressed with the way Marston handled Erin's case?' asked Norman.

'Handled it? He didn't handle it, did he? Once he knew about the CCTV footage showing her getting on a train to London, he handed it over to the Met like it was the hottest potato ever. Why do you think I spent all that time there searching for her? No one else was going to bother, were they, certainly not Marston.'

'And you didn't see him after that?'

'Oh, he was always looking in to see if Dilys was okay, but that was usually when I wasn't around. And did he ever bring any news about Erin? What do you think?'

* * *

'What did you make of that?' asked Norman as they drove away from Ross Watkins's house.

'I get the feeling he's being economical with the truth,' said Southall.

'Yeah, that's what I thought,' said Norman.

'But I can't wait to speak to Graham Watkins,' said Southall. 'I've definitely got at least one burning question to ask him.'

'You think he could be Erin's father, right?' asked Norman.

'Maybe he was hanging around Dilys so he could see Erin,' said Southall. 'Or, perhaps he had something going with Dilys for years and was trying to persuade her to leave Ross and bring Erin with her.'

'What about this friend of Ross's, Glen Matthews?' said Norman.

'We don't know anything about him, do we?' asked Southall.

'I can rectify that easily enough,' said Norman. 'And I'd like to check out the factory where they both work. Ross makes it sound like Fort Knox, yet the night we told him about Dilys, he asked Glen to clock him in so it would appear he'd been at work. If they have no qualms about clocking each other in, it follows they clock each other out, too.'

'But wouldn't it be obvious he hadn't been operating his machine?' asked Southall.

'Not necessarily,' said Norman. 'I've known guys who worked night shifts. If all they have to do is watch machines all night, a single guy can watch two or three while the other guys sleep or even leave the premises. It would keep the man doing the watching busy, but as long they take it in turns, and nothing breaks down, who's to know?'

'So, does that mean it's possible for someone to be clocked in and out without even showing up?' asked Southall.

'When I was a young PC I used to patrol an industrial area. I soon learned which factories would offer me a cup of tea on a cold night. There was one place that had a night staff of ten, but there were never more than eight on site. They worked an unofficial rota where two were off every night but still got clocked in and out. It meant everyone on nights worked four nights but still got paid for five.'

'And the boss never knew?' asked Southall.

'Oh, he knew all right,' said Norman. 'But, as I recall, he found it hard to get people to do the night shift. So there was an unspoken agreement that as long as everything ran smoothly, he would turn a blind eye.'

'And did it work?'

'I was only on that patch for a few months, but I seem to remember it was a very happy workplace. I guess the boss there was a pioneer for the four-day working week thirty or forty years before anyone else thought of it. Anyway, my point is, if there's anything like that going on where Ross Watkins works, his alibi could be a complete fabrication.'

'We need to check it out sooner rather than later then,' said Southall.

'What about Marston and Dilys?' said Norman. 'You know, that guy leaves a real bad taste in my mouth.'

'Would he really behave that badly?' asked Southall.

'I told you I thought he had a thing for Dilys,' said Norman. 'And what Ross just told us rather confirms it. But the way Marston tells it, Dilys was the one chasing him. "Sexy, and she knew it" were his exact words. Listening to him gave me the creeps!'

'Remember that ambush we talked about arranging for him?' said Southall. 'I think you should give him a call and arrange it.'

Norman smiled. 'I would be happy to do so,' he said, 'but I doubt he's going to be too keen on letting me have another crack at him.'

'Then perhaps we need to think of another way of getting to him,' said Southall.

'I've been thinking about that,' said Norman. 'Now I know where he has lunch most days, I could just turn up unannounced. I was thinking I could tell him we spoke to Ross Watkins about the stalking accusation, and that Ross is now considering making a complaint about the way it was handled. I could also mention that Ross is so angry he's considering complaining about the way Marston behaved towards Dilys when Erin disappeared. If he thinks I can offer him an escape route out of that mess, he might jump at the chance.'

Southall looked across at Norman. 'You can be quite devious at times, can't you?'

Norman smiled. 'Only when I have to be.'

'Changing the subject,' said Southall. 'When I went through Dilys's phone records there was one number that called her a lot.'

'Did she answer those calls?'

'Not many, which makes me think it was someone she didn't want to speak to, though I haven't yet been able to identify who it is. And she made a call the night she died. It was the last call she ever made but, again, I've yet to identify whose number it is.'

'That's not like you,' said Norman.

'I'm afraid, just like the younger members of our team, I don't have enough hours in my days either. I just didn't have the time to pursue it.'

'Have you asked Judy? She seems to have a knack for that kind of thing,' said Norman. 'And while we're on the subject of time management, I've been thinking about ways we might make the hours we have between us go a little further.'

'Does it involve magic?' asked Southall. 'Because I can't see how we can get more done without there being more of us, unless we work longer hours.'

'I'm afraid I lost my magic wand when I moved here from England,' said Norman. 'I'm not suggesting we can save hundreds of hours, but do you think it would help if maybe you and me spent more time working alone? I mean, we do a lot of stuff together which is great, and I love it, but I also think there are times we could just as easily use the other guys as our partners. Obviously, we'd need to team up when we're making arrests or for formal interviews, but when it's just asking a few questions, we could even work on our own.'

'Is it something I've said?' asked Southall.

'What? No, of course not, it's just . . .' Norman glanced at Southall, who had a big grin on her face.

'Ha ha, yeah, right, very funny.'

'I had you there, didn't I?' she laughed.

'Okay, I'll let you win that one, but seriously, what do you think?'

'As you said, it won't save us a great deal of time, but I suppose every little helps. We could certainly give it a try, so long as it doesn't mean anyone taking unnecessary risks.'

CHAPTER FOURTEEN

'I've got the results of that ANPR search we requested,' said Judy Lane as Norman followed Southall into their office. 'They have enough motorway images to show Dilys making her way up to Scotland through the day on the Monday as we thought. They don't spot her on Tuesday or Wednesday, but she does appear again on Thursday heading south down the motorway network.'

'She didn't go home on Wednesday night, then,' said Southall.

'My guess is she spent Wednesday night in a hotel and didn't trigger any cameras,' said Lane. 'It fits in with what we know and explains why she's off grid until she pops up on motorway cameras around mid-morning on Thursday.'

'Did she come straight home?' asked Southall. 'No detours to Yorkshire?'

'The last image was taken on a dual carriageway near Carmarthen late on Thursday afternoon.'

'She must have come straight home then,' said Norman. 'There's no way she would have time to go off-piste and still be back here that early.'

'What about after that?' asked Southall. She walked across to the large map pinned to the wall.

'After that the car doesn't show up again,' said Lane.

'Which means what?' asked Southall, staring at the map.

'It means she didn't use any major roads after that last sighting near Carmarthen,' said Norman, joining her by the map. 'That doesn't necessarily mean she stayed at home, but she was probably in the area and didn't go far.'

Southall placed a finger on the spot where Dilys's body was found. 'So, why were you there, Dilys, and how did you get there?' she mused. 'If you drove there, where is the car now?'

'We searched the whole development site,' said Norman. 'Traffic have covered the entire area, the registration number is in circulation, and the ANPR database is ready and primed. If it appears, it'll get spotted.'

'I don't think it's going to appear, Norm,' said Southall. 'I think whoever killed her has hidden it or, even worse, it could have been fitted with false number plates and driven away before we even found the body. It might even have been sold to some unsuspecting punter on the other side of the UK.'

'Why don't we put out a request for information like we did with the handbag?' asked Lane.

'Now that's an idea,' said Norman. 'What do you think, boss?'

'I think that's an excellent idea,' said Southall. 'Let's get it done today. The car could be the key that unlocks this whole case.' She turned to Norman. 'We need to speak with Graham Watkins, but first I want to get some background on him.'

'Is there anything in particular you want me to do?' asked Norman.

'Do you have something in mind?'

'I thought I might see if I can speak with Glen Matthews. It might be easier to get him to talk if Ross Watkins is well out of the way.'

'You think he's got something to tell us?' asked Southall.

'It's just a hunch,' said Norman, 'but I figure if Glen has been mates with Ross for years, he must have got to know

Dilys pretty well, so he might be able to tell us what she was really like. I mean, was she the nice person we've been led to believe, or was she a flirt like that creep Marston claims? I'll try and pin him down about Ross's alibi, too.'

Southall nodded.

'Good idea. We can catch up later.'

* * *

Norman found Glen Matthews in his garage, tinkering with what appeared to be an ancient car — or at least its chassis. There were car parts everywhere, including bits of bodywork piled high in one corner, along with an engine in a hoist, waiting to be manoeuvred into place.

'Hi, Glen,' said Norman. 'I wonder if I could have a quick word?'

'What about?'

'Well, you see, Ross told us he was working every night last weekend — the weekend Dilys died. Can you confirm that?'

'Yes, that's right, we both were. We'd got behind with a big order and we were asked to work over the weekend to catch up.'

Now Norman's eyes had adjusted to the poor light in the garage, he could make out more of the vehicle Matthews was working on.

'Is that an old Land Rover?' he asked, nodding towards the car.

'That's right,' said Matthews. 'Early 1960s. I'm restoring it. It's a hobby of mine.'

'You mean to say you can strip down one of these and rebuild it from scratch? Wow, that's clever. I wouldn't know where to start.'

'I've done a few now, so I can almost do it with my eyes shut,' said Matthews. 'It's not so difficult once you know what you're doing. They're pretty basic machines to work on, so it's like playing with a giant Meccano set. Even the bodywork is held together with nuts and bolts.'

'Yeah, but engines must be tricky to strip down and rebuild,' said Norman.

'I cheat when it comes to engines. You can buy them already reconditioned. If I can get that engine installed and make this thing roadworthy, I can sell it on for a profit. Then I'll buy another one and do it again.'

'Really? People still buy these old things?'

'You'd be surprised. Enthusiasts are willing to pay good money for a nice recon. And there's nothing like a hobby that makes a profit.'

'I think if I worked nights, I would need to sleep during the day,' observed Norman.

Matthews winked. 'Not if you were sleeping for a good part of the night shift.'

'That happens a lot, does it?' asked Norman.

'Well, you know. If you run the machines faster you get the work done quicker. As long as the work gets done, what the boss doesn't know about, the boss doesn't worry about.'

'How many of you work that shift?' asked Norman.

'There are four of us.'

'Do you have a rota?' asked Norman. 'I used to know some guys who took it in turns to sleep while they were supposed to be working. They even clocked each other in and out so they could have nights off. Do you guys do that?'

'Yeah, sometimes,' said Matthews. Then he seemed to suddenly remember that Norman was a detective and his smile vanished.

'You're not going to tell the boss, are you?' he asked, looking alarmed.

'Relax, Glen,' said Norman. 'I have enough to do without worrying about whether you're working or not. As long as it's not illegal, I'm not interested.'

'That's all right then,' said Matthews, the smile now restored.

'There is one thing I am concerned about though. If you guys have such a relaxed working regime that you can sleep when you like, and come and go when you like, how can you be so sure that Ross was at the factory all night at the time of Dilys's death?'

'What are you saying?' asked Matthews.

'Well, you just told me Ross was at work the night Dilys died, but how can you be sure? If you were asleep, he could have gone out for a while and you wouldn't have known. But then there's the other two guys, aren't there? I suppose they could tell me, right?'

'Er, no, they couldn't. One was off sick, and the other one was on leave.'

'Oh, is that right? Well, isn't that convenient?' said Norman.

Matthews shrugged. 'It's not convenient, it's just one of those things.'

'Oh, it's one of those things all right,' said Norman. 'But, in that case, Ross's alibi for that night hinges on you being able to verify it, and before you say anything, I'll remind you that perverting the course of justice is a serious offence.'

Matthews stared at Norman and licked his lips.

'So let me ask you again, Glen. Did Ross Watkins leave the premises during that Saturday night shift, or not?'

'No, he didn't.'

Norman sighed. 'Let me get this straight. Are you now saying you were awake all of that night, and you know for sure that Ross was there all the time?'

'Yeah.'

'And if you were being questioned in court, you'd be happy to testify to that fact?'

'Well, I suppose I could have been asleep for some of the time,' said Matthews nervously.

'In that case you can't be sure Ross was there, can you?'

'Well, no, I suppose not.'

'So, he could have gone out.'

'I guess he might have, without me knowing, like.'

'Does that mean he might have left the premises, or does it mean he did leave?'

'I dunno for sure, but I think he might have gone out for a while.'

'D'you know where? Or for how long?'

Matthews shook his head. 'Look, I admit he might have gone out for a couple of hours, but I dunno exactly. I would have been asleep when he came back.'

'What time did he go out?'

'I can't say for sure. Probably around ten.'

'Did he have his car with him that night?' asked Norman.

'He never brings it to work. He prefers to walk. Anyway, didn't he lend it to Dilys so she could go away?'

'Oh yeah, that's right,' said Norman. 'Has he got it back yet?'

'Not as far as I know,' said Matthews.

'And he didn't borrow one from anyone?'

'Like who?'

'You don't have one?' asked Norman.

'You're looking at it,' said Matthews.

'You've known Ross for a long time, right?' asked Norman.

'Since we were teenagers. We played in the same football team.'

'So you must have known Dilys.'

'Yeah, I knew her.'

'What was she like?'

'How do you mean?'

'Well, we've heard she was nice, and we've heard she was flirty—'

'Flirty? What, Dilys? Who told you that? She was never like that.'

'That's what we thought, but when we hear something like that we have to check it out, in case it has a bearing on the case. So, what did you think of her?'

'She was a good mate,' said Matthews. 'And she was a bit special.'

'Special? In what way?'

'She was a good listener. You know how when you speak to some people you can see they're not listening to you, they're just waiting for their chance to speak? Well, Dilys was the exact opposite. She had a way about her when she spoke to you that made you feel as if you were the most interesting person in the room. It was like she was focused on every single word that came out of your mouth.'

'Would it be fair to say you were very fond of her?' asked Norman.

Matthews smiled ruefully. 'Yes, I was. Believe it or not, it could just as easily have been me she married. I went out with her before Ross.'

'And she dumped you for him? That must have been awkward,' said Norman.

'Oh no, Dilys didn't dump me. It was my fault we split up. For some stupid reason, I thought I could do better than her. Ross had always fancied her and he was on hand to pick up the pieces. By the time I realised what a fool I was and tried to win her back, the wedding was all planned and I was too late.'

'And that didn't cause a problem?'

'I was jealous at first, but then I thought, well, why would Dilys want to come back to me after I dumped her for no good reason? It was my own fault. You have to be an adult about these things if you want to stay friends.'

'So, Ross got the girl,' said Norman.

Matthews nodded.

'They only got married because she was pregnant,' he said. 'She never would have chosen to marry him if she'd had a choice.'

'Why not?' asked Norman.

'He's always been the jealous type, you know? She once told me that being married to Ross made her feel like being a bird in a gilded cage.'

'Can you tell me anything about why they split up?' asked Norman.

'You know he's not Erin's father, right?' said Matthews.

Norman merely smiled.

'Yeah, of course you know,' said Matthews. 'Anyway, they split up after Ross found out.'

'That must have been a shock,' said Norman.

'Yeah, it was for Ross, especially when they'd only got married because he'd been led to believe he was the baby's father. Mind you, I actually knew a long time before they split up. It got a bit awkward when he told me and I had to pretend I didn't know.'

'You knew before Ross did?' asked Norman.

Matthews nodded. 'Dilys told me.'

'Did she tell you who the father was?'

Matthews shook his head. 'She didn't say, and I didn't ask.'

'That's a rather private thing to tell you, before her husband even knew,' said Norman.

'Yeah, well, sometimes Ross got her down, and when she needed a mate to talk to, I was always there for her.'

'And there's no other reason why she would have told you?'

'What's that supposed to mean?' asked Matthews.

'I'll spell it out for you, Glen, if you want to play dumb,' said Norman. 'Are you Erin's father?'

'Like I said, we were a couple a long time ago, but when that ended we remained mates, but that's all we were,' said Matthews. 'I'm also mates with Ross, and I'm not the sort to stab a mate in the back like that.'

'You're sure about that, are you? Only someone did.'

'Look, I'll admit I wouldn't have said no if she'd asked me,' said Matthews. 'But the question never arose. Dilys wasn't like that.'

'Does Ross know how close you were?'

'Obviously he knew I was going out with her before him.'

'But did he know you had stayed such close friends?'

'I'll tell you this, he didn't trust her with anyone, and that included me.'

'Yeah, but that's not an answer,' said Norman. 'Did he know you and Dilys were such close friends?'

'I dunno. You'll have to ask him.'

'Oh, I will,' said Norman. 'You can count on it. One more thing. Do you have a mobile phone?'

'Why do you want to know that?'

'In case I think of any more questions. It'll be quicker than coming out here to see you.'

'No, sorry, I don't have one.'

'Really?' said Norman. 'That's unusual these days.'

'I used to have one but I kept getting all these spam calls. You know the ones, asking you to claim compensation for the car accident you never had, or trying to sell you this, that and the other that you don't want. I couldn't stop the damned calls, so I ditched the phone when the contract ran out.'

'Don't you find you miss it?'

'No way,' said Matthews. 'It's the best thing I've ever done. Those things demand your attention twenty-four seven. I've got my life back now.'

'Well, good for you,' said Norman. 'I wish I could get rid of mine, but I have to have one for work. Anyway, I'll leave you to your hobby.'

Norman was just turning to leave when Matthews suddenly said, 'I'll tell you one thing about Ross and Dilys that you probably won't know.'

'What's that?' said Norman, stopping in his tracks.

'Whatever Ross might tell you about them hoping to get back together, it was never going to happen. Dilys was actually relieved when it came out into the open about Erin, because it gave her a chance to escape.'

'You'd be surprised how many families break up after something like that,' said Norman. 'Even the closest ones find it's hard not to start blaming each other.'

'Obviously, Dilys didn't want Erin to run away, and she could have done without all the crap that Ross gave her for that but, believe me, when he said he wanted to separate, she couldn't believe her luck. She couldn't wait to get away from him.'

* * *

Norman was on his way back to his car when his mobile phone rang. 'Hi, Sarah. Are you calling to tell me there's been a change of plan?'

'Hi, Norm. No, you carry on and interrupt Marston's lunch. I just thought you might want a bit more ammunition to use against him.'

'I'll not say no to that,' said Norman, sliding into the driver's seat of his car. 'What have you got?'

He sat back, to listen as Southall told him what she had.

'And there's no doubt about it?' he asked.

'Absolutely not,' said Southall.

'He'll deny it.'

'If he does, you tell him we've got concrete evidence.'

'Are you going to charge him?'

'I'd really love to, but we've got enough to do as it is. I'm going to pass it all on to Professional Standards and let them deal with it.'

'Wow!' said Norman. 'I knew the guy was a creep but I didn't think I'd ever be able to prove it.'

'Well, there you are then,' said Southall. 'I'll text you the number. Enjoy your lunch.'

'Oh, I will. What are you up to?'

'I'm still trying to identify the last number Dilys called. I'll catch you later.'

'Bye, Sarah.'

Norman stared unseeing at his phone, considering what he had just heard. Then it pinged, making him start. He took a quick look at the message Southall had sent and, shaking his head at the sheer stupidity of some people, he started the car and set off to find Marston.

CHAPTER FIFTEEN

As he had hoped, Norman found Marston sitting at the table he had occupied before, masticating like some bulky ruminant, with ketchup and grease oozing down his chin.

Norman sat down opposite. 'Didn't anyone ever tell you it's bad manners to eat with your mouth open? Jeez, look at the state of you. You're worse than a toddler.'

Marston stared angrily at Norman, still chewing. 'Oh, great. It's Mr Prefect Cop. What the hell do you want?'

Norman leaned back to avoid getting hit with morsels of food. 'Do you always speak with your mouth full? Jeez, you're spraying it everywhere. No wonder no one wants to have lunch with you.'

'Can't I even have my lunch in peace?'

'Not when you're up shit creek and I know where to find you,' said Norman.

Finally, Marston managed to swallow the mouthful of burger. 'What are you on about? I told you I wasn't in charge of that case. I was just following orders.'

'Which case are you talking about?' said Norman. 'The one where you didn't try very hard to find a missing girl because you were more interested in her mother?'

'What?' said Marston. 'This is bullshit. I never—'

'Or the one where you wrongly allowed Dilys Watkins to believe her husband was stalking her when it was actually you?'

'You're talking bollocks!' snarled Marston, jabbing a finger at Norman. 'You can't prove any of this.'

Norman produced his phone and showed Marston the phone number that had been texted to him. 'Is this yours?'

'No, it isn't.' Marston produced his phone. 'Here, you can check the number for yourself.'

'Of course, it's not the phone you use every day,' said Norman. 'Even you wouldn't be that stupid. This number — he tapped the screen — is for the phone you use when you want to harass women like Dilys Watkins.'

'Oh yeah? Well I've got news for you, Mr Smartarse Clever Dick from London. You can't prove anything without evidence, can you, and Dilys Watkins won't be accusing me of anything now.'

'Is that why you killed her?'

'Jesus! Are you bloody mad? I didn't kill her! It's been two years since I've even set eyes on her.'

'But you were calling her, weren't you?'

'Bollocks.' Marston jumped to his feet. 'I don't have to put up with this crap. I'm leaving, and I'm going to call Professional Standards and register a complaint against you. You can't just go around trashing the reputation of your fellow officers whenever it suits you. Especially when you haven't a shred of evidence—'

Norman aimed a pitying smile in Marston's direction.

'It's the phone you used when you were harassing DC Judy Lane during your time at Llangwelli, you moron.'

Marston stood with his mouth opening and shutting, like a fish dragged from the water. Norman watched his expression slowly change from indignation to realisation, and finally to resignation.

'Unless you want everyone to continue gawping at you, you should sit down,' said Norman. 'There again, if you really want to cause a scene, I can arrest you. That will get everyone's attention.'

Marston looked around. There weren't that many people sitting outside the cafe, but every one of them had their eyes on him. Slowly, he sank back into his seat.

'You can't arrest me,' he hissed.

'Oh, trust me, I could,' said Norman. 'But the fact is, I can't be arsed. I've actually got better things to do. Anyway, Professional Standards will be dealing with you and I wouldn't want to get in their way.'

'You bastard!' snapped Marston. 'I could get the sack!'

'I don't think anyone but you would have a problem with that,' said Norman. 'But if I were you, I'd be more concerned about how you'll cope with being a police officer in prison. Even coppers who've been fired aren't welcome inside.'

'You've got no proof,' said Marston, desperately. 'You can't prove that phone is mine, and without it you've got nothing.'

'We do have proof though,' said Norman. 'You see, we got hold of Dilys's phone records, and we can see that she was getting call after call from the number I just showed you. She never answered those calls, and we figured out that the reason she didn't answer was because she knew who was calling, and she didn't want to speak to them.'

'You can't prove it was me.'

'Oh, but we can,' said Norman. 'As I said just now, you remember a young detective called Judy Lane, don't you?'

'No.'

'Sure you do. She worked at Llangwelli station when you were there. Nice looking girl. Kinda quiet but super-efficient and, unfortunately for you, she has a great memory.'

Marston shook his head. 'She must have been really quiet, because I don't recall her at all.'

'No? Well that's kinda funny, because when she saw that mobile phone number, she knew straight away that it was yours. And do you know how come? Because she's got old text messages from you on her phone.'

'You're bluffing,' said Marston.

Norman smiled. 'You wish.'

'I never sent her any messages. And why would she keep them anyway?'

'So you admit you did send her messages?'

'I'm saying nothing of the sort,' snapped Marston. 'What I'm saying is if I had sent messages, why would she keep them?'

'Judy kept those messages because she was hoping that one day she would have the courage to come forward and use them against you. Since she's been working with us, her confidence has grown. And now, guess what?'

'But it's an unregistered phone. You can't prove anything.'

'You admit it's your phone then?'

'I repeat, I admit nothing,' said Marston.

'Ross Watkins tells me you were more interested in Dilys than in finding her daughter,' said Norman. 'I suppose you're going to tell me that's more bullshit, are you?'

'Balls. He's a fantasist. You can't believe a thing he says. According to him every bloke was after his missus. I mean, it's not as if she was anything special.'

'That's not quite what you told me before,' said Norman. 'Didn't you say she was "sexy and she knew it"?'

'Look, I took a professional interest in her well-being. That's all it was.'

'Ross also tells me he wasn't stalking Dilys, he just bumped into her one time by accident, and we've got witnesses who can confirm his story. So now I'm wondering who was really stalking Dilys.'

'You can't be serious,' said Marston.

'Can't I?' said Norman. 'I mean, you could have found out all this about Ross at the time, and I'm sure Dilys probably told you when she discovered the truth, but it was much more convenient for you to quietly write a report that blamed Ross and recommend no further action, wasn't it?'

'Look,' whined Marston. 'We can sort this without getting Professional Standards involved, can't we? I mean, we're all on the same side.'

'Don't insult me, Marston. We've never been on the same side. And you don't seriously think I'm going to cut you some sort of deal, do you?' asked Norman. 'You have to be kidding. I'm not here to cut any kind of deal. I'm here because Dilys Watkins is dead, and you have a motive for killing her. You're now a murder suspect.'

'You can't pin that on me,' pleaded Marston. 'I might have fancied her, but I never touched her. Honest!'

Norman's phone started ringing. Irritated, he looked at the caller ID, then at Marston. 'I have to take this, but you wait here. I haven't finished with you yet.'

He moved away from Marston and raised his phone to his ear.

'Hi, Sarah, is this important?'

'I'm afraid it is,' said Southall. 'We've just had a call from the Operations Centre. A body has been found at Nantwygil landfill site.'

'Jeez, are we the only detectives in Wales?' said Norman. 'Can't they send someone else?'

'It's less than ten miles from us, and apparently the chief constable has said he wants us to attend.'

'Is that right?' said Norman. 'How the heck are we supposed to handle two murders at once?'

'Superintendent Bain tells me the chief constable has been very impressed with our performance.'

'That's all very well, but he does realise we're only detectives, and not robots, does he? Is he even aware of just how small this team is?'

'I admit I sometimes wonder,' said Southall, 'but I'm sure he realises.'

'Well, if he knows we're such a small team, why is he pushing additional work on to us? I mean, why the hell doesn't he kick some arses over at Region and get them working?'

'I'm not sure what exactly is going on, but as he's the big boss, I'm not about to argue with him. However, I will ask Superintendent Bain to point out to head office that if we're going to be asked to handle more work, we're going to need a lot more staff.'

'I take it that means we are going to take on this new case then,' said Norman.

'I understand what you're saying, Norm, but do you honestly think it would be right for us to refuse to go and look at a murder scene?' said Southall.

Norman sighed. 'I suppose you're right. Do you want me to head out there?'

'Can you go and check it out for me? At least then no one can say we refused,' said Southall. 'In the meantime, I'll speak to Superintendent Bain and tell him we're going to struggle unless we get some help. I'll be there as soon as I can.'

'Where is this place?'

'I've sent you the address and a map,' said Southall. 'It doesn't look far.'

'Around here, nowhere looks far on a map,' said Norman, 'but you can't get anywhere in a hurry—'

'Because of the crappy roads,' finished Southall.

'Yeah, of course I forgot, you know that, too,' said Norman.

'I found it out the first week I was here,' said Southall.

'I admit I've got used to it now,' said Norman. 'I suppose it's one of the things you have to accept when you choose to live out here, a bit like the rain.'

'Ah, yes. I'm glad you mentioned that,' said Southall. 'It's just started pouring down over here, so you'd better make sure you've got a hat, a coat and a pair of wellies.'

Norman ended the call, squinted up at the sky and smiled ruefully. Small spots of rain were just beginning to fall and the sky was full of ominously dark clouds which promised much worse to come.

'Just what I needed,' he muttered. 'As if a landfill site wasn't going to be mucky enough already.'

He slipped the phone into his pocket and headed for his car.

'Oi! Hang on a minute,' shouted Marston. 'You can't just walk off like that. What about me?'

Norman turned and shrugged. 'I guess you'll keep until later. Right now, I've got something more important to deal with. But don't worry, I know where to find you when the time comes.'

* * *

Seething with impotent rage, Marston stood and watched Norman turn and walk to his car. Easily outsmarted by the older detective, he was now trapped between a rock and a hard place. If he admitted to Professional Standards that he had been stalking Dilys, he could get fired. There again, he could get lucky and end up with a slap on the wrist and a suspension from duty.

The bigger fear was Norman, and that jumped-up DI Southall. If they had already identified him as a murder suspect because they believed he had been stalking the victim, admitting to it would make him an even bigger suspect.

CHAPTER SIXTEEN

Ten miles from the roadside café where Norman was inter-
rupting Marston's lunch, Terry Reynolds sat watching the
rain and patiently munching his sandwiches while he waited
for a mechanic to finish working on his vehicle. A driver of
fifteen years' experience, Terry knew there was no point complaining about the length of time it was taking, because if he
did, the mechanic would almost certainly take even longer.

Back in its heyday, Nantwygil had been the biggest open-
cast coal mine in West Wales. Following the mine closures of
the eighties, it had stood unused until, in 2005, desperately
short of a place to deposit the area's burgeoning heaps of waste,
the county council stepped in and took it over as a landfill site.

Heroic efforts by the council to encourage recycling
had drastically reduced the amount of household waste that
went to landfill, but even so, a steady flow of lorries carrying skips full of assorted rubbish, especially builders' rubble,
rumbled to and fro. Each lorry-load would be scrutinised on
entry, and the driver directed to the correct part of the site
in which to offload. When this was done, huge bulldozers
would spread and crush the waste.

Terry's job for today was bulldozing the builders' rubble, but that morning, his bulldozer had suffered a hydraulic

failure, so the twelve loads that had been tipped so far that day remained untouched.

As he watched another two lorries arrive and dump their loads, Terry realised he would probably have to work late to catch up. He wasn't that bothered, however, since the overtime would bring him a little extra money as compensation.

The mechanic finally emerged from beneath the machine and gathered up his tools, giving Terry a thumbs-up and a gap-toothed smile.

'All fixed now!' he shouted.

Terry gave him a cheery wave and fired up the engine, which coughed and spluttered a couple of times before roaring into life, belching clouds of black diesel fumes over the hapless mechanic, who shook a fist at him as he moved away. Laughing, Terry put the huge machine into gear and turned his attention to the waiting piles of rubble.

He had spread and flattened the first five piles when his bulldozer's blade inadvertently caught a long piece of timber jutting from the next pile as he was reversing. Cursing the idiots who should know better than to put timber in with rubble, Terry braked hard. But a bulldozer weighing twenty tons isn't a car that responds instantly to the touch of the brake pedal. Terry watched, helplessly, as the long timber, acting like a huge lever, sent a huge dust-filled cloud of debris in all directions before it finally split in two.

Terry thought he caught a glimpse of something vaguely familiar through the cloud of dust but put it down to imagination. Nevertheless, curiosity got the better of him and he pulled on the handbrake and watched as the swirling dust slowly began to settle. As it did so, Terry realised that what he had seen had been no trick of the eye.

At first he could only stare, uncomprehending, at the dust-covered human arm that seemed to slowly rise from the rubble. It was only when he realised that the arm must still be attached to a body that he came to life and acted.

Switching off his engine, he grabbed his radio. 'I need help! And an ambulance. Call an ambulance.'

Then he jumped from the cab and ran through the rain to see if he could do anything to help whoever was buried there, under the rubble.

* * *

As Norman had feared, the gentle rain had become a heavy downpour by the time he arrived at the Nantwygil landfill site. On the positive side, he was pleased to find that the entire site had been secured. A uniformed officer stopped him at the gate, checked his ID, wrote his details on a clipboard and explained where he should park his car. Then he pointed in the direction of a cordoned-off area and a small pop-up tent that had been erected about a hundred yards away.

'They've got forensic suits in the tent, sarge,' he was told. 'The body is just beyond that.'

Norman parked his car, looked up at the sky and realised there was no way the rain was going to ease off any time soon. But at least this time he was prepared for it, having taken the precaution of removing his coat and wellington boots from the boot of his car and placing them in the passenger footwell before setting out.

Knowing he was for once going to be correctly dressed for the weather felt like a small victory to Norman and, buoyed by this rare triumph over the elements, he was able, with the use of some nifty in-car gymnastics, to change into his waterproofs reasonably quickly.

Before he left his car, he looked across the site to the first tent, where he would have to change into a forensic suit. A short distance beyond, he could see a second pop-up tent, which he knew had been erected to protect the body and its surrounding area from the elements. This meant that the scenes of crime officers were already on the site, and quite possibly a pathologist too.

Keen to make sure he didn't miss anything important, he stepped out into the rain and set off for the site.

Norman had purchased his wellington boots many years ago when he worked in London. They hadn't seen much use during those years, and he was still using the same ones now. Catren Morgan had on more than one occasion pointed out to him that modern wellies weighed almost nothing and were much more comfortable but, loath to spend his money, Norman had stubbornly held on to his heavy, old-fashioned boots.

From his first step away from the car, Norman began to regret having been so tight-fisted. The Nantwygil clay, already churned up by bulldozers trundling backwards and forwards, was rapidly being transformed into a gloopy morass by the heavy rain. At every step, it pulled and sucked at Norman's wellingtons and he feared it was only a matter of time before it stole one from him.

By the time he reached the first small tent, his already heavy footwear felt like lead diving boots, and he was sweating from the huge effort required just to put one foot in front of the other.

A young PC waited at the entrance to the tent, unable to suppress a smirk as he watched the approaching detective struggle through the mud. Norman thought he looked about fifteen years old.

'Not the best day to be ploughing your way through the mud in your wellies, sir,' said the officer cheerily.

'You don't say,' said Norman testily.

'This area is notoriously bad for clay.'

'No, really?' said Norman, his voice laden with sarcasm. 'I would never have guessed.'

The officer pointed into the distance.

'They say there's evidence there was once a pottery over that hi—'

'Look, no offence, son,' said Norman, 'but right this minute, I really don't need to hear about the history of clay. Can I just have a forensic suit so I can go and look at the body?'

'Oh. Right. Yes, sir. Sorry, sir.'

Crestfallen, the young officer reached into the box of suits, his face a deep shade of red. Norman immediately felt ashamed of himself.

'Hey, look, I'm sorry,' he said. 'It's not your fault I'm getting old, or that I'm tired, or that my boots weigh a ton. I had no right to bite your head off, and I apologise for behaving like an arse.'

'That's okay, sir. Everyone tells me I talk too much when I'm under a bit of stress.'

'What's your name, son?' asked Norman.

'Hopkins, sir.'

'Is this your first dead body, Hopkins?'

'No, sir. I've seen a couple before, but this is the first one I've seen dumped in a rubbish tip. He's in a bit of a state.'

'Well, even if you've seen a hundred dead bodies, it's not okay for me to snap at you like that. We all have different ways of coping with the shitty parts of this job, and if yours is talking, who am I to stop you?'

Hopkins, obviously taken aback by the apology, was suddenly at a loss for words. He also seemed to have forgotten what he was supposed to be doing.

'And you don't have to call me sir every time you open your mouth,' said Norman. 'We're not in the army.'

'Yes, sir.'

'Now, are you going to give me one of those suits?' asked Norman.

'Yes, of course, sir. I mean . . .' Hopkins fished a bright blue forensic suit from the box.

'Jeez. Are you kidding?,' said Norman. 'We have to wear Smurf suits?'

'I'm afraid that's all we have,' said Hopkins. 'Can you sign the clipboard, please?'

Reluctantly, Norman signed for his suit. A tarpaulin had been placed on the ground to try to keep the floor of the tent dry. Unfortunately, everyone who had been inside the tent before Norman had also walked across a hundred yards of sticky clay in their wellies, and then trodden it onto the tarpaulin. Consequently, there was little difference between it and the morass outside.

Norman stepped away from Hopkins to give himself some room, found a small, almost clean, patch of floor and toed his wellington boots off. For a moment he struggled to get into his forensic suit, then realised he couldn't do it while he was still wearing his coat.

Muttering under his breath, he slipped off his coat but now realised there was nowhere to hang it. As he angrily threw it onto the floor, he slipped and had to hastily adjust his stance to regain his balance, not realising until too late that he had stepped onto a particularly muddy part of the floor.

'Holy crap. Can this day get any worse?' he muttered, as the cold mud soaked into his socks.

'Are you all right, sir?' asked Hopkins, turning to see what was wrong.

Norman pulled on the forensic suit, zipped it up and slid his now mucky feet back into his even muckier boots.

'Don't you worry, Hopkins, everything is hunky dory over here, even if I do look like old Father Smurf.'

'You should get a pair of wellies like these,' said Hopkins, raising a foot so Norman could see.

'I have a detective constable who tells me the exact same thing every time it rains,' said Norman.

'There we are then,' said Hopkins. 'We can't both be wrong.'

'I'm beginning to think you're probably right about that,' conceded Norman, looking down at his own boots. 'Anyway, I'd better get on. I don't think my boss will be too impressed if I tell her I spent half an hour talking to you about the merits of modern wellington boots.'

He gave Hopkins a faint smile and trudged from the tent. The second tent was barely twenty yards away so he ducked under the cordon tape and set off, his feet now making wet, fart-like noises inside his wellies, a fitting counterpoint to the squelchy, sucking noises they were already making in the mud.

Under the cover of the second tent, a forensic technician, also in blue, was taking photographs of the body, directed by another blue-suited figure kneeling over the body. Norman recognised the pathologist, Dr Bill Bridger.

'Is this the right place for the Smurf convention?' called Norman as he approached.

Bridger looked up. 'Hi, Norm. I was wondering who was to blame for calling me out here on a day like this.'

'Sorry, but I am genuinely not guilty,' said Norman. 'If I had my way, someone else would be dealing with this, but when the chief constable requests that no one but us is to come out in the rain, it's kinda hard to say no.'

Bridger studied Norman's awkward, heavy-booted gait and began to laugh.

'Next time they make a film about someone walking on the moon, I'm going to recommend you for the part.'

'To be honest, I'm getting a little tired of all these welly jokes at my expense,' said Norman. 'Can't we change the record?'

'It would probably be better if you changed your wellies,' said Bridger.

Norman had now reached the tent. 'How close can I come? I mean, I wouldn't want to destroy any evidence with my diving boots.'

'I don't think you need to worry too much about that,' said Bridger. 'Between the rain, the mud and the bulldozers, I can't imagine we're going to find anything that could be used as credible evidence. And, anyway, I'd stake my reputation that this isn't the crime scene.'

'Are you sure?' asked Norman.

'My guess is that the guy was brought here inside a skip full of rubbish, and he could have been lying in the skip for a day or two before that. I would imagine that whoever dumped him in the skip intended him to be buried by the bulldozers, and he probably would have been but, luckily for us, he was discovered before that happened.'

'Any idea how long he's been dead?' asked Norman.

'My best guess? No more than three or four days.'

'Cause of death?'

'The body is in such a state and has so many injuries that, at this stage, it's difficult to work out which ones are ante-mortem, and which ones are post-mortem.'

'Any ID on him?'

'No, but I think I might know who he is.'

'You do? Is he a friend of yours?'

'More like a friend of yours,' said Bridger. 'Or, at least, a friend of your department.'

Norman frowned. 'What does that mean?'

'Aren't you looking for a young man who's gone missing?'

'Well, yeah,' said Norman, 'but this can't be him. We think he's either in Llangwelli, or he may have even gone back to London.'

'Are you sure about that? Only one of the PCs who was first on the scene said he thought this dead guy looks like the one in the photo you circulated.'

'Holy crap! Are you sure?'

'I'm just telling you what I've been told.'

'What's he wearing?' asked Norman.

'Jeans and a blue T-shirt,' said Bridger.

'No coat?'

'Not on him. Of course, if it was in the skip, it'll be around here somewhere.'

'What about tattoos?' asked Norman.

'He seems to be well decorated, but that's not uncommon these days,' said Bridger. 'Have you got the photograph with you?'

'I've got it on my phone,' said Norman.

'Well, why don't you bring it over here, take a look, and see what you think?'

Norman squelched his way over to the body, fumbled in his pocket for his phone and found the photograph. Bridger stepped aside so Norman could hold the photo alongside the dead face.

'It's one hell of a coincidence if it's not him,' said Norman. 'He's got the same long hair, and the same earring. But it's hard to say for sure with his face being all dirty and scratched like that. And him being dead doesn't make it any easier.'

'Can I see?' asked Bridger. 'I'm more used to dead people's faces.'

Norman passed him the phone and Bridger studied it for a moment.

'We'll know for sure when we get him to the lab and clean him up, but I'd say, with reasonable certainty, that this is your missing man,' said Bridger, handing the phone back to Norman.

'Shit,' muttered Norman. 'This wasn't supposed to happen.'

'What's that?' asked Bridger.

'Remember the girl Sarah stopped from jumping off that roof?'

'The fragile one whose mother's body was found in the old mining village?'

'That's the one,' said Norman. 'Well, this here is the body of a guy called Wozzy. He was her boyfriend.'

'Oh, hell. That really is shit,' agreed Bridger.

'I'm not sure she's even been told about her mother yet,' said Norman. 'How the heck is she going to deal with losing her boyfriend as well?'

'I'm glad I don't have to break it to her,' said Bridger.

'I'd better call this in,' said Norman.

* * *

Southall answered his call at once. 'Whatcha got, Norm?'

'A situation that says we can't hand this murder over to someone else,' said Norman.

'Why is that?'

'Because our case just got bigger,' said Norman. 'We have a second murder on our hands. This time it's Erin's boyfriend, Wozzy.'

'Oh, no! Are you sure?'

'One of the first responders recognised him as the guy we're searching for, and now me and Bill have compared the photo I had of his face, I'd say we're as sure as we can be,' said Norman.

'I'm on my way,' said Southall.

'Honestly, Sarah, I'm not sure you're going to achieve a great deal by coming out here. The torrential rain would be bad enough on its own, and the bulldozers churning up the clay wouldn't be very helpful either, but put them both together and we have a whole site knee-deep in thick, sticky clay.'

'What about the crime scene?' asked Southall.

'Bill and the forensic guys are here. They say if there was ever any useful evidence, there's zero chance they're going to find it in this mess. And Bill's pretty sure this isn't the murder scene anyway.'

'Do you think it was his blood at number nineteen?'

'We'll know for sure when they get the body back to the mortuary, but that's my best guess,' said Norman. 'I reckon Wozzy was murdered there and then his body was dumped in a skip. There are plenty of skips scattered around that site to choose from. All the killer had to do was find one that looked ready to go to the tip, cover the body with rubble, and who's going to look close enough to notice?'

'Do you think one of the lorry drivers picked up the skip on the back of his truck, drove it out there and tipped it without realising there was a body on board?' said Southall.

'That's what I reckon,' said Norman. 'I can't imagine a driver would take a good look at what's inside a skip so long as it looks like a safe load.'

'Are you sure you don't need me to come out there?'

'I think you'd be wasting your time. There isn't anything you can do here that I can't, and you'll just end up getting covered in this crappy clay for nothing.'

'If you're sure, Norm.'

'I'm positive.'

'When you get back, I'd like to see Ross Watkins again and ask him why he gave us a false alibi.'

'No problem,' said Norman. 'But I'm going to have to go home and clean up before I come back to the office.'

CHAPTER SEVENTEEN

Ross Watkins opened his front door to Southall and Norman looking tousled and sleepy.

'Hi, Ross,' said Southall. 'Sorry if we woke you.'

'You guys again?' he said. 'Is this important? Only I'm just about to get ready for work.'

'It's up to you how long it takes,' said Southall. 'We just have a couple of questions.'

'I suppose you'd better come in then.'

Watkins stepped back to let them in and followed them into his living room. 'What's so important that you need to make me late for work again?'

'Won't Glen Matthews clock you in?' asked Norman. 'You guys always cover for each other, don't you?'

'Well, yeah, I suppose we do.'

'Like he covered for you the night Dilys died?' asked Southall.

Watkins drew in a sharp breath. He stared at them. 'What?'

'I went to see Glen,' said Norman. 'We had quite a chat about the night Dilys died, and where you were. Then I explained to him how obstructing a murder investigation was a criminal offence, and how it wouldn't be a good idea to commit perjury. After that, he decided to change his story. He now says you did leave the building that night, and he can't say for sure how long you were gone.'

'That means you no longer have an alibi, Ross,' said Southall.

'I don't need an alibi. I already told you, I didn't kill Dilys. I hadn't set eyes on her since I let her borrow my car, and I didn't see her that night.'

'So, where did you go that night?' asked Southall.

'If you must know, I went to the pub.'

'Which pub?'

'The White Hart.'

'Can anyone confirm that?' asked Southall.

'The landlady, and the regulars,' said Watkins. 'I go there two or three nights a week.'

'Oh, you do, do you?' asked Norman. 'Is there any particular reason why you go there?'

'It's five minutes' walk from work,' said Watkins.

'And how long were you there that night?' asked Norman. 'Glen couldn't say for sure because he thought he was asleep when you got back.'

'That's bullshit. He was definitely awake that night. He was the only one watching the machines, so he had to be. Anyway, he knows what time I came back from the pub because he was waiting to go out as soon as I got back.'

'Where did he go?' asked Norman

'He's got some woman he meets in Carmarthen.'

'Does his girlfriend know?'

'I wouldn't think so, would you?'

'Do you always go out and come back at the same time?' asked Southall.

'More or less,' said Watkins. 'I usually go down there at about ten p.m., and stay until closing time. I can't tell you to the exact minute what time I left that night, but I'm usually back at work around eleven forty-five or midnight at the latest.'

'Isn't it risky drinking while you're operating machinery?' asked Southall.

'I don't go there to drink,' said Watkins, adding hastily, 'what I mean is I don't drink alcohol when I'm working.'

'Soft drinks only,' said Norman.

'Yeah, something like that. Now, have you got any more questions, or can I get ready for work?'

'Have you seen Erin?' asked Southall.

'I'm seeing her tomorrow as it happens.'

'Does she know about Dilys?'

'Yes, the doctors told her, but it should have been me. I'm her dad.'

'I'm sure they did what they thought best,' said Southall. 'Don't forget she had told them she didn't want to see you. What were they supposed to do?'

'Yes, I suppose you're right. It wouldn't have been right to keep her in the dark, would it?'

'So how come she changed her mind about seeing you?' Southall asked.

'Her doctor contacted me and asked me if I was willing to see her. Apparently, she had asked the doctor if she thought I would take her back now she's all on her own. Can you believe that? I never wanted her to go in the first place.'

'What does the doctor think about Erin? She's been through a lot, especially losing her mum.'

'The doctor says she's made of tough stuff. She thinks Erin will be fine so long as she has someone to support her. I'm hoping we can get over this DNA thing so I can bring her home.'

'Every daughter needs her father,' said Southall.

'Fingers crossed, that's how it's going to be,' said Watkins.

* * *

'That didn't sound like the voice of a man who's a hardened killer, did it?' said Southall when they got back to their car.

'He's not in the clear yet,' Norman said, and started the engine.

'Fancy a drink on the way back?' asked Southall.

'I take it you want to go to the White Hart,' said Norman.

'It's less than five minutes from here,' said Southall.

'I know. We passed it on the way,' said Norman. 'You're hoping this new alibi checks out, aren't you, and Ross is in the clear. Especially now he wants to play the good father.'

Southall sighed. 'After what she's been through, that girl needs her dad. Anyway, I think Ross is already in the clear if you're right about both murders being committed by the same person. Even if Ross had a car we don't know about, it would be totally unrealistic to think he could have met Dilys, killed her, driven several miles to hide her body, got in a fight with Wozzy, killed him and hidden his body, hidden Dilys's car, and then driven back to work, all within the space of a couple of hours. He'd have had to be out half the night to accomplish so much.'

'And don't forget the handbag,' said Norman. 'He would have needed to make the trip to the woods to dump that, too.'

'I think we can agree that Ross Watkins is rapidly slipping down the list of suspects, and if this alibi checks out, we can cross him off completely.'

A few minutes later, they were knocking on the door of the White Hart.

'What sort of pub is this?' asked Southall. 'It's nearly six p.m. Shouldn't they be open by now?'

'I think you'll find that these days most pubs won't open unless they know they're going to be busy,' said Norman. 'And the way their costs keep on rising, I can't say I blame them.'

'You seem to know a lot about the costs of running a pub. Is that your retirement plan?'

'No way,' said Norman. 'Twenty years ago maybe, but not now. There's a reason so many pubs have closed, and I have no intention of becoming another statistic. Besides, I've spent my working life serving the public. When I retire for good I want to enjoy a bit of peace and quiet.'

The sound of a bolt being drawn back and a key turning in a lock was followed by a muffled curse. The door opened a crack and an eye looked them up and down through thick-lensed spectacles. 'We open at six, so you can sod off until then.'

Southall held up her warrant card over the security chain. 'DI Southall and DS Norman. We're from Llangwelli station. If you can spare a couple of minutes, we'd like to ask you a few questions.'

'But I haven't done anything!'

'We're not accusing you of anything,' said Southall. 'We just have some questions about one of your customers.'

'Well, if you come back at six, I'll answer them.'

Norman looked at his watch. 'Are you seriously going to make us wait here for four minutes?' he asked. 'It'll take you longer than that to lock up again.'

'We don't start serving until six.'

'Fine,' said Norman. 'We were planning on having a drink, but now we've sampled your hospitality we've changed our minds about that. Now we'll settle for asking a few questions. It'll take about five minutes of your precious time and then we'll be gone.'

After a lot of muttered grumbling and complaining, the door closed. They heard the chain being released, and then the door swung slowly open. The woman waiting defiantly inside stood less than five feet tall. She was of indeterminate age, but the lines on her face and the colour of her long silver-grey hair suggested she had been around the block more times than either Southall or Norman, and possibly more times than both put together.

Having unlocked the door, the old woman shuffled across the room, ducked under the flap, and took up position behind the bar. The detectives followed and stood by the stools on the customers' side.

'I didn't catch your name,' said Southall.

'That's because you didn't ask what it was,' said the old woman.

'I'm sorry,' said Southall, patiently. 'What is your name?'

The woman sniffed haughtily. 'It's Nina, if you must know.'

'Does Nina have a surname?' asked Southall.

'She might have.'

'Look,' said Norman. 'I don't know what's eating you, Nina, but we're not here to cause trouble or accuse you of anything, it's just that one of your customers told us he was here at a certain time, and we need to know if he's telling us the truth.'

Nina's eyes narrowed. 'You mean he wants an alibi? Why? What's he done?'

'If he was here like he said, then he hasn't done anything,' said Southall.

'When was it? asked Nina.

'Saturday,' said Southall. 'Around ten p.m.'

'I wouldn't have been here,' said Nina. 'I open the pub at six for my granddaughter, but I only work for a couple of hours, then I'm back upstairs, out of the way.'

'We need to speak to your granddaughter then,' said Southall.

'Sounds like it,' said Nina.

'Is she here?'

'She's upstairs.'

'D'you think you could call her?' asked Southall.

'Well, yes, I suppose I could,' said Nina without moving.

'Let me rephrase that,' said Southall. 'Will you please call your granddaughter and let her know we'd like to ask her some questions?'

'You're a bossy cow, ain'tcha?' said Nina.

Norman winced as he saw Southall's face darken.

'Yes, I am,' said Southall testily. 'And if you don't call your granddaughter now, I'm going to come behind that bar and find her for myself.'

'There's no need to be like that,' said Nina. 'I've just pressed the bell. She'll be down in a minute. Now, if you don't mind, I've got a kitchen to prepare for the evening meals.'

As she shuffled off through a door behind the bar, Southall turned to Norman.

'Was there really any need for her to be quite so rude?'

Norman couldn't hide his smile. 'She's just a tetchy old dear, looking for someone to wind up. And it looks like she struck gold with you. Jeez, did you bite, or what?'

'It's not funny,' said Southall.

'I'm sorry, Sarah, but I'm afraid it is if you're watching from here.'

'You're supposed to be on my side,' argued Southall.

'Oh, I am, you know that. The thing is, I can't help but admire a feisty old lady who doesn't give a damn who we are.'

A woman suddenly appeared behind the bar. 'My gran says the police are looking for me.'

'That depends who you are,' said Southall.

'I'm Alice Durham. I own the pub.'

Southall produced her warrant card and made the introductions again.

'If that was your gran we were speaking to, Alice, she wasn't very helpful.'

'I'm sorry about that. She's a sweet old thing really, but she thinks I need protecting. She doesn't seem to realise she can be quite offensive.'

'She must lose you some customers,' said Norman.

'She insists on helping out to pay her way, so I let her open up at this time of day when there are usually no customers to upset. Anyway, what can I do for you?'

'Do you have a customer called Ross Watkins?' asked Southall.

'Yes, I know Ross. He comes in most nights.'

'He told us he comes in two or three nights a week.'

'More like five nights. Is this about his wife's murder?'

'Was he here last Saturday night?' Southall asked.

'Yes, he was.'

'Can you remember what time he came in?'

'Not to the minute. We were quite busy, but it would have been around ten p.m.'

'And can you recall what time he left?'

'That would have been about eleven forty-five'ish. He likes to be back at work by midnight.'

'So, you know he's supposed to be working when he's here?' asked Southall.

'I'm not his keeper. If he wants to spend his money here when he should be at work, that's not my problem, is it?' said Alice.

'Don't you close at eleven?' asked Norman.

'What of it?'

'I'm just wondering how come Ross is here so late,' said Norman. 'Isn't it ten minutes' drinking-up time? I'd have thought everyone would be gone by eleven fifteen, and yet you're saying Ross is usually here for another half hour after that.'

Alice planted her hands firmly on her hips.

'Look, we're consenting adults, right? I'm divorced and he's separated. There's no law against it, is there?'

'And you're quite sure Ross was here on Saturday night? Didn't you think it was odd he was working over the week-end?' asked Southall.

Alice stared defiantly at Southall. 'He told me they'd got behind with a big order and they were working over the weekend to catch up. I don't think there's anything odd about that. I can tell you two don't run a business and have to make ends meet. Now, is there anything else, or can I get back to my dinner?'

'No, I think you've told us what we needed to know,' said Southall. 'We'll go now. I'm sorry about your dinner.'

'Feisty like her grandmother,' said Norman once they were outside. 'She just managed to give Ross an alibi and a motive for murder at the same time.'

'It's not him,' said Southall. 'It can't be, unless he's superhuman.'

CHAPTER EIGHTEEN

Friday, 17 March

Norman hated post-mortems at the best of times, and first thing in the morning was definitely the worst. Thus, he was relieved to find the pathologist had made an early start.

'You've done all the gory stuff already? Now, this is the kind of post-mortem I like.'

'I hate to disappoint you, Norm,' said Bridger, 'but the only reason I started so early is that we happen to be busy today. I'm not going to make a habit of it just so you can keep hold of your breakfast.'

'Trust me, I didn't for one minute think you'd done it for my benefit.' Norman looked down at the body. 'Jeez, he looks like he was trampled by a herd of elephants.'

'He is a bit of a mess, isn't he?' said Bridger. 'But that's what happens if you're dumped in a skip full of builders' rubble, buried by that same rubble when it's emptied at a landfill site, and then shifted by a bulldozer.'

'When you put it like that, who needs elephants?' said Norman.

'And, of course, there's no way of telling if more rubble was being dumped on him while he was in the skip,' added

Bridger. 'Frankly, I think it was a stroke of good fortune that the bulldozer driver was sharp-eyed enough to spot the protruding arm, or this body may have been crushed by the machine, or even buried and lost forever.'

'I hope you're not going to tell us the poor fellow was alive when he was tipped out of the skip,' said Southall.

'I can't rule it out at this stage, but I think it's highly unlikely,' said Bridger.

'Does that mean you think all these injuries were inflicted post-mortem?' asked Norman.

'The vast majority are,' said Bridger.

'But?' asked Southall.

'But there are enough tell-tale signs to indicate he was beaten about the head and torso and also strangled,' said Bridger, pointing to the neck area. 'Now we've cleaned him up a bit, you can see there's a ligature mark around his neck.'

'So, which do you think was the cause of death?' asked Southall. 'The beating, or the strangulation?'

'I can't confirm one way or the other without further tests, but I would say that if the beating didn't kill him it would have left him severely weakened, and possibly unconscious,' said Bridger. 'In that condition, it would have been relatively easy to strangle him just to make sure.'

'Is there anything else you can tell us?' asked Southall.

'Not right now. I'll let you know as soon as more comes to light.'

'Right, we'd better get going then,' Southall said.

Norman had been studying the vague mark around the body's neck. 'That looks to be quite a hefty ligature, Bill. How wide is that? I'm guessing it must be, what, an inch or so? Any idea what it was?'

'My best guess at this stage is some kind of polypropylene rope about thirty-five millimetres in diameter. That's about an inch and a half in old money, Norm.'

'Right. That's interesting,' said Norman.

'Come on, Norm, we've got to get a move on,' said Southall.

* * *

Norman was unusually quiet on the way back to their car.

'What are you thinking?' Southall asked, starting the engine.

'Well, it's possible you might be carrying a thin length of twine in your pocket, or you might be wearing a belt, either one of which could be used to strangle someone, but who the heck carries around a polypropylene rope as thick as that?'

'You think the killer came prepared?' asked Southall as she drove away from the mortuary.

'Yeah, that's a possibility, but I'm thinking polypropylene rope is something that would be useful on a building site, and if someone knew where it was kept, they wouldn't need to come prepared.'

'Who have you got in mind? I'm thinking it's Joe Harding.'

'Not necessarily, although I realise we haven't completely ruled him out yet.'

'He's still a suspect in my eyes,' said Southall.

'Oh, for sure,' said Norman. 'But, thinking about it, he's the boss on that site, isn't he? He doesn't strike me as the sort of guy who likes to get his hands dirty, so would he actually know which materials are kept on site and where to lay his hands on them?'

'So you think one of the builders committed both murders?'

'Well, why not?' said Norman. 'Whoever dumped Dilys's body had to know the site was there, and now it looks as if Wozzy has been murdered on the same site.'

'I agree it's possible that someone who works on the site killed Wozzy,' said Southall, 'but what about Dilys? She was murdered elsewhere and her body was then hidden in one of the houses. Surely someone who worked on the site would be aware the houses were coming down and that the body would be found.'

'That rules out Harding then,' said Norman.

'You're right, it does, doesn't it?' said Southall. She thought for a few seconds. 'No, hang on, that's not right. Dilys was murdered before the planning committee granted

198

permission for the demolition to go ahead, so the murderer wouldn't have known the houses were coming down.'

'That still rules out Harding,' said Norman. 'If we're saying he bribed the committee to grant planning permission, he would have known the houses were going to be coming down on the Monday.'

'Yes, but he hadn't bargained on the houses being searched before they were demolished,' said Southall. 'If you recall, the site foreman made that decision without asking Harding. What if Harding thought Dilys's body would be lost under the debris? Even if it had been found later, everyone would have assumed the house had collapsed on top of her.'

'Don't you think that would be a huge risk for a guy like Harding?' asked Norman. 'I mean, whatever Dilys might have suspected him of doing, we haven't found a shred of evidence to prove she was right. And the fact is, the guy appears to have a squeaky clean reputation. Why risk it all by dumping a body on his own doorstep?'

Southall drove on in silence. Much as she disliked Joe Harding, she had to admit Norman could be right.

'Okay, so let's talk about Wozzy's murder,' she said. 'Do we even know why he was killed? And before you mention Erin, can we ignore her as a suspect for now.'

'You're not ruling her out altogether?' asked Norman.

'We both know we can't do that, don't we? Just indulge me for a few minutes, and let's explore other possibilities.'

'Okay,' said Norman. 'Do you want me to suggest a scenario that suggests a motive?'

'Yes, but keep it simple, and keep it plausible. I don't want you to go off-piste and dream up some wild theory we can't prove.'

'Okay, I can do that,' said Norman. 'So, what if Wozzy is in number nineteen, on his own, and he hears a noise outside. Curious, he looks out of the window and sees someone carrying what looks like a body into number nine.'

'Okay, I'm with you so far,' said Southall. 'but it only works if the blood upstairs at number nineteen is Wozzy's.'

'That's true, but let's assume it is his blood.'

'Okay, so how did it get there?'

'Maybe he goes down to take a look, the killer spots him and chases him back into number nineteen. Or perhaps he accidentally knocks something over and alerts the killer to his presence. The killer hasn't finished disposing of Dilys's body yet, but he can't afford to have a witness to what he's doing, so he rushes into number nineteen, finds Wozzy hiding upstairs and beats the crap out of him.'

'That would explain the blood,' said Southall. 'Then what happens?'

'Wozzy passes out,' said Norman. 'The killer knows where the rope is kept, so he goes to get some, comes back and strangles Wozzy, carries his body to the nearest skip and dumps it.'

'How far away is this skip? Wozzy's bigger than Dilys. He'd be much heavier.'

'Good point,' said Norman. 'I actually have no idea where the nearest skips were, but even if there wasn't one nearby, maybe Wozzy escaped from number nineteen while the killer went to get the rope. But he's been weakened by the attack and he doesn't get far before the killer spots him. Maybe he's even trying to hide behind a skip when the killer sees him. By now he's pretty much done in so he can't fight back when the killer uses the rope to finish him off. After that, the killer dumps his body in the skip.'

'You said the killer hadn't finished disposing of Dilys's body,' said Southall. 'What do you mean by that?'

'When me and Frosty first searched the houses, we found a can full of petrol at number nine. I thought maybe the builders were going to use it to start a fire, but they told Frosty that wasn't the case and they had no idea why it was there. I pushed it to the back of my mind after that, but now I'm thinking perhaps the killer's original idea was to dowse Dilys's body in petrol and burn it.'

'So why doesn't he go back and finish doing that after he killed Wozzy?'

'I dunno. Perhaps he's been spooked by finding Wozzy there, and now he's worried that if he's found one squatter, there could easily be more. Or maybe all that fighting and chasing has scared him and in his haste to get away, he forgets to finish the job.'

Southall said nothing.

'Well, what do you think?' asked Norman. 'Does it work?'

'It's certainly plausible,' said Southall.

'I thought so too,' said Norman. 'And it doesn't rule out Erin.'

'I still think you're barking up the wrong tree,' said Southall.

'Yeah, quite possibly,' said Norman. 'But we'll see.'

'Have you got anything planned for today?' asked Southall.

'You mean apart from trying to solve two murders?' said Norman.

'I mean anything specific to do with the case.'

'No, I haven't,' said Norman. 'Your wish is my command.'

'Let's go back to that building site then. I'd like to speak with the foreman, Tom Fletcher. It might help if he could tell us where the skips were. And I think it's high time we had a chat with Graham Watkins.'

'That sounds like a plan to me,' said Norman.

* * *

They found Tom Fletcher in the small wooden hut he used as an office. Disappointingly, he couldn't offer any concrete help with the skips. They were distributed randomly, he said, literally scattered all over the site.

'I thought you would have had an office like Joe Harding's,' said Southall.

Fletcher laughed. 'Oh no, not me. I know my place. Anyway, I'm happier being one of the workers. You have to earn the respect of the guys who do the actual work, and you don't do that by being flash and behaving as if you're somehow above them.'

201

'You mean like Joe Harding?' asked Southall.

'Joe's not so bad. He's the boss, so he's allowed to tell us what to do. And he's been around long enough that he doesn't need to go out of his way to impress anyone.'

'What's he like as a boss?' she asked.

'He doesn't suffer fools, and he hates it when things go wrong, but apart from that I can't fault him. He's hard but fair, and he makes sure the guys get paid what they're worth.'

'What about the Rolls Royce? That's a bit flash for a building site, isn't it?'

'That's not flash, that's just Joe. When I said flash, I was talking about the other guy, Graham Watkins.'

'What's wrong with Graham?' asked Southall.

'For a start, he's an arrogant sod. I mean, he's from around here, the same as the rest of us, but he thinks that because he's got a fancy job title and he lives in Yorkshire, it somehow makes him superior.'

'I'm getting the impression you don't like him much,' said Norman.

'I don't have to like him, do I?' said Fletcher. 'Don't get me wrong, Graham's very good at his job, it's just a pity he has to be such an arse.'

'Is he here?' asked Southall. 'Only we'd like to speak to him.'

Fletcher glanced through the shed window towards Harding's portacabin.

'His Mercedes is over by the boss's office so he must be here somewhere.'

'You didn't mind Harding's Rolls but it sounds like you don't approve of the Mercedes,' Norman said.

'With Graham it's just a status symbol, like that bloody Range Rover he drives.'

'He has a Range Rover?' asked Southall.

'That's what he was driving when he went away for the weekend, then he comes back in the Merc. Next time he goes back home I expect he'll return in the Range Rover again.'

'Does he go back to Yorkshire very often?' asked Southall.

'So far he's only been here when he's had to, and then he stays in a hotel for two or three nights. But now the project has started for real, I believe he's booked in at the hotel from Monday to Friday every week.'

'Was he here last week?'

'Yes, he was here for most of it, making sure he had everything ready to go.'

'And did he go back to Yorkshire last weekend?'

'He left here on Friday afternoon, and didn't come back until Tuesday evening. He said he was going home, so I assume that's where he went.'

'But you don't know for sure?'

'Look, I don't like the man, I don't socialise with him, and I'm not his keeper. I'm assuming he went home because he changed cars, but if you want to know for sure, you'll have to ask him.'

Fletcher glanced out of the window and pointed to a man who had just emerged from the portacabin.

'Talking of the devil, that's Graham there, if you want to speak to him.'

'Excellent,' said Southall setting off through the door.

'Thank you for speaking to us,' said Norman. 'You've been very helpful.'

'Have I?'

'Perhaps not with the skips,' said Norman. 'But otherwise, more than you know. We may have some more questions.'

'If you need to speak to me again you can usually find me here, in my hut. If not, I'll be on the site somewhere.'

'Great,' said Norman, scuttling off after Southall. He caught up with her just as she was making themselves known to Watkins.

'What can I do for you?' asked Watkins.

'I'm sure you're aware that a woman's body was found on site earlier this week,' said Southall. 'We've spoken to everyone else on site. We just have a few questions for you.'

Watkins gave Southall a patronising smile. 'I don't see how I can help. I wasn't here when the body was found.'

'I hear you were in Yorkshire. Is that right?' asked Southall.

'That's correct. I left on Friday afternoon and got back on Tuesday evening. So, I don't really see how I can help you.'

'But you knew the victim, didn't you?' said Southall.

The smile disappeared. Watkins's eyes darted back and forth between the detectives and he licked his lips nervously.

'Wasn't she married to your brother, Mr Watkins?' asked Southall.

'My brother and I haven't seen or spoken to each other for years.'

'But the victim was married to him, wasn't she?' Southall said.

'Yes, she was. You know she was.'

'Can you tell us why you fell out with your brother?' asked Southall.

'Just silly family stuff. You know the sort of thing.'

'No, I don't know the sort of thing,' said Southall. 'Perhaps you could explain what you mean by "silly family stuff".'

'Is this really relevant to your investigation?' asked Watkins.

'It could well be if the silly family stuff has anything to do with you being Erin's father.'

Watkins took a step back and his mouth dropped open. 'Whatever makes you think that?'

'According to Ross, the reason you fell out was because you kept pestering Dilys, and he didn't like it,' said Norman.

'Rubbish,' said Watkins.

'How did you break your nose?' asked Norman.

'I'm sorry?'

'I've seen enough broken noses to know when I'm looking at another one,' said Norman. 'Ross said he had to break your nose to convince you he didn't want you hanging around Dilys. We wondered if maybe the reason you were hanging around her was because Erin was your daughter and you wanted a turn at playing happy families.'

'This is ridiculous,' said Watkins. 'I'm not Erin's father. Ross is her father.'

'Ah, I'm afraid that's not true,' said Southall.

'What?'

'You mean you didn't know?'

'Know what?' said Watkins. 'What are you talking about?'

'Then let me explain,' said Southall. 'You see, Erin thought it would be a bit of fun to send off DNA samples from Ross, Dilys and herself to be analysed. But she didn't bargain on the results showing that Ross wasn't her father. That's why she ran away.'

'Erin ran away? I didn't know that. Why didn't someone tell me?'

'Why? Did you know where she was?' asked Norman.

'Well, no, of course not.'

'She wasn't up in Yorkshire with you then?' asked Southall.

'With me? That's ridiculous. Why would she be with me?'

'You'll be telling us next that you didn't know Ross and Dilys had separated,' said Norman.

'They're separated? No, I didn't know.'

'Aw, come on,' said Norman. 'Do you really expect us to believe that?'

'But how could I know? I live two hundred miles away and, as I've already said, me and Ross haven't spoken in years.' He looked at his watch. 'Look, I'd love to help you but I really don't see how I can. Anyway, I'm late for a site meeting, and Joe Harding hates it when things don't go to plan.'

Southall studied Watkins's face for a moment.

'Where are you staying?' she asked.

'The Lifeboat Hotel.'

'Okay,' she said. 'You get off to your meeting, Mr Watkins. But don't go too far from the hotel, or this site. I think we'll be speaking again.'

Southall and Norman watched as Watkins climbed into his Mercedes and hurried off to his meeting.

'What do you think, Norm?'

'I got the feeling we didn't tell him anything he didn't already know,' said Norman. 'In my opinion, he's lying through his teeth.'

'Yes, I agree, but was it all lies, or just some of it?' said Southall, thoughtfully. 'Did you make a note of that registration number?'

'Yeah, I got it,' said Norman. 'I'm going to get the registration number of his Range Rover too. Once we've got that we shouldn't have any trouble tracking his progress up to Yorkshire on Friday through the ANPR cameras.'

'Good,' said Southall. 'Let's start there and see if any of it's true.'

CHAPTER NINETEEN

Shortly after lunch, Norman sidled over to Southall's office. 'Tom Fletcher was right. Graham Watkins does own a Range Rover as well as the Mercedes.'

'So we should be able to track his movements over last weekend,' said Southall.

'I've made a request to the ANPR database, and I've asked them to make it a priority. They say they'll do their best but they're as short-staffed as we are. I did stress we were in the middle of a murder case so I'm hoping we won't have to wait too long.'

Judy Lane entered the office, waving a handwritten note. 'I think we may have found Ross Watkins's car.'

'Fantastic,' said Southall. 'Is it still in the area?'

Lane nodded. 'Apparently, a farmer has been complaining to Traffic for a couple of days about a Ford Kuga that's been abandoned behind one of his field shelters. Someone noticed that the description and registration number match the one we circulated for Ross Watkins's car.'

'Oh, Jeez, really?' said Norman. 'I hope they haven't destroyed any evidence—'

'They haven't been near it yet, Norm,' said Lane. 'I get the impression they'd like us to deal with it so they don't have to.'

'As if we don't have enough to do,' said Norman.

'No, it's okay,' said Southall. 'So long as the farmer hasn't interfered with it there could be some vital evidence just waiting for us to discover.'

'In that case, I take it you'd like me to get out there and take a look,' said Norman.

Southall nodded. 'Take Catren with you. I'll get on to Forensics and have them meet you out there.'

Norman hurried off, calling out to Morgan, 'Come on, Catren, we think we've found the car, and I need someone with a bit of local knowledge to help me find it.'

Morgan grabbed her jacket and rushed after him.

* * *

'Are you sure this is the right place?' asked Norman, twenty minutes later. 'I can't see anything but hedges and trees.'

'I thought you told me you were adapting to life in the country,' said Morgan.

'I am,' said Norman.

'Then why are you complaining about seeing trees and hedges?'

'Because I can't see any barn and I'm beginning to think we must be in the wrong place.'

'We're not looking for a barn, we're looking for a field shelter. There's a difference.'

'And you know this because you're a farmer's daughter, right?'

'Correct,' said Morgan gleefully. 'Didn't you bring me along for my local knowledge?'

'Well, yeah, that was one reason.'

'In that case I think you should trust that knowledge, don't you?' said Morgan. 'All the land around here belongs to Osterly Farm, which is owned by Old Farmer Aaron, and—'

'Old Farmer Aaron?' echoed Norman. 'Is that really his name?'

'That's the name everyone knows him by.'

'Is Aaron his Christian name, or his surname?'

Morgan thought for a moment. 'Now you've asked me, I realise I don't actually know.'

'How long have you known this guy?'

'I don't really know him, but I know of him. Everyone around here does.'

'Even though no one knows what his real name is,' said Norman.

'But they don't need to.'

Norman considered for a moment. 'I suppose, in some weird way, there is a sort of rural logic behind that.'

'Obviously,' said Morgan. 'Anyway, I promise you the field shelter we're looking for is in a field along this lane. Just because you can't see a massive arrow with a sign saying *This way to the field shelter* doesn't mean it's not here. I promise you it'll be along here somewhere. It's probably hidden behind the trees. Keep driving nice and slow, and look for a five-bar gate.'

'You mean like this one?' asked Norman pointing to a gate twenty yards ahead of them.

'Well, there we are then,' said Morgan. 'Isn't this just what your friendly local expert said you would find?'

'Okay, local expert, this is all well and good, but where the heck am I supposed to park?'

'You want a car park too?' said Morgan. 'Wow! You really are a city boy, aren't you?'

'No, I don't want a car park, but you have to admit this road isn't exactly a motorway, is it? I mean, it's not as if I can pull onto the verge, because there isn't one.'

'The reason the road is so narrow, Norm, is because there's almost zero traffic along here. You could probably leave your car where it is for a couple of hours and the chances are no one would want to get through, but if it's worrying you, let me get out, and then you can park nice and tight to the hedge. Trust me, it'll be fine.'

Grudgingly, Norman accepted Morgan's suggestion. While he was edging the car close to the hedge, she leaned over the gate and looked around.

'What are you waiting for?' he asked when he caught up. 'Can't you open the gate?'

'Well, yes, I can,' she said. 'But I'm just wondering why it's closed.'

'Aren't gates supposed to be closed?'

'Normally, yes,' said Morgan. 'But I would say this one is usually open.' She pointed to a big clump of grass with a gate-shaped gap in the centre. 'You can see where the grass has grown around it. That couldn't happen if it was normally closed.'

'Okay, fair enough,' said Norman. 'But it is closed and, right now, we need it open.' He reached forward, but before he could do anything, Morgan placed a hand on his arm.

'Whoa,' she said. 'Not so fast.'

'Why not?' said Norman. 'We need to get in there to have a look at this car, don't we?'

'Yes,' said Morgan. 'But at least one of us has to be aware of where we are.'

'What's that supposed to mean?'

'This is farming country, right?'

Norman nodded. 'It may surprise you to know but I don't actually need a local expert to help me work that one out.'

'Your sarcasm is noted,' said Morgan. 'But I suggest you humour me for a minute.'

Norman sighed. 'Okay, Catren, I'm listening.'

'Right. Now, you just said gates are supposed to be closed in the country, which is normally how it should be. However, you can see this one is usually open, but now it's closed.'

'Yeah, and?'

'The question you should be asking is, why is the gate closed? We know the farmer came here and found the car, but why did he come here in the first place?'

'Jeez, this is like being back in school,' said Norman. 'Does it matter why he came here? Let's just be grateful that he did.'

'Well, it might matter if he brought livestock up here,' said Morgan. 'Haven't you ever heard stories about people walking into a field where there was a bull, and how the bull wasn't too impressed by their intrusion?'

Anxiously, Norman looked over the gate, then took a hasty step back from it.

'Holy shit! There's a bull? Where?'

Morgan laughed. 'Relax, Norm. I hate to disappoint you but there is no bull in this field.'

'I suppose you think that was funny.'

'I wasn't doing it to be funny,' said Morgan. 'It worries me that you didn't even consider the possibility.'

'Don't they have to put signs up to warn people about bulls? Isn't that a health and safety thing?'

'There are lots of things that should be done, Norm, but do we all do them?'

'Right, I get it,' said Norman. 'So what animals are in the field?'

'None that I can see,' said Morgan. 'But you should always check before you go opening gates and charging into fields. Even cows and sheep can be aggressive if they have young to protect.'

'Really? They don't look as if they could do you much harm.'

'Don't be fooled by the way cows amble around,' said Morgan. 'They have a surprising turn of speed when it comes to protecting a calf, and three quarters of a ton of angry cow can do you a lot of damage. Even a sheep butting your backside can be a painful experience.'

Norman smiled at the idea.

'Seriously, Norm. Don't forget their ancestors had big horns. Even modern breeds have very bony heads, and they know how to butt.'

'Okay, Catren, I get your point. I need to be more careful when I'm out and about.'

'I'm only telling you this because I like you and I want you to stay safe,' she said.

'It's very sweet of you to look out for me, and I do appreciate it,' said Norman. 'But don't you think that's enough countryside code for one day? I want to have a look at this car before Forensics get here.'

Morgan opened the gate and followed Norman through.

'And always close the gate behind you, right?' said Norman.

'That's right,' said Morgan, closing the gate. 'But do you know why?'

'I'm guessing that would be to make it harder to escape from the bull you didn't spot before you opened the gate?'

Morgan laughed. 'Come on,' she said, pointing to a dilapidated field shelter about fifty yards away to their right. 'It's over there by those trees.'

The field shelter had a roof but was open on two sides, and years of tractor access had worn a rough, muddy track across the grass from the gate.

Norman pointed at the track. 'It looks as if these aren't all tractor tyre marks. We'd better keep to the grass until Forensics have taken some casts.'

'I'll make sure they do,' said Morgan.

'How many more of these disused barns are there around these parts?' said Norman as they walked towards the shelter.

'Field shelters,' corrected Morgan.

'Whatever the correct name is, from what you were saying earlier they seem to be everywhere.'

Morgan smiled. 'Says the man who didn't believe there was one here.'

'But that's my point,' said Norman. 'It was right next to the road but you couldn't see it for the trees.'

'They're here to provide the animals with shelter from the rain or to store hay. They build them behind the trees to provide a bit of protection from the weather and to hide them from vandals.'

'I can understand that if you were building one now,' said Norman. 'But no one even knew what vandalism was when some of these old things were built.'

'Maybe they were future-proofing,' said Morgan.

'You have an answer for everything, don't you?' said Norman.

Morgan winked. 'Isn't that why you love me so much?'

Norman rolled his eyes. 'Yeah, right. Of course it is.'

As they neared the shelter they could see there was nothing inside except a few bales of hay, but two lines of flattened grass showed where a vehicle had been driven off the track and around the back. They found the car tucked in between the shelter and the trees.

'Well, this didn't get here by accident,' said Norman.

He slipped on a pair of latex gloves and tried the car door. 'It's unlocked,' he said, opening the door and peering inside. 'No keys, and nothing immediately obvious to suggest anything bad happened in here.'

Morgan was squinting over his shoulder. 'Dilys wasn't very tall, and that driver's seat is pushed all the way back.'

'Good observation,' said Norman. 'So, either she moved it back for some reason, or it could well have been driven here by someone else. I can't see any reason why she'd need to move it back, can you?'

'It could have been driven here by a man then,' said Morgan.

'That would be my guess,' said Norman. He stepped back from the car. 'Let's leave it to the forensic guys. If someone else has driven this car, I don't want to contaminate the interior. Take a look in the boot. Let's see if there's anything to suggest there was ever a body in there.'

Morgan slipped on a pair of latex gloves, walked around to the back of the car and popped open the boot. The only things inside were a wheel with a flat tyre, a jack, and a wheel brace.

'That's interesting,' she said.

'What's up?' asked Norman.

'Dilys obviously had a flat tyre at some stage.'

Norman peered into the boot. 'I've never managed to change a wheel without getting my hands covered in crap. Even a relatively clean wheel is usually covered in brake dust

213

that turns your hands black. I don't recall Dilys's hands being particularly dirty when we found her. So, I'm wondering exactly when that happened.'

'Maybe while she was away,' said Morgan.

'I'm assuming Dilys wouldn't deliberately mess up Ross's car before she gave it back to him but, look, the boot is filthy from that wheel. Whoever put these things in here didn't give a damn,' said Norman. 'And, anyway, wouldn't she have had a suitcase in the boot while she was travelling? You wouldn't dump a dirty old wheel on top of that.'

'What if she had the case on the back seat?' said Morgan.

'Yeah, I suppose that's a possibility,' said Norman.

'But you're not convinced, are you?' said Morgan.

'It bothers me that these things have been chucked in there without a thought. I mean, who does that?' Norman said.

'Someone in a hurry?' suggested Morgan.

'Exactly.'

'So, what do you think happened?'

'Now that's a question with numerous possible answers,' said Norman. 'Did it happen when Dilys was away, or after she got back? Did it happen here, or somewhere nearby? Maybe I'm wrong about her and she was the sort who wouldn't care about giving Ross his car back in a filthy state. Or, was it already like this when Ross let her borrow it?'

'Would he let her drive it all the way to Scotland with a punctured spare wheel?' asked Morgan.

'Good point,' said Norman. 'It wouldn't seem to fit with how much he says he cares about her, would it?'

As they spoke, they heard the sound of car doors slamming, and now voices could be heard heading their way.

'It sounds like Forensics are here,' said Morgan. 'Do you want me to stay here with them?'

Norman looked around.

'I don't think that's necessary,' he said. 'Yes, the car's been dumped here, but I'm pretty sure this isn't a crime scene. I won't be surprised if they do a quick search of the area and then put the car on a trailer and take it back to their workshops. Just make sure they take some casts of those tyre tracks.'

Morgan had a quick word with the forensic team and then joined Norman at the car. She waited while he pulled out into the lane before opening the passenger door.

'Are they okay?' he asked as she climbed in beside him.

'Yeah, fine. As you said, they're going to take the car away once they've finished checking out the scene.'

'In that case we may as well head back to the ranch,' said Norman.

* * *

Norman hadn't been back at his desk for more than a few minutes when he announced that he'd received an email from UK Traffic.

'What does it say?' asked Southall.

'It confirms that Graham Watkins came back down from Yorkshire on Tuesday afternoon in the Mercedes, just as he told us.'

'Yes, but what about the previous Friday? Does it confirm his alibi?'

'Yes, and no,' said Norman, reading through the email.

'What does that mean?'

'It means yes, he did drive to Yorkshire, but not when he said. He's not caught on any cameras until three thirty-eight a.m. on Saturday morning, when he's photographed heading north on the A483 just past Llandrindod Wells.'

'But that's not far from here, is it?' asked Southall.

'You could drive there in little more than an hour at that time of the morning,' said Morgan.

'Well,' said Southall, 'that blows rather a big hole in his alibi. He told us he set off for Yorkshire on Friday afternoon. What else can they tell us, Norm?'

'Going by the ANPR cameras they reckon he didn't stop on the way and was home in Holmfirth by seven thirty a.m. They can't be exact because they don't have cameras everywhere, but they reckon it's a five-hour journey and at the speed he seemed to be averaging he appears more or less where they would expect him to be if he left here at around two thirty a.m.'

'And this is in his Range Rover?'

'That's what they're saying,' said Norman. 'They say they're sending photographs but they're not here yet.'

'It would be nice to have one or two to show him, but even without them, we've got plenty of reasons to bring him in.'

'Can I go and get him?' asked Morgan. 'He was such an arrogant sod I'd love to be the one to spoil his day.'

'Yes, okay,' said Southall. 'Take Frosty with you. It would be better if he came in with you voluntarily, but if he tries to fob you off with some excuse, you have my permission to arrest him.'

As Morgan and Winter set off for the car park, Norman reached for his phone.

'I'd better call Faye and tell her not to expect me home for dinner anytime soon.'

* * *

It was almost seven p.m. by the time Norman and Southall finally settled into their seats opposite Graham Watkins.

'Thank you for volunteering to come in and speak with us,' said Southall.

'Volunteering?' said Watkins. 'Is that what you call it when one of your young detectives threatens someone with arrest? It seemed to me I had no choice. That young woman was itching for an excuse to attack me.'

'I presume that by "attack" you mean arrest,' said Southall. 'Or are you making a complaint against DC Morgan?'

'Complaint?' said Watkins.

'Are you suggesting that DC Morgan assaulted you?'

'She was dying for an excuse—'

'But she didn't attack you, did she, or even touch you?' said Southall.

'Well, no, she didn't.'

'So, are you making a complaint or not?'

'No. I'm not,' said Watkins, grudgingly. 'But why exactly am I here?'

'You mean you didn't expect us to check your alibi?'

'What's wrong with my alibi? And why do I even need one?'

'You need one because you knew the victim, and you were in the area at the time of her death,' explained Southall. 'As to what's wrong with the alibi you gave us, well, surely you don't need me to tell you that.'

'But I said I went home to Yorkshire, and if you have checked you should know that's what I did,' said Watkins.

'Yes, Mr Watkins, you did tell us you went to Yorkshire, but I'm afraid the devil is in the detail. You see, you told us you left on Friday afternoon, yet you don't appear on our traffic cameras until three thirty-eight on Saturday morning, by which time you had only just passed through Llandrindod Wells.'

'I went back to my hotel before I left. I had intended to nap for an hour but I must have fallen into a deep sleep. By the time I woke up it was well after one a.m. so I had a shower and a few cups of coffee before I left.'

'And what time did you leave?' asked Southall.

'It must have been about two thirty.'

'So why didn't you tell us this when we spoke before?' asked Southall.

'Because you didn't ask me for a minute-by-minute account. You asked me where I went, and I told you.'

'If you didn't leave here until two thirty in the morning you would have had plenty of time to meet Dilys Watkins,' said Norman.

'I already told you I didn't meet Dilys. Why would I?'

'To rekindle an old relationship?' suggested Norman.

Watkins sighed. 'Did you people listen to anything I said last time? I can't be Erin's father because I never, ever had a relationship with Dilys. I didn't meet Dilys. I haven't seen her or spoken to her in years!'

'How well do you know Joe Harding's redevelopment site?' asked Norman.

'I know my way around, if that's what you mean.'

'So, you would know where different types of equipment are stored, right?'

'I know it's all stored in containers,' said Watkins. 'But as for what's in which container, I have no idea. I don't need to know that. I'm a consultant, not a navvy.'

There was a knock on the door.

'Excuse me a moment,' said Norman. 'I'd better see what that is.'

He went over to the door and stepped out into the corridor. Judy Lane was waiting for him, clutching a sheaf of printed papers.

'What's up, Judy?'

'These just came through from Traffic,' she said. 'They're the ones you've been waiting for. I was in two minds about disturbing you, but when I saw them I knew it couldn't wait, so I printed them out.'

She handed them to Norman, who stared open-mouthed at the topmost page.

'Jeez!' he said, looking up at Lane. 'Is this for real?'

'It looks real enough to me,' she said. 'And they say the camera never lies.'

Norman glanced through the other photographs and directed a beaming smile at her.

'I thought you'd be pleased,' she said.

'Pleased? Judy, you've just made my day. I can't wait to see how he gets out of this!'

'I'll leave you to it then,' said Lane and headed back to the office.

Norman wiped the smile from his face, went back into the room and very discreetly handed Southall the top photograph. She did a double take. Clearing her throat, and with her eyes on Watkins, she very deliberately placed the first photograph on the table, turned it around and slid it across to him.

'This is a photograph taken at three thirty-eight a.m. on Saturday by an Automatic Number Plate Recognition camera just north of Llandrindod Wells. Is this your car?'

Watkins stared down at the photograph and licked his lips. 'I'm sure you know it's my car, or you wouldn't be asking me.'

'You're right, we do know it's your car,' said Southall. 'But what we'd really like to know is how it came to be so badly damaged.'

'You see that damage to the windscreen?' said Norman. 'In the emergency services we call that a bull's-eye. It's caused when a pedestrian is hit by a car, flips over the bonnet and hits their head on the windscreen. And, coincidentally, that's exactly what happened to Dilys Watkins.'

Watkins sat for a few seconds, opening and closing his mouth. Finally, he managed to say, in a strangled voice, 'I'm not prepared to say another word without a solicitor to advise me.'

'I think that's probably a very good idea,' said Southall, standing up. 'In the meantime, Graham Watkins, I'm arresting you on suspicion of the murder of Dilys Watkins. You do not have to say anything, but it may harm your defence if you do not mention when questioned something you later rely on in court. Anything you do say may be given in evidence.'

Silent, Watkins gaped at Southall.

'DS Norman here will arrange for you to be taken into custody where you will stay overnight,' said Southall. 'We'll organise a formal interview for the morning, so you'll have plenty of time to think about your situation and what you've told us so far, and to speak with your solicitor.'

* * *

Norman and Southall were having a cup of tea before they went home. 'D'you think we've got our man?' Norman said.

'Don't you?'

'It explains why Judy hasn't been able to find anyone around here requesting a replacement windscreen,' said Norman. 'He's certainly got some explaining to do.'

CHAPTER TWENTY

Saturday, 18 March

At ten a.m. the following morning, Southall and Norman sat down opposite Graham Watkins and his solicitor. Norman started the recording, and they made their introductions.

Southall was about to begin when Watkins's solicitor said, 'Before you ask any questions, I'd like to put on record that my client withdraws anything he may have said during informal questioning yesterday.'

'You mean he lied to us yesterday,' said Southall.

'He may have omitted one or two facts that may be pertinent to your investigation.'

'So, he did lie to us.'

'My client feels he was placed under extreme duress and that you were trying to coerce him into saying things that weren't true.'

'He wasn't under any pressure,' said Southall. 'He was asked to come in voluntarily, which he did. He could have refused to answer our questions and left at any time, but he chose not to.'

The solicitor shook his head. 'Under such pressure anyone would feel intimidated and could easily say things that weren't accurate.'

'Or lie,' said Southall.

'I've stated our position, Inspector. My client is willing to answer your questions so long as the slate is clean. Of course, if you won't accept our position . . .'

Southall stared at the solicitor, gathering her thoughts. She could feel Norman tensing next to her, and with good reason. If she accepted his statement as it was, she would be admitting to having bullied Watkins. There again they needed answers to their questions.

'I'm afraid I can't accept Mr Watkins's suggestion that he was under duress,' said Southall. 'In fact, I was even considering charging him with wasting our time. However, if your client is prepared to answer our questions truthfully, I am prepared to forget about him wasting our time in the previous interview.'

The solicitor whispered something to Watkins, and he nodded.

'Very well,' said the solicitor. 'We're willing to proceed on that understanding, but before you start, I would like to read a statement prepared by my client.'

'A statement?' said Southall.

'Is there a problem with that?' asked the solicitor. 'He's done it to help you.'

Norman sighed impatiently.

'He could have helped by—'

Southall coughed.

'I'm sorry, Sergeant. Did you want to say something?' asked the solicitor.

'No, no, I'm sorry. Definitely not,' said Norman.

'Please read your client's statement,' said Southall.

'Very well . . .'

* * *

The solicitor set down the page and sat back.

'You're saying your car was damaged because you hit a deer?' said Southall.

'That's correct,' said Watkins.

'Why didn't you tell us that yesterday?'

'Because you didn't give me a chance,' said Watkins, turning his gaze on Norman. 'If you recall, your partner, Detective Sergeant Norman, seemed to be convinced I'd run down Dilys Watkins.'

'How did you manage to hit this deer?' asked Southall.

'I couldn't avoid it. It ran out in front of me without warning. The damage to my windscreen came about because, when I hit it, it went up in the air and over the bonnet.'

'Did you kill it?'

'There was blood everywhere and it didn't seem to be breathing, so I'm pretty sure I did. It was lying by the side of the road when I left the scene.'

'What speed were you doing when you hit it?' asked Norman.

'I don't remember. About fifty miles an hour, I guess.'

'What time did this happen?' Norman said.

'Around eleven p.m.'

'Can anyone verify this?'

'It was dark. I didn't see anyone else around.'

'Where did it happen?' asked Norman.

'In one of the lanes. I don't recall exactly.'

'If you seriously want us to believe you, you're going to have to do better than that,' said Norman. 'If you could show us where the accident happened, we might be able to find some evidence that will corroborate your story.'

'Where is your car now, Mr Watkins?' asked Southall.

'What? My car? Er, it's in a body shop near Holmfirth, waiting to be repaired.'

'I'd like the address of that body shop,' said Southall.

'Yes, of course. I'll write it down for you.'

Southall slid a piece of paper and a pen across the table and Watkins wrote down the name and address.

'I'm afraid I can't remember the phone number,' he said, passing the paper back to Southall.

'I'm sure we can manage to find it,' said Southall.

'Does this answer all your questions?' asked the solicitor.

'What do you think?' asked Southall. 'It answers the one about the damage to the car, that's all. And then only if we can find some proof.'

'You don't accept my client's word?'

'This is a murder investigation,' said Southall. 'You know very well I'm allowed to have doubts if there's no proof.'

'But surely there will be DNA evidence on the car,' argued the solicitor.

'Which is why I want to know where the car is,' said Southall. 'But, as Sergeant Norman said, if Mr Watkins can show us where the accident happened, we may be able to find proof at the scene.'

Watkins glanced at the solicitor, who nodded.

'Okay,' said Watkins. 'But I can't guarantee I'll be able to take you straight there.'

'That's okay,' said Norman. 'I'm sure if we drive you around for long enough, we can find it.'

* * *

'You know, Graham, I already thought this story of yours was a pack of lies,' said Norman. 'And the longer you have us driving around in circles like this, the more I become convinced that I'm right.'

'I swear I'm telling the truth,' said Watkins from the back seat of the car.

In the passenger seat, Morgan's phone began to ring. She held a mumbled conversation, while Norman continued speaking to Watkins.

'And yet here we are,' said Norman. 'You have a golden opportunity to prove your version of events, and you can't. I mean, even you must agree the damage to your car is compelling evidence.'

'It's circumstantial at best, unless you're trying to frame me for Dilys's murder.'

'Why would I need to frame you, Graham? The evidence is right there in the photographs of your car.'

'You're making the evidence fit the crime.'

'But the evidence does fit the crime,' said Norman.

'I'm telling you I hit a deer!'

'So, show me where it happened and maybe I'll believe you,' said Norman. 'I don't understand why you can't remember where it happened. I mean, a thing like that — it must have been one heck of a bang.'

'Yes, but all the lanes look the same in the dark, don't they?' said Watkins angrily. 'Anyway, I'm not worried. The DNA evidence from my car will prove I'm right.'

Morgan had just finished her call.

'I'm afraid that's not going to happen, Mr Watkins. Your car has already been steam-cleaned ready for repair. If there was any DNA evidence, it's gone now.'

Norman was watching Watkins's reaction in the rear-view mirror.

'Oh dear, that's not good news, is it, Graham?' he said. 'I really think you need to start remembering exactly where you hit this deer if you want us to believe your story.'

Watkins stared out of the window. 'This bit seems familiar.'

'That's because we came past here fifteen minutes ago,' said Norman. 'I wasn't kidding when I said you'd been directing us around in circles.'

'Perhaps if you could stop yapping all the time, I might be able to concentrate.'

Norman bit back the retort that was on the tip of his tongue. Watkins had a valid point, he supposed. And as the senior officer, he wasn't exactly setting a good example in front of Morgan.

'It's just up here,' said Watkins, now distinctly perky. 'By that old oak tree up ahead.'

'You said that last time,' said Morgan.

'That's because the deer ran out from behind an oak tree. I just got the wrong oak tree.'

'And is this the right one?'

'I think so. The problem is they all look the same.'

'And that's your observation as an environmental expert, is it?' asked Morgan. 'Didn't you say we were looking for one with branches that spread right across the lane?'

'Yes, that's right.'

'So they're not all the same then,' said Morgan.

Norman brought the car to a halt about twenty yards in front of an ancient oak tree with branches hanging over the lane. Southall was following in her own car, along with Winter. She pulled up behind them and jumped out.

'Is this it?' she asked Norman as he climbed from his car.

'He says the deer ran out from behind an old oak tree with branches that spread across the lane.'

'Let's take a look around,' said Southall.

Ten minutes later she called out, 'Anyone found anything?'

A chorus of 'no' echoed in reply.

'What do you think, Norm?' she asked.

'It was a week ago and, as usual, it's been raining. If there was any blood it would have been washed away by now. Likewise any evidence of a crash.'

'Yes, but what about the body?' said Southall impatiently. 'He said he left it by the side of the road. That wouldn't have been washed away by the rain, would it?'

'I guess not,' said Norman. 'Do you think this story about the deer is bullshit?'

Southall looked at Norman in surprise. 'Don't you?'

'The thing is, I was watching his face when Catren took a call about the DNA evidence being steam-cleaned off his car. He looked genuinely dismayed. I think he was relying on the car to prove he's telling the truth.'

'You mean you actually believe him?'

'Let's say I'm beginning to think it's possible he really did hit a deer.'

'But he's got motive, he's got opportunity, and he's got the damage to his car. What more do you want?'

'If you're saying his motive for killing Dilys is that he's Erin's father, we don't actually know that for a fact, do we?' Norman said.

'DNA will prove it,' said Southall.

'Or it will prove he's not,' said Norman.

'You think he's innocent then?'

'I'm not saying he didn't kill Dilys, I'm just saying maybe we've got the scenario wrong. When we spoke to him yesterday evening he told us that he had been asleep in his hotel room all evening, but if he was out here colliding with a deer, he couldn't have been asleep, could he?'

'Of course,' said Southall. 'So the question we need to ask is, what was he doing out here?'

'Exactly,' said Norman. 'This isn't the way to Yorkshire, so where was he going?'

'I'm glad you're in my team, Norm,' said Southall. 'I was getting blinkered, forgetting to look at other possibilities. You're right, Watkins has a lot more questions to answer, and I think he's deliberately wasting time.'

'What do you want to do?' asked Norman.

'What do you suggest?' she said.

'If we can't find the dead deer, he can always claim he was asleep like he said before. He might even claim he dreamed about the deer. If we can find it . . .' Norman said.

'Why don't I take him back along with Frosty, and start asking some awkward questions?' Southall said.

'And you want me and Catren to keep looking for a suitable oak tree? There must be dozens around here. It could take months.'

'You need to learn your trees, Norm. There aren't that many oaks, and they don't all hang over the lanes, but I take your point. Give it half an hour and then come back. If Watkins has us in the right area, you might get lucky.'

'Half an hour works for me,' said Norman. 'But don't hold your breath.'

CHAPTER TWENTY-ONE

As Southall and Winter headed back with Watkins, Norman started his car and continued slowly along the lane.

'Don't forget we're only going to spend half an hour on this and we're looking for an old oak tree with spreading branches, close to the road,' he reminded Morgan.

'The words needle and haystack . . .'

'Yeah, I know,' said Norman, 'but it is what it is, unless you've got a better idea.'

'And we're not going to find it if he's been feeding us more bullshit,' said Morgan.

'I don't think this is bullshit,' said Norman.

'What makes you so sure? Is this one of your famous gut feelings?' she asked.

'It's got nothing to do with gut feelings or hunches. I was watching his face when you told him the car had been steam-cleaned, and it wasn't the face of a man who had just outwitted us.'

'Don't you think it's a bit too much of a coincidence?' Morgan asked.

'Yes, I was thinking that, but then I saw his face.'

'Does this mean you think he's not guilty?' Morgan said.

'Oh, he's definitely guilty of something. Even if we can prove he did hit the deer like he said, it doesn't mean he didn't murder Dilys. Let's face it, he had plenty of time before he left for home. Plus, this is nowhere near the route back to Yorkshire, so he must have come out this way for a reason.'

'And it's not a million miles from where Dilys was found,' said Morgan.

'Right,' said Norman. 'And that's the coincidence the boss is going to be questioning him about when they get back.'

Morgan pointed along the road. 'There's a suitable oak tree up ahead.'

Norman slowed the car and stopped a few yards away from the tree.

'Okay, let's try this one,' he said, and opened the car door.

They walked to the tree, scanning the road, the narrow grass verge, and the hedge alongside the road. As they reached the oak, Norman began studying the ground in front of the tree while Morgan walked around to the other side. Eyes on the ground, they hardly heard the vehicle approaching. It slowed, drew to a halt next to Norman and a window slid down.

'Lost something?' asked the driver.

Norman produced his warrant card. 'Police. We heard there was a deer knocked down near an old oak tree somewhere out here.'

The man grinned. 'Hoping for a free supply of venison steaks, were you?'

Norman smiled. 'Yeah, something like that.'

'Well, I'm afraid you're looking in the wrong place,' said the driver. 'And, anyway, you're too late. The local roadkill hunters have already taken it.'

'So someone really did collide with a deer?' asked Norman.

'I'll say. Poor bloody thing looked as if it had been hit by a train.'

'But you say it wasn't here, right?' said Norman. 'Do you know where it was?'

'Why are you so interested in a dead deer? Accidents happen, you know, and it's not always the fault of the driver.'

'I suppose that's because the animals don't know their green cross code,' said Norman.

The man frowned. 'I'm sorry?'

'Don't worry, it's not important,' said Norman. 'Just my little joke. I don't suppose you know where the accident did happen, do you?'

The driver pointed back the way he had come.

'About two hundred yards further down the road. You can't miss it, there's a big old oak tree on the left.'

'I don't suppose you saw what happened?'

'No, sorry. It must have happened during the night. I saw the body next morning as I was passing. The deer was just lying there at the base of the tree. I stopped, but when I got to it I could see it had lost a lot of blood. I think I already knew it was dead but, even so, I couldn't just drive by and ignore it. Mind you, I don't know what I could have done if it had been alive.'

'And you say these roadkill hunters took the body away?'

'Aye, that's right. It was gone by that evening. None of the roadkill around here gets left for long.'

'Oh, right,' said Norman, thoughtfully. 'Do you come this way a lot?'

'Most days. Back and forth to work.'

'You haven't seen any suspicious vehicles in the last few days, have you?'

'What sort of vehicles? Suspicious how?'

'We believe the deer was hit by a dark green Range Rover. Have you seen one like that?'

'I can't say that I have. Mind you, I wouldn't if it was during the night. I don't often drive along here at nighttime. In fact, I can't remember the last time I did.'

'Okay, no worries,' said Norman. 'Thanks for your help. Do you have a contact number? Just in case we need to ask you anything else.'

'I can give you my mobile phone number if you want.'

Norman found his notebook and made a note of the man's name and number.

'Thanks again,' he said. 'A couple of hundred yards along the road, by the old oak tree on the left. Is that right?'

'You've got it,' said the driver. He winked at Norman. 'Now I must be off,' he said. 'Places to go, people to see, you know the sort of thing.' And with that, he slipped his car into gear and drove off.

Morgan had been standing back, listening to the conversation.

'We've got the wrong oak tree,' Norman told her.

'So I heard. But don't feel too bad, Norm. It's an easy mistake to make when there are so many along these lanes.'

'Actually, I've spent so many hours of my career searching for things through the process of elimination that I rarely feel anything but indifference when I get it wrong.'

'What about when you get it right?' she asked.

'Ah. Now, that's when I get the buzz,' said Norman. 'And now we know how close we are, I can feel it coming on already. Come on, jump in the car and let's go check it out.'

* * *

'Are you still buzzing?' asked Morgan a few minutes later.

'Not so much,' said Norman. 'I don't know what I was expecting, but I'd be a lot happier if we had something concrete to show for it.'

'But this tree fits the description, and we've got these,' said Morgan, holding up a small evidence bag filled with glass fragments.

'Yeah, but they could have come from a million different cars,' said Norman.

'We also have a witness who saw the dead deer the next morning,' said Morgan. 'And we've got the damage to Watkins's car. I reckon that's more than enough to create reasonable doubt if we were trying to convince a jury that Watkins hit Dilys and not the deer.'

'Yeah, you're probably right,' said Norman. 'What about these roadkill people? If they took the carcass, they co—'

'If you're suggesting they could be witnesses, I wouldn't bother unless it's a matter of life or death,' said Morgan. 'And, trust me, even then they probably wouldn't help us just on principle.'

'Why? What did we ever do to them?'

'Come on, Norm, we're the police. That's enough for them.'

'Yeah, of course. Why would anyone want to help the police solve a crime?' Norman sighed. 'Come on, let's get out of here before I lose my spark altogether.'

The already narrow lane appeared to get even narrower up ahead where it disappeared around a bend, and as Norman started the car another vehicle appeared, heading towards them.

'Crap,' he muttered, putting the car in gear. 'Now I'm going to have to drive into the hedge to let them pass.'

He expected the other car to slow and allow him to pull over and make room for it to pass, but the car just kept on coming, finally pulling up right in front of his vehicle, so they were bumper to bumper with barely two feet between them.

'Oh, jeez, what's this idiot doing?' said Norman, as a man emerged and walked towards Morgan's side of the car.

Morgan wound down her window. 'Hello there.'

'What's going on here then?' asked the man.

Morgan produced her warrant card. 'Detective Constable Morgan. And this is Detective Sergeant Norman.'

'If you're looking for something, perhaps I can help. I'm up and down this road all the time.'

'Oh really?' said Morgan. 'Did you see any vehicles that you don't recognise around here last weekend?'

'Is this to do with that lady who died? I heard you found the car you were looking for,' said the man.

'What makes you think that?' asked Morgan.

'I saw all the police vehicles parked by the gate. They weren't there for a picnic now, were they?'

'I can see there are no flies on you,' said Morgan.

'I hear it's a grey Ford,' said the man.

Up until this point Norman hadn't been paying much attention. Now, he leaned across to get a better look at the man. 'How did you know that?'

'Old Farmer Aaron told me,' said the man.

'Oh, right, I see,' said Norman.

'I don't know if it's important but I think I might have seen the same car the night that woman got run down.'

'You did?' Norman felt his heart begin to pound. 'Could you possibly spare a few minutes to tell us about it?'

'Do you think it's important?'

'I won't know that until you describe what you saw,' said Norman. 'Why don't you jump in the back and tell us about it?'

The man got in and settled himself on the back seat behind Morgan, who had armed herself with a notebook and pencil.

'What's your name?' asked Norman.

'Ivor Heath.'

'Okay, Ivor, tell us what you saw.'

'I'd been in Carmarthen having dinner with some friends, and I was on the way home.'

'And this was on the Friday night?' asked Norman.

'That's right. Although it was after midnight so I suppose, technically, it was early Saturday morning.'

'Do you remember exactly what time it was?'

'Not exactly, but it wouldn't have been much before two a.m.'

'Okay,' said Norman. 'So, what did you see?'

'I was driving along and there was this car pulled over with the boot wide open. It was on the wrong side of the road, and it seemed to be sitting at a funny angle. I thought the driver might be in trouble so I stopped next to the car, thinking I'd ask if they were all right, only I couldn't because there was no one inside.'

'The car was empty?' asked Norman.

'That's right, but then this man's head appeared from the other side of the car. I asked him if he was in trouble and he said he'd got a puncture, but he'd just finished changing the wheel. I think it was because the car was jacked up that it seemed to be at a funny angle when I first saw it. And he must have been on his knees tightening the wheel-nuts when I stopped. Anyway, he thanked me for stopping but said he didn't need any help, so I drove on.'

'And that was it?' asked Norman.

'He said he was okay so I left him to it.'

'Are you sure it was the same car?'

'Well, I didn't get the full registration number, and it was dark, so I couldn't swear to it, but it was grey, it was a Ford and it was less than half a mile from where Farmer Aaron found it.'

'And it was definitely a man you saw?' asked Norman.

'I think I can tell the difference.'

'And there was no sign of a woman? No passenger?'

'If she was there she must have been hiding,' said Ivor. Then, a look of horror spread across his face. 'Oh, God. You're asking me if I saw the woman who was murdered, aren't you? Does that mean the man I saw was the killer? Could I have saved her?'

'Hey, calm down, Ivor,' said Norman. 'You couldn't have stopped what happened. We don't know if you saw the killer, and even if you did, we think she was dead before you came across the car.'

'Are you sure?'

'As sure as we can be, yes. Now, are you okay?'

'Yes, of course. It's just a bit of a shock to think I . . .'

'Try not to dwell on it,' said Norman. 'And remember you couldn't have stopped what happened.'

'No? Well, if you're sure.'

'I take it the car wasn't stopped along here,' said Morgan. 'It would have blocked the whole road.'

'No, it wasn't here. The road was a bit wider where I saw him. It was near the entrance to a car park.'

'Can you remember exactly where it was?' asked Morgan.

'I think so. If you follow me, I can show you if you like.'

'If you're sure you don't mind, that would be very helpful,' said Norman.

'Of course I don't mind. If I can help you catch whoever did this I'm not going to say no, am I?'

'Is it far?' asked Norman.

'About a mile. You'll need to turn around because we have to pass the field where you found the car.'

CHAPTER TWENTY-TWO

Norman managed to make enough room for Ivor to pass him but then, because the lane was so narrow, he had to negotiate practically a nine-point turn before he could follow.

'At first I thought this guy was being really helpful, but now I'm beginning to think he's having a laugh,' said Norman, panting slightly as they finally got moving.

'How do you mean?'

'Well, come on. A car park? Out here in the middle of nowhere? Why would there be a car park out here?'

'If it's where I think it is, there's a viewing point,' said Morgan.

'A what?'

'A viewing point. You know the sort of thing, where you can stop and admire the view. If it's the one I'm thinking of you can see for miles, even though it doesn't seem that high up.'

Norman gave her a sideways look.

'Local knowledge,' Morgan said with a grin. 'Isn't that what you brought me along for?'

'Yeah, right. You've got me there, for sure,' said Norman.

'It was a piece of luck he came along though,' said Morgan.

'Yeah, it's amazing how often luck plays a part in helping to solve a case,' said Norman. 'But, I wonder, would he have come forward if we hadn't been searching the roadside just as he happened to be driving past?'

'Is this your cynical side speaking?' asked Morgan.

'No, seriously, I'm not being cynical. I just wonder, would the guy have put two and two together if we hadn't been there? I mean, we're trying to make connections because it's our job, but it's not his job, so why would he?'

'I know you've been doing this a lot longer than me,' said Morgan, 'but I think perhaps you underestimate the public's willingness to help.'

'They may be a bit more willing to help around these parts,' conceded Norman. 'But, believe me, I've worked in a lot of places where the public never helps.'

Up ahead the road had widened somewhat, and they could see a sign indicating a viewing point up ahead.

'See that sign?' asked Morgan.

'Okay, so I accept you were right about that,' said Norman, grudgingly.

Ivor had slowed to a crawl, stopping every few yards so he could look around. Fifty yards ahead, a huge arrow pointed to something on their side of the road.

'Here we go,' said Norman. 'My cynical self can't decide if he's genuinely having trouble remembering exactly where he saw the car, or he's made it all up and he's doing this for effect.'

'Give him a chance, Norm,' said Morgan. 'That big arrow up ahead is pointing to the car park, so his story checks out so far. Don't forget it was dark when he saw it, and he's probably feeling a bit of pressure with us two on his tail. I think he's just trying to make sure he gets it right.'

'I hope you're not wrong about that. I'm not going to be too happy if he's a time waster.'

'Stay here and let me go and talk to him.'

Morgan stepped from their car and hurried after Ivor, waving her arms to catch his attention. Soon he stopped and lowered his window.

'It was along this stretch that you saw the car, right?' asked Morgan.

'I know it was along this stretch before the car park,' said Ivor, 'but I was driving in the other direction so we might have already passed the spot. Now I'm here, I'm not sure.'

'Was he heading towards the car park, or away from it?'

'He was heading this way,' said Ivor. 'He must have been because I was heading home and I came up behind him.'

'Don't worry if you can't recall exactly where you saw it,' said Morgan. 'If you're sure it was along this stretch, we can walk it.'

'Yes, but I wanted to help—'

'Trust me, Ivor, you've been an enormous help. If we need you to make a statement, would you be willing to do so?'

'Oh, yes, definitely.'

'Okay. We've already got your details so you can get on your way.'

Morgan walked back to join Norman, who was talking on his phone. She waited for him to finish before she opened the car door and slid into her seat.

'I've just been bringing the boss up to speed,' said Norman.

'What does she think?'

'She thinks that if this guy Ivor's for real, this could be our breakthrough moment. A description would have been the icing on the cake, but because we don't have one, we need to prove beyond reasonable doubt that it was Dilys's car before we can use it against anyone.'

'She doesn't want much then,' said Morgan.

'It's too vague without any proof,' said Norman.

'I think Ivor definitely saw the car somewhere along this stretch of road.'

'I'm not disputing that,' said Norman. 'But unless we can be more definite, a decent defence lawyer will simply argue that it could have been any grey car with any driver.'

'Yeah, I know,' said Morgan, wearily.

'So what else did Ivor tell you?'

'He thinks he saw it between here and the car park, but it could have been a bit further down the road.'

'Which way was it heading?'

'It was heading back the way we've come.'

'So it could have come from the car park,' said Norman.

'Is that what the boss thinks?'

'We've got to start somewhere, and she thinks it's an assumption we can't ignore.'

'Do you think Dilys met someone there?'

'She must have been out here for a reason, so that's one possibility,' said Norman. 'There again, if she wasn't driving the car when Ivor saw it, it could suggest that whoever was driving had already disposed of her body and was taking the car to hide it and just happened to be here when he got the puncture.'

'So this might not get us anywhere,' said Morgan.

'Let's take a look at the car park before we decide,' said Norman.

'But what if we can't find anything?'

'Then we work our way back down the road to see if we can find out where this car was when Ivor saw it. If we can identify the spot, we might just find some useful evidence. Anyway, what's with the negative vibes? That's not like you.'

'I dunno. I'm not sleeping well worrying that I might fail my sergeant's exam.'

'You'll be fine,' said Norman. 'Just remember, we don't do negative, and we don't give up.'

He drove up the road and stopped just past the car park entrance. From the car they could see a few wooden picnic tables at the back of the car park overlooking a spectacular view that stretched away into the distance.

'Well, there's the view,' said Norman. 'And you were right about being able to see for miles. Jeez, look at it.'

'That's why it's a popular spot,' said Morgan. 'Imagine sitting at one of those tables having a picnic with a view like that in front of you.'

'I might just try that one day,' said Norman. 'Come on, let's take a walk around the car park. If this spot gets lots of visitors, I don't suppose we'll find anything we could use as evidence, but you never know your luck.'

Together, he and Morgan took a look around the car park, paying particular attention to any tyre marks they could see.

'There must be a hundred different tyre tracks in here,' said Norman. 'We'll need to get a forensic team down here to take some casts but I'll be surprised if we get any conclusive evidence.'

'What's your theory then, Norm?' asked Morgan as they ambled along. 'You think Dilys came here to meet someone, right?'

'I can't see any other reason for her to be out here that late at night,' said Norman. 'It would be a great place to meet someone in secret.'

'You think she had a lover?'

'From what we've heard, I'm not so sure about that,' said Norman. 'If she had a lover, and a place of her own, would she really need to meet him out in the middle of nowhere?'

'That might depend on who he was. Isn't Ross the jealous type?'

'Yeah, so we've been told, but we've yet to see any solid evidence that proves he ever followed Dilys to spy on her. And don't forget, Ross has an alibi that puts him in the White Hart up until nearly midnight, and then he was at work for the rest of that night. Also, the post-mortem said there were no signs Dilys had engaged in sexual activity that night, so I'm inclined to believe there was a very good reason it had to be in secret, but she wasn't meeting a lover.'

'You have someone in mind, right?'

'You mean you don't?' asked Norman.

'There's a long list of potential suspects.'

'Yeah, but there's only one who claims to have been out of the picture for years and would really be worried that Ross might find out he had seen Dilys.'

'You mean Graham Watkins?'

'I think it's safe to say he's at the top of my list,' said Norman.

'I understand what you're saying,' said Morgan, 'but what about his car?'

'I'm sorry?'

'Well, Ivor says he saw a man fixing a puncture. If that man was Graham Watkins, and he had used Dilys's car to hide her body, and was on the way to hide the car, where was his Range Rover?'

'I don't know,' said Norman. 'If he met Dilys here, maybe it was in the car park. If it was dark, Ivor wouldn't have seen it.'

'But that means Watkins would have to drive the car to the field where we found it, and then walk all the way back here in the dark, and, trust me, it gets seriously dark out here where there are no streetlights.'

'I admit I don't have all the answers,' said Norman. 'Anyway, whose side are you on?'

'It's not about sides, is it?' said Morgan. 'I'm just pointing out the issue of reasonable doubt. Isn't that what you're always telling me to watch out for?'

They had walked round the perimeter of the car park and were now back at the entrance.

'Yeah, that's a good point,' admitted Norman. 'But that's also why we're out here searching for evidence. Anyway, as we've found nothing useful in the car park, let's walk down the road. Maybe we'll have more luck along there.'

They turned right at the road. Both the road and the roadside verge widened as they walked away from the car park, a thick hedge denoting where the verge ended.

'It can't be far along here,' said Morgan. She pointed along the road. 'Ivor said the road was wide enough to stop alongside the other car, and you can see where it begins to narrow up ahead. How far away is that, do you think — seventy-five metres?'

'How far is that in old money?' asked Norman.

Morgan smiled. 'Oh yeah, sorry. I forgot you're stuck in the land of old-fashioned, imperial measurements.'

Norman smiled too. 'Says the woman who walks in metres but drives in miles. At least I'm consistent.'

'Ah, yes, but I'm a woman,' said Morgan, 'which means I'm versatile and capable of multitasking.'

She laughed as Norman rolled his eyes.

'Yeah, right, of course you are,' he said. He stopped and pointed to the side of the road. 'Now, what do you think caused that?'

Morgan followed Norman's gaze. There, barely ten yards ahead of them, was a ragged, scuffed, wheel-sized mark along the edge of the verge.

'Someone has driven over it?' said Morgan.

'I reckon,' said Norman. 'It's the sort of thing that might happen if you had a sudden front wheel puncture. It would take you by surprise and the car would veer to the right before you got it back under control.'

'It would tie in with what Ivor said about the car being on the wrong side of the road, and about the driver popping up from behind the car,' said Morgan. She pointed to another area a few yards further on. 'And, look just there. I reckon this is where he had just finished changing the wheel when Ivor came along.'

'I think you're right,' said Norman.

'Shall we take a look?' asked Morgan. 'He might have thrown some evidence over the hedge.'

'I think we should get a forensic team out here,' said Norman. 'This is too important to risk contaminating evidence. You call them while I ring the ranch to let the boss know what we've found.'

CHAPTER TWENTY-THREE

Back at Llangwelli station, Southall and Winter sat facing Graham Watkins and his solicitor across a table.

'Now then, Mr Watkins, let's go back to the night in question,' said Southall. 'When we first spoke you told us you had fallen asleep in your hotel room and you didn't wake up until after one a.m.'

'Did I?'

'Yes, you did, and now you're telling us you hit a deer at around eleven p.m. I'm sure you can see the discrepancy.'

'But I withdrew everything I told you previously,' said Watkins.

'Oh yes, that's right,' said Southall. 'All previous lies were withdrawn.'

'Inspector, I really don't think your attitude is helpful,' said the solicitor.

'You're right,' said Southall. 'It's probably about as helpful as your client's lies. If he wants us to believe what he says, perhaps you should advise him to tell the truth. Wasting our time will only keep him here longer.'

Watkins and the solicitor exchanged a look.

'So, Mr Watkins,' said Southall. 'Were you asleep until one a.m., or were you killing a deer at eleven p.m.?'

'I did fall asleep as I said, but I woke at about nine thirty, had a shower, a sandwich and a cup of coffee and then set off for home. I'd hardly been on the road ten minutes when I hit the deer. I was pretty shaken up, so I went back to the hotel to get myself together and assess the damage to my car. I eventually left for home at about two thirty.'

'You're saying you were on the way back to Yorkshire when you hit the deer?'

'Yes.'

'And am I right in thinking this isn't the first time you've made this journey? In fact, you've made it several times, isn't that right?'

'Yes, that's right,' said Watkins.

Southall turned to Winter. 'DC Winter, would you say the lane where Mr Watkins claims to have hit the deer is the most direct route from the Lifeboat Hotel to the A483?'

'Definitely not,' said Winter. 'He would actually have been heading in completely the wrong direction. Most people would take the bigger roads, which lead the other way.'

Southall turned back to Watkins and smiled. 'Now, you're an intelligent man, Mr Watkins, so you'll understand why I'm asking this next question, which is why would someone who regularly makes a journey set off in the opposite direction to where he's going? And, please, don't waste any more of my time. My team is small but thorough, and if you are lying, I guarantee they will find out. And, just so you know, we've found the car park where we believe Dilys met someone that night.'

'Can I speak with my solicitor in private for a minute?' asked Watkins.

Southall considered for a moment. 'Why don't we take a twenty-minute break?'

* * *

'I'd like to tell you what really happened that night,' said Watkins, when they resumed.

243

'Hold on, I'm losing track,' said Southall. 'Will this be version number three, or is it number four?'

'Look, I know you think I killed Dilys, but I honestly didn't.'

'When you keep coming up with different versions of your story every time we speak, it's difficult to think anything else,' said Southall.

'Which is why I've decided to tell you the truth.'

'Oh, such a magnanimous gesture,' said Southall. 'How gracious of you.'

'Really, Inspector,' warned the solicitor.

Southall sighed theatrically. 'Okay, Mr Watkins, go ahead, let's hear this latest version.'

'On that Friday afternoon I left work and went to the petrol station near my hotel to fill up ready for the journey home. While I was there filling up my car, Dilys drove in and stopped on the other side of the pump from me. I hadn't seen her in ten years or more, but I knew it was her straight away. She hadn't changed a bit, and there she was with just the width of a petrol pump between us.'

'What time was this?' asked Southall.

'Around three thirty.'

'What car was she driving?'

'I didn't take much notice. It was a grey Ford but I couldn't tell you the model.'

'Did she recognise you?' asked Southall.

'Not at first,' said Watkins. 'Not until I spoke to her, and then we got talking. But she was in a hurry, so we agreed to meet up later that night in the car park at this viewing point we used to go to when we were kids.'

'What time did you meet her?'

'Ten p.m.'

'Was she still driving the same car?'

'Yes, I think so.'

'Why would she agree to meet up with you?' asked Southall.

'Why shouldn't she?'

'I thought you moved away because Dilys complained about you pestering her?'

'I expect that's what Ross told you, isn't it? The real reason I moved away was because things were getting a bit too hot between me and Dilys. Ross was my brother. I didn't want to be the one to break up his marriage.'

'Were you two having an affair?'

'Ross thought we were, but no, we weren't, although I think we would have if I'd stayed.'

'So, when you met Dilys in the petrol station, you were hoping to carry on where you left off ten years ago?'

'When she told me she and Ross had separated, of course I thought there might be a chance.'

'But why meet at a car park in the middle of nowhere?'

'It was her choice. We went there a few times when we were younger, before she met Ross. When she suggested we meet there, I assumed she was hoping the same as me, but it turned out she only suggested that place because I'd know where it was.'

'So things didn't go according to plan?' asked Southall.

'It wasn't really a plan, was it? I just got the wrong end of the stick. I thought this was it, the big, happily ever after thing, but she just wanted to catch up. When she realised I still had ideas about us being a couple, she told me she still loved Ross and there could never be anything between me and her.'

'That must have upset you,' said Southall.

'I was disappointed, of course, but I know what Ross is like. She didn't love him, she was frightened of him. He would have killed her if he'd known she was meeting me. That's the real reason we were out there in the middle of nowhere.'

'But Ross couldn't have seen you. He was at work,' said Southall.

'Apparently, he can come and go from work whenever he pleases,' said Watkins. 'He's like her own personal stalker.'

'And Dilys told you this?'

'I know it from ten years ago, when he thought he'd caught us having an affair.'

'And you weren't?'

'Of course we weren't. I've just said so — I wouldn't do that to my own brother.'

'And you weren't trying to rekindle an older affair? Like from before Ross and Dilys married?'

'You mean you still think I'm Erin's father? I've already told you I'm not, but if you really don't believe me, why don't you take a DNA sample? That'll soon prove it.'

'That can be arranged,' said Southall.

'Then I suggest you arrange it, Inspector,' said the solicitor testily. 'My client has told you more than once he's not the girl's father. I can't think why you haven't done it before now.'

'Getting back to that night,' said Southall. 'What happened after Dilys told you she wasn't interested?'

'We'd been sitting in my car while we were talking. After she told me that, Dilys went back to her own car.'

'Is that when you ran her down?' asked Southall.

'Wouldn't you have found some evidence?' asked Watkins.

'What happened?' asked Southall.

'She went back to her car, and I drove back to my hotel to collect my things. It was while I was on the way back that I hit the deer.'

'And what about Dilys? Did you see her drive off?'

'No. I left first.'

'We found her car,' said Southall. 'You probably thought you had it well hidden, but we did.'

'I don't know what you're talking about,' said Watkins.

'So, we're not going to find your fingerprints inside her car, or on the wheel brace?' asked Southall.

Watkins turned to his solicitor, looking genuinely confused.

'Wheel brace?' he echoed.

'From when you had the puncture and had to change the wheel.'

246

'I didn't change a wheel on her car,' said Watkins. 'If she had had a puncture I would have happily changed her wheel for her, but the last time I saw Dilys, she was sitting in her car as I drove away. Believe me, if I'd known what was going to happen to her, I would have escorted her home.'

* * *

Five minutes later, Southall had decided the interview was going nowhere and called a halt.

'What do we do now, boss?' asked Winter as he and Southall walked back to their office.

'We need Forensics to tell us they've found his finger-prints in the car,' said Southall. 'And I'd like you to see if there's any CCTV footage at the petrol station that confirms he saw and spoke to Dilys.'

'Do you still think he did it?'

'You've seen the evidence, and now you've heard the man. What do you think, Frosty?'

'What do I think? I'm just a lowly DC at the bottom of the food chain,' said Winter. 'It doesn't matter what I think.'

'Of course it matters,' said Southall. 'One day it could be you making these decisions, so you might as well get some practice in. Come on, I'm not asking you to run the case but I am interested in what you think.'

'Really?'

'Yes, really.'

'And you don't mind if I disagree with you?'

'We won't know if we disagree if you don't offer an opinion.'

'Right. Of course,' said Winter, nervously. 'Well, we know he has a motive, he's admitted he had the opportunity, and his car is the means. The damage to his car suggests he could have run Dilys down, and the fact he keeps changing his story doesn't help.'

'Right so far,' said Southall. 'Go on.'

'However, in his favour, we know a deer was hit and killed by a vehicle that night. He might not have been able to take us to the exact spot, but he wasn't far out, and he was right about there being an oak tree where he hit it. He also admitted he met Dilys at the viewing point car park. And, what clinched it for me is that he genuinely didn't seem to know the car had been hidden, or about the puncture.'

'So, what's your verdict?' asked Southall.

'Well, it's not really for me to say, but in my opinion I think we might have got the wrong man. I'm sorry if that's not what you wanted to hear.'

'We really need to work on your confidence, Frosty,' said Southall. 'When I ask for your opinion, I don't want you to tell me what you think I want to hear. I want you to tell me what you think, and you don't have to apologise if you disagree with me.'

'Oh, right. Well, that is what I think.'

'As it happens, and much as I hate to admit it, with what little evidence we've got at the moment, I think you're right,' said Southall.

Winter couldn't hide his surprise. 'You do?'

'We've got no real proof, have we?' said Southall. 'Yes, there is plenty of circumstantial evidence, but without something concrete we'd never get a conviction. Unless they've got at least one fingerprint from Dilys's car that matches Watkins's prints, I think we'll have to let him go.'

As soon as they entered the office, Lane announced that the blood results from number nineteen had come through.

'And about time too,' said Southall. 'What does it say?'

'It's definitely Wozzy's blood.'

'Which means he was attacked in that bedroom,' said Southall.

'I've also got the forensic report from Dilys's car,' Lane said.

'I can tell from your face that they didn't find Graham Watkins's fingerprints,' said Southall.

'They've only got prints from Dilys and Ross Watkins inside the car,' said Lane, reading from the report.

'It's Ross's car, and Dilys had been using it all week, so that's to be expected,' said Southall.

'Whoever drove the car to its hiding place must have been wearing gloves,' Lane said. Then she looked up. 'But there is a print on the wheel brace that was in the boot.'

'Don't tell me, they're Ross's,' said Southall.

'No, they don't match Ross, or Graham Watkins. The problem is, they don't match anyone on the database either.'

CHAPTER TWENTY-FOUR

'That's two hours of my life I'll never get back,' said Norman as he started his car.

'Now who's being negative,' said Morgan. 'They have enough evidence to prove a puncture was repaired there.'

'Yeah, but we already knew that. I was hoping for something more.'

'Well, you never know, they might still find something else.'

'Yeah, I suppose they might, but it's not likely to be anything major, is it?'

'Ah. I see. This is about you being pissed off because you didn't find anything,' said Morgan.

'Catren, you know very well I don't care who finds the evidence. I never have. It's a team game, and there's no "I" in team.'

'Relax, Norm. I'm just teasing.'

Norman reversed the car and headed back past the forensic team who were still searching the verge. He waved to them as he passed and then put his foot down, until a hundred yards further on, he braked hard. Morgan, who had been gazing out of her window, would have been thrown from her seat if she hadn't been wearing her seatbelt.

'Jesus, Norm, what's up?' she asked, as the car skidded to a halt.

'It's probably nothing,' he said, opening his car door and jumping out.

With Morgan following, Norman trotted back along the road a short distance, then slowed. He walked on, staring at the verge, scanning the grass.

'What are we looking for?' asked Morgan as she caught up.

'As I said, it's probably nothing,' said Norman, looking closely at the verge, 'but something shiny caught my eye in the grass around about here. Knowing our luck today it's probably just an old drinks can someone's tossed from their car window.'

Morgan walked a few yards further along the verge and began in turn to search, heading back towards Norman. Less than a minute later, she called out, 'Okay, Eagle-eye, I think I've found it.'

'What is it?' called Norman, hurrying up to join her.

Morgan pointed at an object lying in the grass. 'It looks like a smashed wristwatch to me. You must have eyes like a hawk. No normal person would have spotted that from a speeding car.'

'I'm sure I wouldn't have noticed something like that normally, but I guess subconsciously I was still looking for clues in the verge.'

Norman slipped on a pair of latex gloves, carefully lifted the watch from the ground and studied it.

'The strap's broken and the face is smashed,' he said. 'The hands read twelve fifteen.'

He turned it over and squinted at the back. 'Can you read these initials, Catren? It's a fancy script and I can't quite make it out.'

He held the watch out to Morgan.

'It looks like a "D" and a "W",' said Morgan.

Norman slipped the watch into an evidence pouch.

'Of course, at this stage we have no way of knowing for sure who it belongs to,' he said.

'Yeah, but it's a bit of a coincidence that it's just down the road from the car park, and even closer to where Dilys's car had a puncture,' said Morgan.

'Yeah, it makes you wonder,' agreed Norman. 'But if it is her watch, how did it get here?'

'Twelve fifteen would fit with the pathologist's window for the time of death,' said Morgan. 'Maybe this is where she was run down.'

'But why was she here?' said Norman. 'Why wasn't she back there in her car?'

'Do you think there might be anything else of hers around here?'

'It wouldn't hurt to ask the forensic team to have a quick look while they're out here, would it?' said Norman.

Five minutes later the forensic team joined them and began a systematic search of the verge. After half an hour, a shout was heard.

* * *

'So what have we got now?' asked Southall.

'We've got the wristwatch which Ross Watkins says he bought Dilys for her birthday five years ago, a story which Erin confirms,' said Norman. 'We've also got a mobile phone Forensics found in the hedge nearby. It's smashed but they're hoping their tech guys can get something from it.'

'What's the story then?' asked Southall.

'Me and Catren have been trying to work it out on the way back here. We think the only explanation that makes sense is that Dilys was walking along the road, got run down and thrown onto the verge.'

'A hit and run?' said Southall. 'That's not quite the crime of passion we envisaged, is it?'

Norman shrugged. 'I'm not saying we've got it right, but you asked what we think happened, and that's it. The time the watch stopped fits with the time of death, and the fact the strap is broken as well suggests a traumatic impact.'

'As it gets so dark out there,' Morgan added, 'we're guessing she may have been using the torch on her phone to light her way.'

'If it is her phone,' said Southall.

'Well, yeah, okay,' said Morgan. 'But it's one hell of a coincidence if it's not hers. Anyway, the tech guys will know soon enough.'

'But if she was carrying a light, why didn't the driver see her?' asked Southall.

Norman sighed. 'I dunno, Sarah. Maybe the driver was drunk. Or maybe he did see her, and that's why she got run down.'

'There is another possibility,' said Morgan. 'Didn't Ross tell you guys that Dilys was always forgetting to keep her phone charged? What if she was using the phone to light her way but then the battery died on her?'

'She'd be up shit creek for sure if that happened,' said Norman.

'And it gets seriously dark out there,' said Morgan. 'If there's no moon, you can't see your hand in front of your face.'

'All right,' said Southall. 'So you're pretty sure it's a hit and run, possibly by a drunk driver.'

'Possibly,' said Norman. 'But if it was a drunk, he or she would have needed to sober up damn quick to then hide the body and the car.'

There was a short, gloomy silence, before Norman spoke again.

'Did Forensics find anything in Ross's car?'

'There's a fingerprint on the wheel brace, but it doesn't match Ross or Graham Watkins, nor anyone else on our suspect list. In fact it doesn't match anyone on the entire national database.'

'What have you done with Graham Watkins?' asked Norman.

'Without any solid evidence, I had to let him go,' said Southall.

'So now we're the ones up shit creek,' said Norman.

'I think we're very close but we're missing something,' said Southall. 'So I suggest we all go home, take tomorrow off, and sleep on it. Maybe one of us will realise what we're missing once we stop focusing so hard.'

CHAPTER TWENTY-FIVE

Monday, 20 March

'Are you sure he won't have destroyed all the evidence by now, Norm?' asked Morgan.

'You know I can't guarantee that, Catren,' said Norman. 'It's a risk with any search. Anyway, since when did you get cold feet about anything? You all agreed with me when I explained why I think it's him. And would the boss have rushed through this search warrant if she didn't think I was right?'

'I don't have cold feet about it, and I'm not disagreeing with you. I'm sure you're right, I just hope we can get enough evidence to prove it.'

Norman stopped his car behind Southall's and, as they gathered by the cars, a marked police car pulled up behind them and a uniformed constable stepped out. Norman recognised him immediately.

'Well, if it isn't PC Hopkins,' he said. 'Last time I saw you we were on a rubbish tip playing at being Smurfs.'

Hopkins smiled. 'And you were wearing diving boots, if I recall.'

'Yeah, well, let's forget about that particular detail,' said Norman. 'I take it you're here to assist us?'

'That's why I'm here.'

Norman quickly introduced the team to Hopkins, leaving Sarah for last. 'And, of course, DI Southall is the boss.'

'Right,' said Southall. 'Once we're inside I want Norm and Catren to head for the workshop. Frosty, you're with me in the house. Hopkins, I'd like you to keep an eye on the suspect.'

'Yes, ma'am,' said Hopkins.

'Everyone ready?' asked Southall. 'Right, let's go!'

She marched up to the front door, rang the doorbell and stepped aside. Norman hammered on the door with his fist, then knelt down and pushed the letterbox open.

'Police. Open up,' he shouted.

They stepped back and waited. After a few seconds they could hear the sounds of movement inside.

'Oh dear, he must have been asleep,' said Norman. 'What a shame we had to wake him.'

Finally, the door creaked open to reveal a bleary-eyed Glen Matthews, who did a double-take at seeing so many people gathered on his doorstep.

'Good morning, Mr Matthews,' said Southall. 'I believe you remember who we are. I'd like to present you with a copy of our search warrant.'

Still half asleep, Matthews took the folded warrant Southall held out to him.

'Search warrant?' he mumbled.

'That's right,' said Southall. 'It gives us the right to come in and search your premises.'

'Search my what?'

'Your house and your workshop,' said Southall.

'But you can't—'

'Actually, I think you'll find that warrant says we can. And we're going to,' said Southall, marching into the house. 'Now if you'd just like to step into the kitchen with Constable Hopkins, I'm sure we can find our own way around.'

'Come along, sir,' said Hopkins. 'Show me where the kitchen is and I'll make us a cup of tea.'

Norman led Morgan out through the back door and across a small yard to a door that led into the garage. He pushed it open and Morgan followed him inside.

'It's a stripped down old Landy,' said Morgan, delighted. 'How cool is that!'

'Before you get carried away and start reminiscing about clapped out old farm vehicles, just remember that if I'm right, this "cool old Landy" as you call it, may be the vehicle that was used to murder Dilys Watkins,' said Norman.

'Ah, yeah. Sorry. For a minute there I forgot why we're here.'

Norman pointed to the small mountain of spare parts piled in one corner.

'Well, now you've been reminded of it, how about you start by going through all that crap over there.'

'Right, no problem. Consider it done,' said Morgan.

* * *

Southall and Norman seated themselves opposite Glen Matthews.

'You understand why you're here, Mr Matthews?' asked Southall.

'Not really,' said Matthews.

'Then let me explain,' said Southall. 'You have been arrested because we suspect you of being responsible for the murder of Dilys Watkins. You will now be questioned about this, and the session will be recorded.'

'You've got it all wrong,' said Matthews.

'You'll get your chance to explain in a minute,' said Southall. 'I take it you've been advised that you are entitled to legal representation?'

'I don't need a lawyer. I've done nothing wrong.'

'Really?' said Southall. 'Let's start with the night Dilys died. Now, you told Sergeant Norman here that you were at work, and that you were asleep when Dilys died.'

'That's right.'

'Can you explain then, why Ross Watkins told us you rushed off out as soon as he got back from the White Hart at about eleven forty-five.'

'He's lying.'

'Why would he lie?' asked Southall.

'He's mistaken then,' said Matthews.

'I see,' said Southall. 'Let's try another one, shall we? Can you explain why your Land Rover appears to have blood on it?'

'I hit a deer.'

Southall turned to Norman. 'With the amount of drivers who claim to have hit a deer lately, it's a wonder there are any left alive around here.'

'It does seem to be a remarkably high rate of attrition,' agreed Norman.

'I dunno what you're talking about,' said Matthews.

'What about the smashed windscreen?'

'I dropped it.'

'That was clumsy,' said Southall. 'But, if you dropped it, how did Dilys's blood get on it?'

'Her blood can't be on it, unless you've planted it.'

'How can you be so sure it's not her blood?'

'Because she nev—' Matthews stopped abruptly.

'Please, go on, Mr Matthews. Finish your sentence.'

'The blood's mine. I cut my hand when I was trying to clean up the broken bits.'

'When we've finished, arrange a blood test for Mr Matthews, Sergeant,' said Southall.

'Yes, ma'am, with pleasure.' Norman beamed at Matthews.

'Now let's get to the real evidence,' said Southall. 'Can you explain why we found a box of latex gloves on the passenger seat of your Land Rover?'

'You probably found three or four boxes of them if you looked around my workshop,' said Matthews. 'Sensible mechanics wear them all the time when they're working, to protect their hands.'

'You worry about getting your hands dirty?'

'It's not just about staying clean. Some of the lubricants are known to be carcinogenic.'

Southall placed a clear evidence pouch containing a mobile phone on the table and described her actions for the tape.

'Who does this phone belong to?' she asked.

'I dunno. I've never seen it before.'

'It was found in your Land Rover.'

'Well, it must belong to the bloke who owned it before me.'

'Buy it locally, did you?' asked Norman.

'What?'

'The Land Rover. Did you buy it locally?'

'No, out Wrexham way.'

'It's a bit of a coincidence that the previous owner, who lived one hundred and twenty miles from here, also knew Dilys, don't you think?' asked Norman.

Matthews swallowed hard. 'I'm not with you.'

'The thing is, Glen, we charged up the phone,' said Norman. 'The last person to call it was Dilys. So either it's your phone, or she knew the previous owner.'

'Well, there we are then. She must have known him.'

Norman sighed.

'I know you think that's a smart answer, Glen, but we also have Dilys's mobile phone records. Now we know for a fact that at eleven twenty-eight on the night she died, Dilys called that very phone. We think she was calling you, and we know you answered the call.'

Matthews looked around, wide-eyed, as if he were looking for a means of escape.

'No. That's not true. I was working. We're not allowed phones when we're on the machines.'

'And, of course, you all follow the rules to the letter, don't you?' said Southall.

Matthews swallowed again, his Adam's apple moving up and down.

'We also know from the mobile phone company that that call was the last one Dilys made. Shortly after midnight, her phone stopped working. The last known location was within a couple of hundred yards of the viewpoint car park.'

'I told you, it's not my phone. You're just trying to trick me.'

'We don't need to trick you, Glen,' said Norman. 'You recall that when you were arrested we took your fingerprints? Well, guess what? Your prints are a perfect match for a print we found on the wheel brace in the boot of the car Dilys was driving. How do you explain that?'

'It's Ross's car. I helped him with a puncture.'

'Yeah,' said Norman. 'We thought you might say that, so we called Ross earlier. He says he's never had a puncture in that car. He also told us you were driving around in that Land Rover of yours during the week Dilys died, and he says you were driving it the night she died.'

'That's a lie.'

'Latex gloves are great. We use them ourselves. The problem is they're very thin, and if you snag one on something sharp they can tear quite easily. If I had to guess I'd say one of your latex gloves tore and that's why you left a single print.'

'It can't be my fingerprint because I wasn't there. My Land Rover was in bits on my workshop floor.'

'Do you know what ANPR cameras are, Glen? The letters stand for Automatic Number Plate Recognition. They're the cameras you see on the side of the road, and on motorways and such. So, when we get the results of the ANPR search we requested for your registration number, it won't show up anywhere, is that what you're saying?'

'I dunno.'

'You thought you were clever taking the Land Rover apart, didn't you? But we've been asking people who have experience of these things, and all of them say that anyone who knows what they're doing could easily strip one down as much as yours is in just a day or two.'

Matthews looked blankly at Norman and then at Southall.

'Look, Glen, we might not know exactly what took place, but we've got enough evidence to charge you with murder,' said Southall. 'It would be much better for you if you told us what did happen that night.'

'I think I need that lawyer before I say anything else,' said Matthews.

'Do you have a lawyer?'

'No. Of course I haven't. They cost money.'

'Don't worry. We can arrange for a duty solicitor to advise you,' said Southall. 'We'll suspend the interview now so you can have a break, and we'll reconvene when you've had a chance to speak with the solicitor.'

* * *

It was six p.m. when the duty solicitor arrived, and it was seven by the time he and Matthews were ready to resume the interview.

'Are you happy you've had long enough with your solicitor?' asked Southall as soon as they started.

'Yes,' said Matthews.

'Okay,' said Southall. 'So why don't you tell us what really happened the night Dilys died.'

'She rang me. She said she'd had a puncture, she didn't know what to do and could I go and help her.'

'Where was she?'

'Close to the viewing point car park.'

'What was she doing out there at that time of night?'

'I don't know,' said Matthews. 'I didn't ask. She was on her way home from somewhere, I suppose.'

'I'm assuming she called you on the mobile phone you said wasn't yours?'

'Well, yeah, okay, it is my phone.'

'And she called you, and not Ross?' asked Southall. 'Is that the sort of thing she would normally do?'

'I told you before, she wanted to keep her distance from Ross, so I'd told her she should always call me if ever she needed anything.'

'Does Ross know you were having an affair with his wife?' asked Southall.

'I'm not—'

'Oh, come on, Glen. Ross might not have worked it out yet, but do we look stupid?'

Matthews said nothing.

'How long has it been going on?' asked Southall. 'Or has it been going on since before Ross and Dilys got married?'

'I'm not going to answer that.'

'You're Erin's father, aren't you?'

'I'm not going to answer that either.'

Southall stared at Matthews for a minute. Things were beginning to add up.

'Okay, so Dilys called you asking for help. Then what happened?'

'I couldn't leave straight away because Ross was down the pub and I had to wait until he came back.'

'How did you get out there?' asked Norman.

'You already know that.'

'We'd like to hear you say it for the tape,' said Norman.

Matthews sighed. 'All right. I was driving my Land Rover.'

'So, what happened?' asked Southall.

'I drove out to where she said she was.'

'What time did you get there?'

'About twelve fifteen.'

'And what did you do?'

'I fixed her puncture for her, she drove off home and I went back to work.'

'And you say Dilys drove home?'

'Well, that's where she said she was going.'

'And you watched her drive off?'

'Yes. I wanted to make sure she was okay, so I waited for her to leave before I did.'

'Did you see any other cars around that area?'

'Not a soul,' said Matthews.

'And what was the time when you last saw Dilys?' asked Southall.

'I got there about twelve fifteen, so I suppose by the time I changed the wheel, it must have been around one a.m.,' said Matthews.

'What time did you get back to work?'

'I'm not sure. It must have been around one fifteen, one twenty, something like that.'

'Tell him, Norm,' said Southall.

'I'm afraid we have a few discrepancies here, Glen,' said Norman.

Matthews licked his lips. His eyes darted from one detective to the other.

'I don't know what you mean.'

Norman heaved a theatrical sigh. 'Really? Then let me help you out a little. You say you fixed the puncture and watched Dilys drive away by one a.m. We know Dilys didn't drive off home, because we now know she was run down less than a hundred yards from where she had the puncture.'

'No, no, no,' stammered Matthews. 'That's wrong. I saw her drive away. She must have come back.'

'Now why would she do that?' asked Norman.

'I dunno. She was stressed about something. Maybe she wasn't thinking straight.'

'Come on, Glen. We both know that's bullshit. The reason we know Dilys was run down is because we found her wristwatch and her mobile phone at the spot where it happened. The watch was smashed and the hands had stopped at twelve fifteen. That's around the time you say you got there. How do you explain that?'

'I can't explain it. I told you what happened.'

'We also have a witness who saw a man changing that same front tyre, on the same car, in the same place, at two a.m. We think that was you, Glen. Are we right?'

'It can't have been me. I told you I was back at work long before then.'

'Oh, yeah, thanks for reminding me,' said Norman. 'I almost forgot. You see, that's another discrepancy. Ross remembers that you didn't get back until almost three a.m.'

Matthews's eyes widened. 'That's a lie!'

'Ross says he remembers because the machines finished running just before two and he had to do all the clearing up himself. Apparently, you're supposed to share that particular part of the job, so he wasn't happy about having to do it all himself.'

Matthews turned to his solicitor. 'What do I do?'

The solicitor merely shrugged his shoulders. In the face of so many contradictions, there was little he could offer in the way of support.

'What you should do, Glen,' said Southall, 'is stop stalling and tell us the truth.'

Matthews stared at his hands for a few seconds and then seemed to come to a decision.

'As I said before, Dilys called me to say she'd had a puncture. So, as soon as Ross came back to work, I drove out there to help her. I found the car, but I couldn't find Dilys anywhere. I assumed she must have started walking and I had missed her somehow.'

'She just walked off on her own, on a dark night, in the middle of nowhere?' asked Norman. 'Really?'

'Look, I was as surprised as you are,' said Matthews. 'I'd told her to wait and not to move.'

'Did you see any other vehicles in the area?'

'Not one.'

'So, what did you do?' asked Southall.

'I drove around trying to find her.'

'You didn't call her?' asked Norman, incredulously.

'Of course I did, but there was no answer. Knowing Dilys, her phone would have been dead. She was always forgetting to charge it.'

'So, then what happened?'

'I drove around for ages, then at about one forty-five, I went back to fix the puncture in case she came back, and then I went looking again before I went back to work.'

'So, you're saying you didn't know where to find the woman you'd been having a long-term affair with, and that you supposedly cared about, so you just took off?'

'Where would I look? She could have been anywhere. She could have got a lift home for all I knew.'

'Well, that's one place I would definitely have checked, more than once,' said Norman. 'And yet you didn't think to try looking there.'

'Look, you asked me what happened, and I've told you. If you don't want to believe me, that's your problem.'

'I'm afraid you're the one with a problem,' said Southall. 'You see, in both versions of your story you told us you rushed out to Dilys's car when Ross got back to work. Now, we know Dilys was run down, barely a hundred yards from her car, at twelve fifteen. And yet in both versions of your story you say you didn't see any other vehicles in the area.'

Matthews looked vacant.

'You're not stupid, Glen, you can see what that suggests.'

'And there's another problem,' said Norman. 'You have previously given us the impression you cared deeply about Dilys, and you say you were having a long-term affair, and yet, throughout this entire interview you have never expressed any concern as to what happened to Dilys that night. It's as if you don't care, and I don't get that.'

For the first time, Matthews lost his self-control. As they watched, his face slowly crumpled and he began to sob uncontrollably.

Southall looked at Norman, who simply shrugged.

'Do you need to take a break, Glen?' asked Southall.

He looked up at her, his expression pitiful, and the words began to tumble out in between the sobs.

'I didn't mean to do it. I just didn't see her. Why did she have to let her phone die? If she'd had a light on, I would have seen her.'

'Holy crap,' muttered Norman. 'He's confessing!'

'Now, wait a minute,' said Southall. 'Are you now saying you ran Dilys down?'

Matthews looked at Southall, tears streaming down his face. 'It was an accident. I only went to help her.'

'Why don't you tell us what happened?' said Southall.

'Dilys called me, just as I said, so I drove out there. I was looking for her car, I didn't see her walking along the verge, and suddenly she stepped out in front of me. I didn't have time to stop or do anything. Next thing I know, she's flying over the bonnet and smashing into my windscreen. I only wanted to help her . . .'

'So, let me get this straight,' said Southall. 'You were driving along, and Dilys stepped out in front of you, is that right?'

'Yes.'

'Didn't she see you coming? Or hear you?'

'She was walking back towards her car, so I was coming from behind her.'

'Didn't you have your lights on?'

'They're not very powerful, and it was really dark.'

Southall exchanged a glance with Norman. He looked as doubtful as she felt.

'Okay,' she said. 'You accidentally ran Dilys down. So why didn't you call the police, or an ambulance?'

'I couldn't call the police, could I? My vehicle is supposed to be off the road.'

'Hang on,' said Norman. 'You've just accidentally run down a woman you supposedly care about and all you're worried about is a possible traffic offence?'

'I panicked,' said Matthews. 'I didn't know what to do.'

'Why did you move the body?' asked Southall.

'I didn't move her body. I didn't go near her.'

'You're telling us you cared deeply about Dilys, and yet when you ran her down you just left her there?' said Norman.

'Well, no, it wasn't like that. I did go to her, but she was dead, I could see that, but I didn't move her. I jumped in my Land Rover and drove around, trying to get my head together before I had to face Ross.'

'Ah, right, I see,' said Norman. 'So, facing Ross was more important than trying to do what was best for Dilys?'

'I couldn't do anything for her once she was dead, could I?' snapped Matthews.

'Jeez, you really are a piece of work,' said Norman, his voice thick with disgust. He turned to Southall. 'Can we take a break for a few minutes, please?'

* * *

'Okay, Glen, while we were taking our break, we received some preliminary results back from our forensics team,' said Southall. 'And just so you know, we have found traces of blood in the back of your Land Rover. Initial tests suggest it's a match for the blood on the windscreen and front panels. So, my first question is, how did that blood get there?'

'It's mine,' said Matthews. 'I told you, I cut myself on the broken windscreen, and I've lost count of the number of times I've nicked a finger while I've been working on that thing. You'll probably find traces of my blood all over it.'

'We'll know for sure soon enough, but my money says it's Dilys's blood,' said Southall. 'We've also found hairs in the back that appear to match the colour of Dilys's hair. A DNA test will prove it, of course.'

'It's not looking good for you, is it, Glen?' asked Norman. 'I don't know if we mentioned it before, but we found some carpet fibres on Dilys's clothes. What's the betting they match that old carpet in the back of your Land Rover?'

Matthews said nothing, but his face spoke volumes.

'I understand they've found some interesting deposits in your tyre treads, too,' continued Norman. 'They suggest you've recently been driving around the old mining village that's being redeveloped.'

'Why would I have been there?' asked Matthews.

'Because that's where you dumped Dilys's body,' said Norman. 'It also seems you keep petrol in jerry cans in that garage of yours. By coincidence we found one just like yours at house number nineteen, where you dumped Dilys's body.'

'I didn't dump Dilys at number nineteen,' snapped Matthews, angrily. 'I left her at nu—'

But it was too late, he'd said too much already.

'That hole you're digging is getting bigger and bigger,' said Norman. 'I had an old boss who used to say, "when you're in a hole, stop digging". I'd offer you the same advice but, the thing is, I think you've just dug a little too deep, and now the sides are starting to fall in on you. The best thing for you now would be to stop lying. It might even help you get a lighter sentence.'

Matthews looked from Norman to Southall.

'He's right, Glen,' she said. 'You know as well as we do that the forensic evidence is stacking up against you, so you might as well come clean and save us all some time.'

Matthews let out a deep sigh and rubbed his face with his hands.

'Okay,' he said, finally. 'I admit I ran Dilys down, hid her body and then hid her car, but I swear it was an accident.'

'Why did you take her body to the village?' asked Southall.

'I don't know why I took her there. I wasn't thinking straight. I'm not even sure I was thinking at all. I was on autopilot, in panic mode or something. I don't know.'

'But you admit you did take her there,' insisted Southall.

'Yes. I didn't want to admit I'd killed her. I mean, how would I ever be able to face Ross? I suppose I thought I could hide her there and she'd stay undiscovered until the houses got demolished. I thought it would be years before she was found. I had no idea it would only be a couple of days.'

'You did realise it was a building site with plans for redevelopment?'

'Well, yeah, everyone knows that, but it's been dragging on for years. How was I supposed to know it had finally got the go-ahead?'

'So, you were just going to leave her body in the house?' asked Southall.

'Yes.'

'Then why did you take the petrol? Were you planning to burn her body?'

'I often have a can in the Land Rover. You never know when you might run short, or come across someone who has run out. I usually have a tow rope on board, too. You never know when someone might need a tow.'

'You weren't planning on burning her body then?' asked Norman.

'Oh, come on,' said Matthews. 'What sort of guy do you think I am?'

Norman raised his eyebrows.

'Why did you take it into the house?' Southall asked.

'I'm not sure you can prove it's mine,' said Matthews. 'There must be hundreds of cans like that in this area. I bet every farmer has half a dozen for a start.'

'If I had to guess,' said Norman, 'I'd say you intended to set fire to Dilys's body so it would be harder to identify.'

'I already said I thought it would stay hidden for years.'

'But someone disturbed you before you could do it,' added Norman.

'Someone disturbed me?' said Matthews incredulously. 'Out there? Who the hell is going to be out there?'

'Erin and her boyfriend were sleeping in number nineteen,' said Norman. 'I reckon it was him that disturbed you. Maybe he saw you, or heard you, and he came to see what was going on. You couldn't risk having someone identify you, so you beat the crap out of him, strangled him with your tow rope to make sure he was dead, and then dumped his body in a skip.'

'I don't know what you're talking about,' said Matthews. 'I admit I ran Dilys down and that I panicked and hid her body, but I did not see anyone else on that building site, and I certainly didn't strangle anyone with a tow rope.'

'We'll see what Forensics have to say about that,' said Norman.

'There must be thousands of tow ropes like mine,' said Matthews. 'They're as common as muck.'

EPILOGUE

Next morning, Southall had her regular meeting with her boss, Superintendent Nathan Bain.

'And he confessed?' said Bain.

'At first he just confessed to running down Dilys. He claims it was an accident.'

'So why did he hide her body?'

'He says he panicked. He claims that if Ross Watkins found out, he'd be a dead man, and if his boss found out, he'd lose his job.'

'Well, that wouldn't really matter if Ross Watkins was going to kill him,' said Bain. 'Do you think he would?'

'I don't know about that,' said Southall. 'A couple of people have mentioned that Ross could be violent, but we've not seen anything to prove it one way or the other. Besides, he's just got his daughter back. I hardly think he'd jeopardise that by killing Matthews.'

'What about the boy who was murdered? Wozzy, was it?'

'Matthews is adamant he didn't kill him. He says he didn't see anyone else on the site that night.'

'Can we prove he's lying?'

'The only evidence we have is the tow rope, and as Matthews says, there must be thousands of those ropes in existence. So, I'm not sure we can make a solid case against him for Wozzy's death.

'The forensic evidence against him for Dilys's murder is strong though. We've got Dilys's blood on the Land Rover body-work, on the windscreen, and on the floor in the back, from where he moved her body. And we've got soil samples from the Land Rover tyres that show he was on the building site. And, of course, we've got DNA — blood and finger-prints that back up our case.'

'Even if we can't prove he committed both murders, that's still an impressive result, Sarah. So, what put you on to Matthews?'

'That was Norm. He'd known for a couple of days that we were missing something, then he remembered that Glen Matthews wore latex gloves. Forensics had said that whoever moved Dilys's car had been wearing gloves. Once we knew a Land Rover could be stripped of enough parts to make it look like a wreck in a couple of days, it all seemed to fall into place.'

Bain smiled. 'I don't know what you and Norm drink, but it must be damned good stuff.'

'We make a pretty good team, don't we? I take it you are aware that Norm's not happy about the idea of moving to Region?'

'He hasn't told me as much, but it doesn't really surprise me. He came here as a favour to me, and now he probably feels I'm reneging on the deal and letting him down. Anyway, we'll cross that particular bridge if, and when, the move to Region happens. Speaking of Region, Professional Standards want Norm to make a statement about Marston if he intends to pursue the complaint against him.'

'He seems adamant,' said Southall.

'Very well. I can't say I'm surprised. Norm's always been pretty hot on that sort of stuff.'

'You said, "if the move to Region happens". Does that mean it might not?' asked Southall.

'Oh, it will eventually, but I wouldn't start packing your bags just yet. I think we'll be here for a while longer.'

'You seem very confident about that, sir.'

'Let's just say I've had the good fortune to stumble across a cupboard full of skeletons, and I know who the owner is. Once you know where the bodies are buried, so to speak, it's amazing how easy it is to persuade people to reconsider their plans.'

'Can I tell Norm?'

'I think that's an excellent idea, Sarah. You do that.'

THE END

THE JOFFE BOOKS STORY

We began in 2014 when Jasper agreed to publish his mum's much-rejected romance novel and it became a bestseller.

Since then we've grown into the largest independent publisher in the UK. We're extremely proud to publish some of the very best writers in the world, including Joy Ellis, Faith Martin, Caro Ramsay, Helen Forrester, Simon Brett and Robert Goddard. Everyone at Joffe Books loves reading and we never forget that it all begins with the magic of an author telling a story.

We are proud to publish talented first-time authors, as well as established writers whose books we love introducing to a new generation of readers.

We have been shortlisted for Independent Publisher of the Year at the British Book Awards three times, in 2020, 2021 and 2022, and for the Diversity and Inclusivity Award at the Independent Publishing Awards in 2022.

We built this company with your help, and we love to hear from you, so please email us about absolutely anything bookish at: feedback@joffebooks.com.

If you want to receive free books every Friday and hear about all our new releases, join our mailing list: www.joffebooks.com/contact

And when you tell your friends about us, just remember: it's pronounced Joffe as in coffee or toffee!

9 781835 260944